*Guru*Cool

*Guru*Cool

Dhananjay Bapat

PARTRIDGE

A Penguin Random House Company

To order additional copies of this book, contact
Partridge India
000 800 10062 62
orders.india@partridgepublishing.com

www.partridgepublishing.com/india

To Sushama, Mitali and Ashwin, for being my motivation.

One

The weary Boeing 747 from Bombay docks, seven hours behind schedule. I stretch my stiff torso, collect my belongings from the overhead bin and disembark. The sight of the magnificent aircraft's regal red and white livery, styled on ethnic Indian motifs, helps ease my irritation at the *en route* hold up in Bahrain. The cause of the unscheduled stopover is unknown beyond the vague 'technical snag', whatever that means. After spending twenty eight hours on a plane crossing ten time zones, my head is swimming. But even to my jaded eyes and jet-lagged brain, New York's John F. Kennedy airport is another planet. The signs at the entrance to the immigration hall guide the arriving throng to split into two categories, one for US citizens or green card holders and the other for aliens. I follow the directions to join the queue for the aliens.

My new description amuses me but I concede its aptness. No sight, sound or smell stored in my mental databank of real life experiences matches these surroundings: multi-racial crowd speaking in obscure accents, women in strange clothes, brightly lit shops replete with dazzling merchandise, automatic doors and escalators, colourful vending machines, squeaky clean surfaces and even the sniff of air-freshener everywhere. I would not find myself more out of place on Mars.

Arun, my cousin, is waiting when I exit the customs area pushing my baggage trolley. He is accompanied by his wife Sujata and their eight-year-old son Anand.

"Happy Birthday." Arun wishes me. Anand hands me a glossy greeting card.

"What a nice gesture! I didn't expect you to remember my birthday."

"I migrated to the US in November 1974; on the eighteenth to be exact. We'd had your twentieth birthday bash the previous night. Can't believe I've completed five years here!" Arun explains.

"Oh, yes. I do remember now."

"In fact, when you informed your arrival date, it struck me as your birthday." He adds.

"Thanks. Such a wonderful surprise!"

We step out of the terminal building into the chill of a windy, early-winter night. I feel as if I have entered a refrigerator, never having faced such a low temperature. And it is yet to drop to freezing level. I wonder how I am going to last the next few months.

"Let me open the trunk for you." Arun offers when we approach his car. My disoriented mind takes a few seconds to realize he is referring to what we call 'carrier' or 'dicky' in India.

As we gather speed on Belt Parkway, I bring Arun up to date on the news of his folks in India. All humanity save the four of us has long disappeared. Apart from the fluorescent green highway signboards, only the headlights of the oncoming traffic and the taillights of the vehicles ahead are visible. I quickly understand why America is called a country on wheels. Clearly, this place runs on automobiles.

Not long into the fifty-minute drive, Sujata and Anand are asleep, Arun concentrates on driving and I have time to think about the purpose of my trip here.

The simple fact is, I am from Pune in west-central India, here to join graduate school and earn a master's in business administration over the next two years. And yes, this is the first time I have really traveled beyond my hometown. But why I have chosen to be here is really a personal matter.

The importance of a professional career is embedded in my psyche. It seems as if it always has been. Indeed, a higher education is considered a basic human need in my family, right behind air, water, food and shelter. I am the youngest in a closely knit family of five: a girl followed by two boys, in addition to parents.

My father studied engineering in the UK, my mother read languages at college and is also a fine painter and fashion designer, my sister has earned a Ph.D. in architecture from London while my brother trained in ceramic technology at Stoke-on-Trent, popularly known in England as 'Chinatown' for the exquisite crockery it is famous for.

At a time when most promising kids in India went on to become doctors, lawyers, accountants, architects or engineers, I was expected to be no different. But my choice of career was more a process of elimination than preference.

The sight of blood turns my stomach. Hair-splitting legalese gives me migraine. Reading balance sheets blanks me out. And I cannot draw to save my life. That left me with engineering. Fortunately, my hometown is famous for one of the oldest engineering colleges in Asia. I did not have to leave home to attend classes.

Half-way through the engineering curriculum though, I started feeling inadequate in the inanimate world of machines. I wanted a future that promised greater involvement with people and their lives. I yearned to study the humanities. In our ossified educational system, however, a quick shift to a different major was ruled out. My only option was to stay the course till graduation and then change track for the master's. But after enduring four tough years of engineering, I considered it a waste to completely abandon the hard-earned knowledge. It was sensible to leverage it to manage a manufacturing business. To qualify for such a job, I needed an insight into the guts of a factory. Equipped with my technical qualification, I chose to take a production engineer's job, supervising the shop-floor of a local steel forge.

It was an arduous learning experience. A supervisor is the pivotal interface between workers and upper management. The two are often at loggerheads. Keeping both groups smiling is a tight-rope walk. As the supervisor, I had to understand the workers' mindset, concerns and motivations to find a way of hitting the management's targets of quality, quantity and cost. It was a balancing act that had to come off without causing friction. Though grueling, this was a great place to get trained. It provided an opportunity to see a manufacturing business ground up.

I worked six days a week in rotational shifts. It was a disruptive timetable one never really got used to. But I adjusted. The day shift had too much meddling from the managers; the night shift was the Twilight Zone of accidents, especially the wee hours. Sleepy workers can kill. And get killed. I needed to be always alert. The swing shift was my favourite. The managers were gone for the day and the workers were yet to get sleepy.

As I gained knowledge of running a production unit, I started thinking about my next career move. Not only did I wish to learn business management but also yearned to taste a different culture. I decided to look for a suitable university abroad.

An American business school was the logical choice: a decent management education system, melting pot for a culture and English the language of instruction. When I was on swing or night shift, I had free time during the day to complete my admission formalities. It was a long and winding process. In the languid world of snail mail, letters between India and the US took ten days with luck, twenty without. But the admission process was eventually completed and it was time to apply for a visa to enter the US.

India's relations with America have been tepid at best and frosty at worst. My country has built a close economic and military relationship with the Soviet Union, an uncomfortable reality for the Americans. The goal of balancing the region's geopolitical equation requires the US to tilt towards India's neighbours, notably Pakistan. The policy of issuing visas perhaps reflects this position.

Applying for an American visa is akin to rolling dice. There are no guarantees.

The consulate is located on Warden Road, an up-market residential locality in Bombay. The handsome cream coloured waterfront structure was built as a palace for the ruler of Wankaner, then a small state in western India. The American government acquired the sprawling property in 1957 and christened it Lincoln House. Its occupants enjoy a breathtaking view of the sun setting in the Arabian Sea every evening.

The visa section occupies the north wing of Lincoln House. It can be accessed from the street without entering the courtyard. Extremists have yet to terrorize the world; the need to convert the consulate into a fortress would arise several years later.

I went to the consulate in the first week of October. About thirty visa aspirants were filling out their applications in a large room furnished with rows of chairs like in a classroom. But in place of a blackboard, the front wall was punctuated with four numbered windows to pass documents through to the office inside. The applicants submitted the documents to the staff and waited.

After half an hour, my name was announced on the public address system. I was asked to enter the office inside through the door in the adjacent wall. It opened into a small hallway lined with a row of three open doors leading to rooms, each occupied by a consular officer. The lady in the hallway directed me to enter the first room.

A young African American sat behind a stout rectangular desk large enough to fill most of his office. He was thin with a narrow face and somber bearing. He must barely be out of college, looking more a student than a diplomat. He bade me to take one of the two chairs facing him. I wished him a good morning, thanked him for the courtesy of offering the chair and took the seat. My file of documents was on the desk in front of him.

"Have any of your family members been to the US?" He came straight to the point.

"Yes. My father and sister."

"Are they still in the US?"

"No. They left after the purpose of their stay was accomplished."

"And that was?"

"Business in my father's case and tourism in my sister's."

"Has anyone from your family lived in any other country?"

"Yes. My father, sister and brother went to college in the UK."

"Do they continue to live there?"

"No. They're all back in India."

"That'll be all. Please wait outside. Thank you."

"You're welcome."

I was back in the waiting room in less than five minutes. The consular officer had given me no clue about his intentions. I had no idea if he had decided to issue the visa. As I waited, I tried to imagine my reaction if he turned down my application. I would certainly feel disappointed at the waste of time and effort invested in the process. But I would not be disheartened. I would continue to work in the forge-shop and perhaps pursue the master's in India or some other country.

My reverie was broken by the mention of my name on the public address speaker. I was to go to window number two in the front wall. When I stepped up to it, the woman on the other side dropped my passport and other papers on the counter. I gathered them, still not knowing if I had been granted the visa.

"Present this at the port of entry." The woman placed a sealed envelope on the counter. Then she disappeared.

It took me a few seconds to grasp the implication of her instruction. She had referred to my entry at a port in the US.

I was all set.

Two

I spend a week roaming New York City in wide-eyed amazement. Sights I had only glimpsed in films or read about in books feel awesome in life size: the Empire State Building, Park Avenue, Times Square, Rockefeller Center, United Nations Headquarters, the Metropolitan Museum of Art, Madison Square Garden, the World Trade Centre. The list goes on and on.

I am also learning a new language: wafers are chips here, chips are fries, scones are biscuits, biscuits are cookies, angry is mad, mad is crazy, rugby is football, football is soccer, directory is phone book, petrol is gas, ring road is beltway, canteen is cafeteria, tap is faucet, cupboard is closet, hostel is dormitory, consecutive is back-to-back, complain is bitch, mistake is goof-up. I cannot fathom why toilets are called restrooms after I find no one resting there. And, to my dismay, a hamburger contains no ham.

Thanksgiving is approaching. Till I arrived in this country, I had no idea a day is earmarked for this purpose.

Happily, it is also a long week-end. That is good news. Shiela and Vinay, our family friends in Virginia, invite me to see Washington, DC. This is an unplanned detour.

The last leg of my air-ticket is from Newark to Kansas City. I get it rerouted from Washington, DC to Kansas City. To my surprise, the change costs nothing. Where I come from, one is charged a fee to alter a confirmed booking. The woman at the airline's Manhattan office not only makes the free change but also issues the boarding pass for the following week's flight.

Shiela and Vinay meet me at the bus station when I arrive on the Greyhound service from New Jersey. Shiela is like an elder sister to me. She and Vinay are very organized hosts. They have drawn up an elaborate itinerary for my three-day visit. We go to virtually every place in the area worth seeing: the White House, the Capitol, Lincoln Memorial, Washington Memorial, Arlington cemetery, the Smithsonian, the NASA Museum, the works.

It is nice to be a tourist but I am also getting a little tired of living out of a suitcase.

Thankfully, the stay in the nation's capital is not long. I am scheduled to leave on the first Tuesday after Thanksgiving. Shiela drives me in the morning to Washington National for the seven o'clock flight.

The five Eastern Airlines check-in counters are open but no passengers have arrived. I am early. The ground staff looks fresh in crisp beige and blue uniforms, ready to attend to the travelers. I pick the counter on the right for no particular reason. A petite young woman wearing a badge marked 'Nancy' is standing behind it.

"Good morning, sir. How're you today?" Her welcome is effervescent.

"I'm fine, thanks." I hand her the boarding pass issued in New York City and place my two suitcases on the weighing scale. One of the suitcases has an old, tattered baggage tag with IA printed on one side, short for Indian Airlines, our domestic carrier.

Nancy looks at the boarding pass, shuffles her feet and seems unsure.

"Please wait, sir. I'll be back momentarily." The sparkle in her manner has dimmed. I make a mental note of 'momentarily' and feel glad my high school English teacher is not around. He would have made her write 'in a moment' one hundred times.

She turns around, walks to a door behind the counter, knocks and enters. The door is fitted with a small brass plaque engraved 'Michael Jones, Manager'. A couple of passengers are now waiting behind me. I wonder if we look foolish queuing up in front of an unattended counter.

Just as I start worrying over the time Nancy is taking, she returns, apologizes and tells me I cannot board the flight. I am flabbergasted.

"You haven't got it right. I'm holding a confirmed reservation." I argue.

"I'm sorry, sir, but we're overbooked today. Have to shut a few passengers out."

"May be, but I can't be on the shut-out list." I smile, hoping to charm her into a change of mind.

"I wish I could help you, sir, but I'm sorry I can't." She chooses not to meet my eyes.

"Actually, I've a boarding pass. If I didn't have bags to check-in, I could've walked straight to the gate and boarded. And don't tell me all the passengers have showed up already." I believe I have a strong case.

"I understand, sir, but I'm really sorry." Nancy's voice begins to quaver and she keeps rolling her weight from one leg to the other as if she is preparing to sprint away. I am making no headway. May be it is sensible to try another strategy. The monitor in the concourse has another Eastern flight to Kansas City listed. I decide to focus on the end, not the means.

"Your next flight to Kansas City is scheduled at nine. Why don't you check me in for that one?"

"Sorry, sir, that's closed too."

I have reached a dead end with her. I am getting impatient, a shade angry too. There is no other way but to go over her head.

"May I see your boss, please?"

My guess is that her boss sits behind the door she had gone through earlier. Nancy picks up the phone, presumably talks to the boss, gets clearance to send me in and points to the door to the manager's office.

I hop across the scale, pick up my suitcases and carry them through the door after hearing a hoarse "Come in" to my knock. I step into a small square office with a narrow rosewood desk in the middle. The desk is uncluttered; just a sheet of paper and two white telephones rest on it. The forty-something man sitting behind the desk has greying hair and sad eyes.

Mike Jones looks up from the sheet of paper that appears to be a passenger manifest. He is obviously not happy to see me but understands that I cannot be wished away. He knows why I am in his office. Reluctantly, he gestures to a chair, inviting me to sit. Then he looks at the manifest again. I follow his gaze. My name is underscored in blue ink. He haltingly pronounces it, mangling it badly, except for the 'Mister'. I let it roll off my back, blaming his unyielding tongue. The windowless room is making me claustrophobic.

Jones has nothing more to add to Nancy's story. Frustrated, I explain to him my need to get to Kansas City today under any circumstances. My first day of college is tomorrow. He claims to appreciate my position but shrugs his shoulders and says he is helpless. Now I am livid.

It suddenly dawns on me to approach Kohinoor Airways. I have paid them the entire fare up to Kansas City while buying the ticket in India. They should be able to find a way of getting me to my final destination if Eastern cannot. I ask Mr. Jones to get me Kohinoor Airways on the phone. My diction is foreign; he is not sure he has understood my question.

"Pardon me?" he says, turning his left ear to me, a bewildered look on his face. I have no difficulty understanding him although I am more accustomed to 'beg your pardon', or simply 'sorry?'

"Will you please get me Kohinoor Airways on the phone?" I repeat slowly, stressing 'Kohinoor Airways' and 'phone' to make myself clear.

"Why Kohinoor Airways?" He is baffled.

"Because I paid money to them for the whole trip from Bombay to Kansas City. Let them figure out how to take me there."

"Where're you from?"

"India."

The sadness in the manager's eyes disappears. So do the creases on his forehead.

"Can I please see your passport and ticket, sir?" He wants to be sure.

I pull out my passport and the crumpled jacket of the Kohinoor Airways ticket from a wallet and place them on the desk. He does not bother to open the passport after seeing 'Republic of India' embossed in gold below the national insignia. He picks up the ticket and looks at it closely. The flight coupons are gone but the last page carries carbon prints of the operative information: Bombay, New York JFK, Newark, Kansas City, flight numbers with dates, fare amount and free baggage allowance.

Satisfied, Jones smiles broadly, apologizes profusely, picks up the phone and calls Nancy in. It is 6:10 a.m.

"We'll put you on the seven o'clock flight, sir. You'll be in Kansas City by eight thirty, local time." He declares very generously, relief evident in his tone.

Now it is my turn to be perplexed. Except for verification of my Indian nationality and Kohinoor Airways ticket, nothing has changed. From my standpoint, that should have no bearing on Eastern's seat availability. And yet the closed flight has miraculously opened.

Jones leans back and stretches in his chair. His taut muscles have visibly relaxed.

"I'm glad you've changed your mind. But I don't see what prompted it." I cannot resist my curiosity.

"We've put you through choppy weather, haven't we?" He uses the airline lingo, ignoring my comment.

"Well, I was getting worried." I admit.

"Let's make up for the inconvenience. We'll upgrade you to first class."

"Wow! That'll be wonderful!" His offer thrills me; I am not used to air travel, much less first class. But it also strikes me that such a gesture would be considered unnecessary in my own country. Back home, we do not much care for the convenience of the user of a product or service. Naturally, the suppliers show no desire to compensate customers for inconvenience. Perhaps that difference in attitude is what separates a free-market system from a planned economy, at least from the consumers' viewpoint.

"There's plenty of time for your flight; can I offer you some coffee?" Mike Jones' question brings me to my present setting. His tone sounds welcoming, even jovial.

"I could do with a cup. Thanks."

"Cream and sugar?" Cream is new for me. We lace coffee with milk.

"Yes please."

He gets up from his chair, walks to the sideboard along one wall and pours coffee from a carafe into polystyrene cups. He brings one over to me along with sachets of sugar and Coffee-mate. Then he walks back to his chair and sits down.

I am dying to know the reasons for the last fifteen minutes' events. I nag him to let me in on the secret.

"You know," he finally begins. His pitch turns conspiratorial, "I shouldn't be telling you this but I guess it's only fair that you know after the trouble you've been through."

"Thanks." I murmur my appreciation for his kindness.

"Do you know about the siege of our embassy in Tehran?" He sips unsweetened black coffee from his cup.

"I read about it around three weeks back." I do not think he would be interested to know that I was in India then.

"Good. So you're aware of the Iranians holding our diplomatic staff hostage. That's illegal but they couldn't care less."

"So?" I fail to connect this international conspiracy to my travel.

"Our relations with Iran have been strained since their Shah's overthrow; now they're broken." He stops to sip from his cup again. I am none the wiser, still not able to see where he is heading.

"I can understand that. But what's international politics got to do with my boarding a plane?" I cannot stop myself from spilling my impatience.

"Good question. There's a connection." He seems to enjoy weaving mystery into the story.

"Really?" I suspect I sound curious when, in fact, I am getting irritated with his preamble. I want him to come to the crux.

"Well, we can't say what'll happen next, but they may put our payments on hold." He stops again, taking his time to finish his coffee. I find it cruel.

"May be, but where do I fit between you and the Iranians?" I feel like physically pushing him to move on.

"So we're tacitly instructed to turn down Iran Air passengers. We thought you were one. Your bag has an Iran Air tag." He pulls the rabbit out of a hat.

"The 'IA' on the tag stands for Indian Airlines, not Iran Air." I clear his misunderstanding.

"Fine, but you also look Iranian, don't you?"

I do not think he expects an answer, but I decide to play the Devil's advocate.

"Let's assume for a minute that I'm indeed Iranian. What's my fault in the hostage drama? I've done nothing wrong."

"You're right, but we run a commercial enterprise. We must take precautions to protect our financial interests." He sounds serious.

There is a knock on the door. Nancy enters without waiting for her manager's clearance. He instructs her to upgrade me to first class and check my bags in for the seven o'clock flight. Her eyebrows jump half-way up her forehead. I turn my head away to hide my amusement.

"His ticket's no problem. He's not an Iran Air passenger." He clarifies.

"Oh, really?" she squeaks before following her orders.

I finish the coffee, get up and start to leave. At the door, I turn around.

"As soon as I land in Kansas City, I'm going to call the press and tell my story."

"If I were you, I wouldn't. What'd you reckon I upgraded you for?" Both of us laugh at the hint of the *quid pro quo*. I step out.

"Have a pleasant flight." Nancy hands me my reissued boarding pass and flashes her sweet yet plastic smile.

"Thanks." I am on my way, again . . . Finally.

Three

The concourse is fairly crowded now. It is easy to make out frequent flyers from their assured gait and brisk pace, needing no directions. Novices like me, on the other hand, stop every few metres to check and re-check the information boards. Almost everyone in view has either a drink or a snack in their hands: soda pop, coffee, shake, juice, sandwich, fries, fruit, chocolate, cookies. Those with no drink or snack are chewing gum. I am not accustomed to seeing people drinking or eating all the time.

The walk to gate B29 is uncomplicated. Americans have yet to feel the need for impervious airport security. The annoying TSA barriers, metal detector door frames, elaborate x-ray screening and obtrusive pat-downs are still decades away.

Eastern's flight 824 to Kansas City is on schedule. My elite boarding pass accords me priority access. The first class section is small, just twelve seats in three rows divided by the central aisle. Only seven are occupied. Each seat is upholstered in deep blue leather, separated from the adjoining one by a wide cushioned armrest. I ease myself into 3A by the window.

The stewardess, smartly dressed in a blue skirt, beige blouse and red scarf, brings a selection of beverages. The rest of the crew is rushing through the pre-departure routine to make sure the flight leaves on time. Unlike in India, punctuality seems to be an obsession here.

When the plane's door is about to be closed, a man in his mid-fifties walks in. He is slim, of medium height and looks fit for his age. His designer grey suit, white dress shirt and expensive silk tie exude affluence and perhaps success. The stewardess welcomes him as if they know each other very well and takes his jacket to hang in the coat rack. May be he is a regular on this run.

He looks at his boarding pass to verify his assigned place and lowers himself in the aisle seat next to me. I cannot but notice the Alfred Dunhill gold and mother-of-pearl cufflinks holding his shirt's French cuffs together. I recall seeing them in windows of designer brand shops on Manhattan's chic Park Avenue. I am impressed.

The DC 8 is pushed back off the stand, then the engines come alive and it starts rolling forward. The gentleman in the next seat buckles his seat belt, turns to me and wishes me "Good morning." He has a charming manner and a nice timbre to his voice. I return his greeting just as the stewardess proffers magazines and morning newspapers. He picks *The New York Times*; I choose *The Washington Post* and *Sports Illustrated*.

The *Post's* front page carries Ayatollah Ruhollah Khomeini's threat of putting the American hostages on trial in the occupied US Embassy and a report on militants planting explosives throughout the embassy compound to thwart any rescue attempt. Clearly, the hostage crisis is turning grim. And I feel inadvertently yet inextricably tied to it.

Elsewhere, Meryl Streep and Don Gummer are blessed with their first child, a son. I am an ardent Streep fan since *Deer Hunter*. Reading the news about her seems like meeting an old friend, suddenly bringing out my feeling of loneliness in this unfamiliar land. In an effort to cheer my mind up, I leaf through *Sports Illustrated*. The popular magazine turns out to be a huge disappointment. It has nothing on soccer or badminton, much less cricket. With the National Football League well underway, the issue is, understandably, devoted to the tournament. But pages and pages of glossy photographs showing football players I do not know fail to hold my interest for too long. I wonder if knowing them would have helped because their faces are veiled behind the shroud of their helmets anyway. While I bend forward to put the periodicals in the seat pocket in front of me, the jet lifts off the ground. The sun is rising in a clear blue sky outside.

As soon as the captain extinguishes the no smoking signs, Mr. French Cuffs folds his newspaper away, takes out a pack of Pall Malls from his shirt pocket, pulls a cigarette out and sticks it between his lips. He has to straighten and stretch his right leg to reach into his trouser pocket and extract a fluted sterling silver DuPont lighter. In one smooth action, he flips its top open, thumbs the flint wheel to ignite the flame and lights the tip of the cigarette jutting from his mouth. He draws a deep swig and exhales a cloud. The nicotine fix visibly relaxes him. Smoking is still fashionable; it would not be passé for another few years.

By the time he is through with the cigarette, the fasten seat belt signs are switched off.

"Nice day." He says, leaning to see the azure sky outside.

"It is. Are you going to Kansas City?" I ask.

"No, no. Las Vegas. I catch a connection in Kansas City."

"On a holiday?" All I know about Las Vegas is gambling. He appears mildly surprised with my question. I wonder why.

"Well, work actually."

"What do you do?"

"I'm in entertainment business." His surprise turns to mild irritation. Again, I do not understand why.

"Wow, that's something. What kind of entertainment? Films, theatre, TV?"

"TV, mostly." Now he is getting more than a little flustered. But I am determined to bring the exchange to its logical end.

"Interesting. What exactly do you do on TV? Act, write scripts, direct?" My question stumps him.

"Well, pretty much everything, I guess."

His voice has developed an abrasive edge now. I am not sure if I should continue this conversation but do not want to let go midway. After all, my teachers and family have always goaded me to bring everything I attempt to its fruition.

"I'm sorry if I sound nosy, but the fact of the matter is that I arrived in this country barely ten days back to join graduate school and haven't had the opportunity to watch TV." I want to sound apologetic, hoping my attempt succeeds.

The explanation causes his demeanour to change; sparkling laughter lights up his eyes.

"Now, that explains your prying questions. I'm Ronny Parton and my show is telecast every evening. Where're you from?" I suspect 'prying questions' is his euphemism for 'naïveté' but decide to give him the benefit of the doubt.

"India. I'll remember to watch your show at the first opportunity." I try to express genuine interest.

"Couldn't imagine having to introduce myself in the US of A. I thought you were trying to be a smart Alec. I'm wondering 'what's this kid up to?' But now I know better." His manner of speaking is transparent. I appreciate his candour.

"We get to see Hollywood films in India but virtually no American TV shows." I offer my alibi.

"I presume your education system would be similar to ours?" He shifts the topic.

"The present system is somewhat like the British system but the ancient Indian practice was very different."

"How?" He turns his head to look at me.

"The kids were sent to the teacher's, that is *guru*'s, abode to be under his tutelage round the clock. The place where they lived and studied for years on end was called *gurucool*."

"I know *guru* is a very knowledgeable teacher. But why *gurucool*?" He enquires with the keenness of a student.

"*Cool* in Sanskrit can be broadly translated as domain. So *gurucool* would be *guru*'s domain."

"A sort of residential school." He interprets my information.

"Far more profound and comprehensive than that. More like a seminary to impart training and administer what is called *sanskar* in Sanskrit."

"What does it mean?" The childlike freshness in his question motivates me to tread on a rather complex notion.

"Actually there is no exact translation of *sanskar* in English. 'Instilling virtuous ethos' would be a loose description of the process that is *sanskar*." I take a stab at explaining a concept that is hard to imagine for the uninitiated, let alone fully comprehend.

"How did they do that?"

"By constantly being in the *guru*'s close proximity for many years. The training and *sanskar* not only imbued wisdom in the student but also helped build his character." I hope he does not ask any more questions simply because I am in no position to provide further insight into the ancient Indian pedagogy.

Luckily for me, the stewardess interrupts the conversation to serve breakfast: orange juice, cereal, omelet, sausages, bread roll and preserves, followed by coffee. The omelet is bland, devoid of savoury filling I like; the sausages taste synthetic. It is easy to guess why my co-passenger has ordered a special meal of orange juice and fruits.

Mr. Parton is more interested in knowing about India than enjoying his breakfast, openly admitting his ignorance of my country beyond the Taj Mahal.

"What's Indian food like?"

"The food in each of our states is different, so there's no single description of Indian food. And many Indians are complete vegetarians." My answer surprises him.

"You mean even chicken's not permitted? I know pork's taboo to some and beef to some others."

"Hard core vegetarians don't touch eggs; chicken's unthinkable."

"That sounds like a sacrifice, doesn't it?" He purses his lips. I decide to take the topic forward.

"Not quite. After all, the human body is designed for vegetarian diet." I share a little known theory.

"Really? Why do you say that?" His twinkling eyes reflect a desire to know.

"Carnivores have short intestines because meat proteins get digested quickly. Herbivores need extended guts because vegetables take more time to break down. Humans have long alimentary canals."

"Actually, I thought it would be the other way around." He is honest.

The discussion then meanders through history and geography to Indian philosophy of life vis-à-vis western.

"The difference between western philosophy and ours is mirrored in our medical sciences." My introduction of the subject leaves him clueless.

"I don't get you." He is all attention now. I feel encouraged to present my argument.

"The ancient Indian life science is called *Ayurved*. Allopathy aims at getting rid of the organism causing the illness; *Ayurved* aims at developing immunity to that organism. The approach of Allopathy is 'germ or me'; implying 'the winner takes it all'. The approach of *Ayurved*, on the other hand, is 'germ and me', seeking co-existence with every species on God's green Earth."

My metaphor takes time to sink in. May be he does not expect a college kid to talk about a profound subject like life's philosophy. Perhaps he is brooding over what I just said. But then again, he may be thinking, 'this guy's crazy'. There is no way to tell.

"Interesting." He remarks, without betraying his thoughts.

The conversation and the breakfast end simultaneously.

As soon as the stewardess clears the trays, the fasten seat belt and no smoking signs light up. The fuselage tilts forward as our descent into Kansas City commences. The increasing pressure at the drop in altitude induces mild pain in my ears. I attempt a yawn to pop them. That helps a little but not much. Luckily, the air traffic control clears the landing without putting us in a holding pattern. Before long, the wheels touch the tarmac with a dull thud, followed instantaneously by a loud wheeze as the pilots employ reverse thrust to slow the plane down.

If I had any doubts about the fame of my co-passenger, they are quickly banished when we step into the terminal building. Noticing the deplaning celebrity, many in the milling crowd mob him, thrusting whatever they can find to get his autograph: boarding passes, calling cards, paper napkins, note pads, books, magazines. Some women want him to sign on their clothing. Mr. Parton is obviously a much sought after megastar. He patiently obliges his fans for several minutes, finally excusing himself at the disappointment of some.

We walk down the concourse together until he sees the arrow pointing to the airline's lounge for first class passengers and heads in that direction. I need to continue on to the baggage claim hall. As we part, Ronny Parton warmly shakes my hand and wishes me success in my studies.

"Thanks for teaching me that a hero is zero without his fans. It'll stop my ego from bloating up." He shares his parting thought, flooring me with his humility.

I wonder if an Indian show business star would react the same way.

Four

I alight from the bus. The stop is a small shop run by a Continental Trailways franchisee. A young man, probably of my age, is occupying the sparsely furnished office, listening to James Taylor's "In My Dreams I Am Going to Carolina" on the radio. I daydream of going back to India, a pang of homesickness searing through my midriff. The thought of not knowing anyone in this small university town adds to my already acute loneliness.

Although I have not had much of an opportunity to know this area, it does seem a little more laid back compared to New York City or even Washington, DC. But the area around downtown Kansas City felt decidedly scary, frequented by drug addicts and petty criminals out to mug unsuspecting travelers. Fortunately, the grandfatherly African American driver of the Greyhound service from the airport was kind enough to drop me at the Continental Trailways terminal, even though it is a little distance beyond his final stop.

A two-hour wait there followed by a ninety-minute ride on another bus has delivered me in front of the young man enjoying his music. Seeing my two heavy suitcases, he realizes I cannot go anywhere without a vehicle, rises from his chair and offers to take me to my destination. I am more than happy to accept his help. The drive to the university's Administration Office is short, barely three minutes. I am not sure how much to pay for it. He asks for a dollar, which I presume is a fair charge. In my mind, however, it works out to eight Indian rupees. A similar cab ride in India would not cost more than a fifth of that.

I find my way to the Foreign Students Department. A tall brunette in her thirties enthusiastically welcomes me with a gleaming smile of orderly snow-white teeth. She has dark eyes, Barbara Streisand nose and a wide mouth of thin lips.

"Good afternoon. I am Gururaj Abhyankar. Here to join the MBA programme." I shake her hand.

"Good to see you. I'm Jane Hunter, assistant in the Foreign Students Department. We've been expecting you. Hope you had a pleasant journey."

"Yes, I did. Thanks." I decide to keep my meeting with Ronny Parton to myself.

"Let me find out if Mr. Copperthwaite can see you." She returns to her seat, calls on the intercom and points to the door to the foreign students' adviser's office. I ask Jane to keep an eye on my bags and step into the adviser's office, noticing the digital clock on the wall showing 2:33 p.m.

James Copperthwaite is nothing like I had imagined from his correspondence. His precise and succinct letters suggested a disciplined bearing.

In person, Mr. Copperthwaite is a fifty-something beanbag dressed in an olive three-piece woolen suit. I am reminded of Sir Winston Churchill *sans* the cigar. He has a wide forehead, small grey eyes and a sagging jowl hiding half the Shell knot of his ochre necktie. The boyish ruffled curls on his pate contrast with his otherwise elderly persona. He peers at me over the half-moon reading glasses slung low on his bulbous nose and pops a peppermint into his mouth from a large glass jar on the desk.

In addition to the jar, the desk is strewn with papers and folders. A thick winter overcoat is huddled in an untidy heap on the sofa by the wall. Evidently his diet, work habits and life style are anything but disciplined. And he does not appear to be the brightest bulb on the Christmas tree.

"Welcome to the campus. Hope you had a good trip." He smiles and extends his hand to shake mine without even an iota of enthusiasm. Somehow his reception sounds hollow, unconvincing. His body language is of a man who finds every new student a burden.

"Oh, yes. Your directions were just perfect." I respond mechanically, not feeling the appreciation my comment conveys. I do not relish the prospect of meeting him frequently, wishing that his role in my campus life would be minimal.

"Good. Jane should be able to help you with the paperwork and guide you to your dormitory. But please feel free to approach me anytime you want."

I am happy to leave his cheerless office and re-enter Jane's vibrant orbit. If she is surprised over the brevity of my meeting with her boss, she hides it.

"Why don't you see one of the faculty advisers in the Academics Department at the end of the hall? In the meantime, I'll call your host family." It is evident that Jane is doing her best to help me adjust to my new environment. But I doubt if she can imagine the void of desolation in my stomach caused by being so far removed from home. It must be approaching two fifteen in the night in Pune, I reflect.

The faculty advisers occupy five small cabins lined along one wall of the Academics Department. I introduce myself to the assistant sitting at the entrance and ask her if I can meet one of the advisers. She places me in a queue. Fortunately, the wait is not long.

"Please see Mrs. Dexter in the second cubicle from left." She directs me after about ten minutes, pointing to the enclosure from where a student has emerged.

"Thanks." I am not sure what this meeting is for.

Mrs. Dexter appears old enough to be a grandmother. She could easily pass as Margaret Thatcher's elder sister. I speculate if she has heard the new British Prime Minister's sobriquet as 'the only man' in the British Cabinet. The world is still tolerant of gender-specific monikers and would remain so for another few years.

Mrs. Dexter looks tired. She smiles at me without compromising the Thatcheresque sternness of her demeanour. I take the chair by her desk and introduce myself. I have to spell my name to enable her punch the correct alphabets on the keyboard in front of her.

"Okay, you're a new graduate student in business administration. Your bachelor's was in engineering." She begins, looking at the computer monitor on her desk.

"That's right." I confirm my background.

"You need to earn fifty four hours of credit to complete your master's programme; eighteen each of background courses, core courses and electives. You can take more if you want, of course, but fifty four is the minimum for non-business background." Her rattling off as if she makes the announcement every so often reminds me of the pre-flight safety briefing on my journey earlier today. I sideline the thought and focus on the topic under discussion.

"Do I need to meet any specific conditions as a foreign student?"

"As an alien on F-1 visa, you've to be a full-time student. That means you've to take courses adding up to a minimum of six credits every term. You can go as high as twelve, but that's uncommon."

She looks at me as if I am a mentally challenged ten-year-old. Her calling me an alien makes me picture myself with moss-green skin, bulging eyes and no hair. I try to imagine Mrs. Dexter's reaction if it were really so. I suppress the burst of laughter and continue the exchange, pretending to be serious.

"All the courses I want to take are of three credit hours, so I can enroll in two, three or four courses every term?" I hope she thinks I am smarter than a ten-year-old dimwit.

"Yes, that's right."

Her introduction is a revelation. Back in India, the courses we take each semester are fixed. No change is permitted till the final term, when students have the freedom to pick one elective from a choice of three. I need to know more about the system here.

"Am I free to choose the subjects for each term?" I ask, incredulous.

"Yes, as long as you cover the background and core courses before advancing to your electives."

I am happy with the flexibility. More importantly, I am thrilled by the prospect of completing my degree at least six months earlier than the two years I expected. My mental high helps in quickly deciding the sequence in which I will take the eighteen courses. But the subsequent interaction pulls down my spirits as rapidly.

"Are you aware of the other requirements graduate students must meet?"

"I'm not sure which ones you've in mind." I try to camouflage my ignorance.

"The ones related to the grades." Her voice has acquired new firmness.

"Not really, except the grade point average." I consider it prudent to find out now rather than later.

"You need to score over ninety points for an A grade, over eighty for a B, over seventy for a C and over sixty for a D. Below that is F or fail territory. Some instructors may grade on percentile but that's not the norm. Graduate students cannot get a D, much less an F. And you're allowed only two C grades in your entire master's programme, no more." Her conditions hit me like a thunderbolt.

Right through my scholastic history, I may have scored more than ninety points once or twice, if at all. Scores over eighty were less rare, but only slightly. I would be ecstatic every time I crossed seventy and very happy beyond sixty. In fact, in the Indian rating system, students are awarded 'first class with distinction' for scoring over sixty six percent overall points, 'first class' for between sixty and sixty six percent, 'second class' for between forty five and sixty and 'third class' for between thirty five and forty five. Students are declared 'fail' if they fall short of the thirty five points threshold in any course.

My final year engineering score was sixty five percent, earning me a 'first class' rating, considered commendable. And now Margaret Thatcher's elder sister wants to throw me out of the master's programme if I score as many here.

I sense strength draining out of my body. All sorts of humiliating scenarios run through my mind. If the school throws me out, my visa automatically expires, forcing me to return home. Going back to India without the degree I came here for would be an utter shame. I would be mortified to show my face to family or friends. And all the effort and money used up on the abortive adventure would be wasted.

"Is there anything else you want to know?" Mrs. Dexter's question shakes me out of my trance. I only need one last clarification.

"What're my options if halfway through the term I realize I'm unlikely to get A or B in any subject?" I ask.

"You can drop it before the assigned drop deadline." I get a feeling from her tone that she wants to add 'elementary, my dear alien' in Sherlock Holmes' style.

My mind goes into overdrive. To avoid the ignominy of getting thrown out, I must steer clear of D and possibly even C. If I take only two courses, I can focus on them and ensure decent grades. But, in case I am unable to score well in spite of the effort, that grade would stick since I would not be able to drop any course. It may be prudent to have a cushion. Taking four courses can provide it; I can drop up to two if I fare poorly. But four courses instead of three or two would allow less time to study for each subject, minimizing the chances of getting desired grades. It is a tough call.

"What're you thinking about?" Mrs. Dexter asks, noticing my stare right through her.

"I'm not able to decide if it's better to take two courses or four." I confess my dilemma.

"If I were you, my pick would be three." She sounds sincere. Even as I balance the pros and cons of her choice, I notice my getting accustomed to 'if I were you' that people back home almost never use.

"I think I'll go by your advice." I take the call.

"It'll be a good idea for you to start with industrial sociology, statistics and principles of marketing. You may've done some statistics in your undergraduate programme so you won't need to study much for it here." Her logic is impeccable; I cannot argue with it.

The process thereafter is quick. Fortunately, the timings of the three courses do not clash; industrial sociology in the morning, followed in the afternoon by principles of marketing and statistics. As I leave Mrs. Dexter's cubicle, the fear of the grading system lingers in my mind. I feel the tension in my limbs.

"What took you so long?" Jane Hunter asks when I return to her office. But before I can respond, her attention gets diverted to the person coming in from across the hallway.

"Ah, here's Edwin McGovern. Ed, Donna and their daughter Anissa comprise your host family. Ed teaches accounting at the B-school, so he may be your instructor sometime later on." She points at a man in his late twenties walking towards us, unbuttoning his quilt-lined hooded winter jacket. He looks like a college student. I am surprised to hear that he is not only married but is also a father.

Thankfully, Edwin is not called my 'local guardian' as he would be in India. That would be a misnomer for someone barely two or three years my elder. And Donna could possibly be younger.

"Everyone calls me Ed." He extends his hand with a smile. His voice is deep; handshake firm. I like that.

"And everyone calls me Guru."

Ed is short, not more than five feet five and slightly built. The straight blonde hair falling on his forehead and neatly trimmed full beard hide his handsome looks; the large blue eyes behind his small wire frame glasses are calm. He is casually dressed in a polo neck jumper and corduroy jeans. His tan Roper cowboy boots and matching leather belt appear new. I find them neat.

"Nice to meet you, Ed. Dashing boots and belt." I complement him, withdrawing my hand from his.

"Thanks. Love them. Hope I didn't take too long to get here." His speech is cultured, suggesting a suave persona.

"Not at all. I just finished enrolling myself in the classes for the first term. Your timing's perfect."

"Good. How's it that you're starting school in winter and not fall?" He poses a question that most would.

"Because of one dollar." I smile, knowing my answer will baffle him.

"One dollar? I don't get it." His forehead gathers creases.

"I sat for my GMAT last year but applied to this school almost a year later. By then, Educational Testing Service up in New Jersey had raised the additional report fee by a dollar."

"What's additional report fee?"

"The fee they charge to send the score to schools other than the ones you list before appearing for your GMAT.

"So?" He still does not get it.

"I didn't know of the change. By the time they informed me, I sent the additional dollar and they confirmed my score to the school, the fall trimester was underway." I clarify.

"Crazy." He shakes his head.

Ed helps me lug the heavy bags to my dorm five hundred yards away across the road. It is an arduous task but Ed is uncomplaining, even after I am allotted a room on the second floor. We haul the suitcases up the stairs and down the long corridor to room two forty nine in the east wing of the building.

It is more spacious than I had expected. The light yellow birch wood furniture is new or recently polished at any rate: a large closet and a dresser with mirror covering most of the south wall, a bunk bed along the north wall and a long desk accompanied by two chairs below the wide sliding window on the east side across from the door. The window overlooks the dorm's parking lot, fast filling up as students return after the brief term-break.

Ed wants to leave before I start unpacking. I let my baggage remain in the middle of the room and go downstairs to see him off. We walk together to the parking lot by the Administration building. I notice his slow waddle and wonder if the new boots have caused it. He is not very talkative but fills me on his family.

"Donna's still an undergrad. She took a year off when Anissa was born in the winter before last. You'll meet them over the week-end."

"That'll be great. Look forward to it."

"That's our home number. Please feel free to call if you need anything." He hands me a slip of paper while getting into his maroon Chevy Citation.

"Thanks, Ed. See you again soon."

Five

When I return to the dorm, mayhem has broken loose in my room. Three guys are loudly abusing the clutter on the floor, using choicest swearwords in English language. The tall, muscular hunk of a man among them is standing in the middle, ready to heave my luggage over the desk and out the window. His boyish features look incongruent on the thick neck and wrestler's physique. He has a triangular face tapering down to a small chin, curly black hair and almond-shaped dark eyes. His nose is the residue of a botched-up repair job after a nasty fight.

"Goddammit, man! What the fuck's this?" He questions me, pointing at my suitcases. Some welcome, I think to myself. His own baggage and an electric guitar with its amplifier are scattered around the room, no less messy than my belongings. But I think it wise to lighten up the mood. It would be foolhardy to take this giant on.

"We're in Seymours Hall dorm. Rearrange the letters in the name and you get 'our messy hall'. That's what this is." I explain with a smile to reduce the tension, extending a hand of friendship to him.

"Smart. Tim Hamilton." He covers half the room in one step to reach me and crush my knuckles. Then he laughs out loud, a raucous chuckle that dimples his cheeks.

"Gururaj. You can call me Guru." I introduce myself, fighting the urge to massage my hurting fingers.

I keep my everyday campus clothes in the closet and push the suitcases under the bed, leaving Tim's property spread out on the floor. Then I repeat his opening words verbatim.

"You got me there, man." He laughs again; this time at himself. He is surely a sport. I like that.

"Where're you from, Tim?" I ask, having got even with him.

"Iowa. On a football scholarship here." That explains the brawn and vice-like handshake.

"I'm from India." I volunteer the information, wondering if he would confuse it with Indiana.

"What are you here to study?" One of Tim's friends wants to know.

"Business management."

"Wow!" I do not understand why my course of study should elicit his reaction. But I ignore it.

"Been here long, Tim?" I turn to my roommate.

"Not really. I'm a freshman. Goddammit man, hate coming back after a break." I tell myself to get used to his frequent swearing. 'Goddammit' seems to be the mildest term in his lexicon.

Tim Hamilton hangs his clothes in the closet, neatly stows his guitar and amplifier away in the space separating one end of the closet from the wall and departs with his friends. It is 4:45 p.m.

When I am alone in the room, I feel engulfed by the pall of loneliness. It is an odd feeling I have never experienced before. I can neither go and meet anyone nor invite someone over. I long for my faraway home, family and friends; my eyes well up. Inexplicably, the fact that my day is their night and my night their day, deepens my sense of solitude.

Once the surge of emotion recedes, I become conscious of my hunger. I have not eaten anything since the unappetizing breakfast on the plane. I do not know where to find food. The best person to ask is Mrs. Kelly, the dorm's house mother. She more resembles a doting grandmother.

"Why don't you walk down to Holden Street? You'll surely be able to get something to eat over there." She proceeds to give me the directions to Holden.

It is nice to walk on clean, broad sidewalks in the crisp evening air, although I would have preferred the ambient temperature to be a few notches higher. Mrs. Kelly's directions are spot on. I find a small restaurant on the corner of Holden and Ming. Aunt Belinda's Eatery is empty. The middle-aged plump lady running the place is happy to see me enter and reaches my table with a note pad and pen as soon as I am seated.

"What'd you like to drink, sir?" She asks. The menu cards are placed under the sheet glass top of each table.

"Water, please." My preference mildly surprises her. I suspect she expected to hear me order juice or soda pop.

"Sparkling or still?"

"Still would be fine."

"With ice?"

"Without ice, please."

"And what'd you like to order, sir?"

"Hamburger and fries, please."

"Regular, double or quarter pounder?

"I think I'll go for a regular."

"With cheese?"

"No cheese, thanks." I think she has asked enough questions for the day.

"Lettuce, onions, pickle and tomatoes?"

"Only lettuce and tomatoes, please. No onions or pickle."

"Fries small, medium or large?" I am getting irritated now, my hunger sharpening the feeling.

"Medium, please."

"Thanks. That'll take about ten minutes." What a relief!

I find it funny that eight questions had to be answered to order three basic items. And even though I am the only diner in the place, the lady wrote down my choice as if she would confuse it with some other customer's or simply forget. I think of it as tyranny of choice and reluctance to depend entirely on one's memory. This is a far cry from the way people work back home. When my six friends took me to a restaurant in Pune last month for my send-off, the waiter served nineteen items without asking a single question or writing down a single word.

After I finish the meal, I ask the lady to fetch my bill. She looks at me with a confused look in her eyes. I act out writing to make myself understood.

"Oh, you mean the cheque?" She sounds amused. I am dumbfounded. We pay a bill with cash or a cheque. I make a note of the new terminology.

The cheque, when it arrives, is in the amount of $2.49. I remember my cousin in New Jersey mentioning that patrons are expected to pay fifteen percent tip for service, calling it gratuity. In my case, the gratuity works out to about forty cents. I am not certain if it will be considered appropriate. I decide to err on the right side and leave a total of four dollars, letting the lady keep $1.51 for serving me. I am sure my friends in India would seriously question my sanity if they ever came to know I tipped sixty percent of the charge for food. I treat it as cost of learning.

I stroll back to the dorm wondering what I am going to do till bedtime. My problem gets solved automatically.

A few minutes after I return to my room, I hear a knock on the door. No one is expected to come looking for me. Must be someone wanting to see Tim. When I open the door, I find two young men from the Indian subcontinent in the corridor.

"Hi, you are Gururaj, right? I'm Atif and this is Aamer. We're from Pakistan." They must have known of my arrival from Jane Hunter.

"Guru to my friends."

We shake hands. Atif is slim, of medium height and fair by south Asian standards. He has an oval face, light brown eyes behind wire rim glasses and neatly groomed hair. Aamer, on the other hand, is short and muscular, darkish with a square face, sporting a thin moustache and disheveled hair.

I have never seen a Pakistani before, let alone met. Our countries have fought three bitter wars in three decades. For every Indian, Pakistan is the enemy. I am sure every

Pakistani also thinks of India the same way. It is both sad and ironic.

Carved out of India in 1947 to give the Moslems across the subcontinent a country they can call their own, Pakistan shares history and many aspects of culture with my country. But India adopted the constitution of a secular democracy while Pakistan chose to be an Islamic state often ruled by military dictators snatching power from elected representatives. The governments of the two countries have rarely seen eye to eye. Naturally, people-to-people contact is all but nonexistent. The relationship between the two neighbours is dictated by distrust, if not downright hatred. The hostility has meant large outlays on both sides for defense expenditure, at the cost of health care, education and infrastructure. The frozen relations have thawed lately but mutual suspicion is still the norm.

On this background, I do not know how to deal with the two Pakistanis standing in the hallway. Atif has no such doubts.

"We're going to the mall. Why don't you join us? You can buy linen and pillows, if you haven't already." I admit to myself that I had forgotten about these and would have found it hard to sleep without them. It makes sense to take Atif on his offer but deep down I am a little apprehensive of foul play. I treat it as nothing more than the fear of the unknown and push myself to go with them.

We get into Aamer's beat-up Oldsmobile Cutlass. Its engine booms through a cracked muffler as soon as Aamer turns the key in the ignition. I doubt if it is good to take us anywhere. Much to my relief though, it does. I get a chance to buy the few items I need: bed sheets, a blanket, pillows, soap and shampoo. When we get back to the dorm and dump my purchases in the room, Atif invites me to go to their home on Highland Avenue. I have nothing better to do so I agree.

They occupy the upper floor of a small two-storey house. It has a narrow sitting room with a Magnavox television in the corner, a large bedroom and a small kitchen. The bathroom is on the ground floor by the entrance. We watch *Hart to Hart* starring Robert Wagner and Stefanie Powers. Sydney Sheldon's name in the credits catches me by surprise. I have read his books but never knew he created TV shows as well.

When the inevitable commercials come on, I bring up the topic that has stressed me up since leaving Mrs. Dexter's cubicle. But I do not want to appear worried.

"How hard is it to get decent grades here?" I ask Atif, making it sound casual.

"Not very, if you attend classes and study regularly." I hear what I want to hear and that eases my tension a little. But I cannot dispel it completely even after deciding to take things as they come.

When I return to my room, Tim is fast asleep. I have had a long day, starting in Washington, DC. In the few hours since my arrival here, I have made new friends. I consider it a day well spent. As I close my eyes on the upper bunk, it must be morning in India.

The grade-phobia continues to haunt me until I eventually fall asleep.

Six

When I open my eyes in the morning, the room's ceiling stares in my face from four feet above. My mind takes a few seconds to recognize the surroundings. I quickly climb down from the bunk bed, feeling enthusiastic at the prospect of attending my classes.

Up until now, it has never been so. Back in India, the first day of school was an event I held visceral aversion for. It always signified the end of a happy break that only masochists would find enjoyable.

My dislike for high school was driven by compelling reasons. Pune, famous for its educational institutions, is home to some of the most renowned schools in the country. Mine has always prided in being the best of the lot. It ranks the students in descending order of their examination scores, placing the first fifty in division A, the next fifty in B and so on. I somehow managed to be in division A, but barely. Within that division, I generally stood in the bottom half, a ground for much displeasure of my parents.

The membership of division A provided a modicum of respect from students in other divisions. But the teachers seemed to consider only the top ten students in the division as rightful members of the august club. The rest were treated like freeloaders and dealt with harshness normally reserved for delinquents.

The school accorded a high premium to scholastic performance. Those who scored well in exams were rewarded with opportunities in dramatics, debates, elocution and inter-school competitions, not to mention access to special training. My name never featured in those lists.

With each school free to set its own curriculum, ours invariably chose the toughest. It included fourteen subjects in addition to drawing and craft: four languages, arithmetic, algebra, geometry, physics, chemistry, botany, zoology, history, geography and civics. I did not like many of these. And just as school children everywhere do, we found much of what was taught irrelevant to our lives. For example, we could never understand how punishment for not memorizing dates by rote would help us learn about how and why events unfolded in history.

We were convinced that all our teachers had to delete the word 'gentle' from their vocabulary before joining the school. Enforcing discipline was their primary duty. They carried it out with missionary zeal sharpened with liberal use of the stick.

The primary school got over after the fourth year and we joined the high school in the fifth. The welcome I got on the first day of high school is still stinging fresh in my memory. I had celebrated my tenth birthday a few months earlier. Reaching that milestone coupled with the extravagance of a different teacher for each subject, made me think of myself as a big boy. The last lecture of the day was physics, taught by Mr. D. S. Pathak, a short, stocky and grim teacher we referred to as DSP, a more widespread initialism for district superintendent of police, a senior position in the force. DSP the teacher was reputedly a more sclerotic disciplinarian than a hardened police officer.

Each school-day ended with the playing of the national anthem on the public address system. During the anthem, we stood at attention in the aisles of our classroom. On this particular day, the boy standing in front of me farted midway through the anthem. I tried the best I could to stifle my laughter but could not completely muffle it. After the anthem ended, DSP walked up to me, let loose a tight slap across my face and walked off without a word. I was left with no choice but to swallow the insult and ignore the injury.

DSP and other teachers after him continued to use their hands, canes and foot-rulers to enforce their control over us. The more ferocious among them even launched the felt-lined wooden brick of a chalkboard duster as a missile to bring our adolescent enthusiasm down. The beleaguered students branded this arsenal 'weapons of class destruction' and bemoaned the United Nations' reluctance to ban it in schools. We remained our teachers' captive targets for seven years till we matriculated and qualified for college.

After the internment suffered in high school, college felt liberating. There was obviously no question of physical torture, but even the attendance was not mandatory. I reacted to the newfound freedom like Champaign in a shaken-up bottle gushing out on popping of the cork. 'Untamed' is the appropriate description of my behaviour then.

The emancipation was short lived, though. Before long, I understood the difficulty level of the pre-engineering course and recognized the need to be serious about my grades. Competition to enroll in engineering school was fierce and I certainly had no intention of failing to qualify.

Once I joined engineering, life turned into drudgery. Uninteresting classroom lectures on cold objects like metals, machines, stones and mortar or hard to imagine concepts like entropy and enthalpy were inter-spread with hours spent in dreary laboratories housing an array of unfriendly equipment. The holidays provided the only respite. Understandably, I never felt ready to relinquish it.

But here in America, I am setting out to study a more interesting side of life. Naturally, I am looking forward to opening a new innings.

My first lecture is on industrial sociology. I have interacted with workers and staff in an industrial unit and gained some knowledge of how they think. Now I hope to understand the reasons behind their behaviour. The prospect seems very appealing.

When I enter the morning class five minutes before nine o'clock, almost all the students are seated. The remaining few arrive in the next couple of minutes. I occupy the tablet-armed chair in the last row by the rear wall. Before I introduce myself to the students on my left and right, the bell rings and Dr. Donald, the instructor, walks in. I am impressed with everyone's punctuality.

Dr. Donald is a dapper man in his fifties, standing on an upright frame supporting broad shoulders. He has large brown eyes, Roman nose and Clark Gable moustache. He wears big black-framed glasses and appears to be the affable

Caucasian version of my father. I take immediate liking for him.

First up, he wants to know how many of us have work experience, either full-time or part-time. Much to my surprise, almost all the students raise their hands. This being my background course, most of the class comprises undergraduate students. And yet pretty much all of them have been working. Back in India, perhaps one or two may have raised their hand, if at all. Indian college kids rarely start work before finishing their education.

Next, Dr. Donald wants to know if anyone has worked in a factory. I am the only one to raise my hand. He asks me to describe the type of factory I worked in.

"Steel forge." I stand up and reply. The young lady on my right tugs the back of my shirt, suggesting I sit down. I am taken aback. In my culture, one must always stand to address one's teacher. Continuing to sit while speaking is considered a mark of disrespect, attracting severe opprobrium. The rules of engagement are different here.

"Did you work full-time or part-time?" Dr. Donald wants to know.

"Full-time."

"And what was your job?"

"Production supervisor."

"All right. So, you worked with blue collar workers."

"Yes, I did."

"Ok. Thanks. I'll be asking you to share your experiences as we go along." He takes out a penny from his trouser pocket and flips it to me over the heads of the students. This is probably the first time I have heard my teacher offer thanks. I am not used to anything but teachers' commands.

The instructor then proceeds to hand out the course sessions plan with a date-wise listing of the topics he intends to cover during the term. The students are expected to familiarize themselves with each day's topic before coming to the class. I need to get used to this system. Back home, the teachers cover the curriculum over the term without committing themselves to a day-by-day schedule. Also, the students study each topic after it is taught in the class. I cannot determine which system is better but the sessions here would be more interactive and that would be fun.

After the class is over, the student on my right introduces herself.

"Hi, I'm Abigail Blum, everyone calls me Gail."

"Good to meet you, Gail." I add after introducing myself.

"We haven't been in the same class before, have we?" She tries to scratch her memory.

"Couldn't have. This is my first term here. I am a graduate student."

"I'm a senior, majoring in sociology." Gail is slender and almost as tall as me. She has a round face covered with flawless pink skin, petite nose and steady mocha brown eyes below delicate eyebrows. She appears an open person, attractive without being beautiful.

"Where did you work in a forging plant?" She enquires as we exit the classroom.

"In India." I don't bother to name the city; she is unlikely to have heard of it.

"Oh, really? I thought there were only elephants, tigers and godmen doing the rope-trick." She instinctively responds but quickly realizes her comment may offend me and hastens to add, "Of course, we're so ignorant about the world beyond our immediate surroundings."

"I'm learning that." I endorse her view as we leave the building and part.

My next lecture is principles of marketing at two in the afternoon. I want to use the time till then to find a part-time on-campus job.

On my walk to the Administration building where the Employment Office is located, I reflect on my first classroom session in America. The fact that I had something different to bring to the interaction is gratifying. And it would be nice if my work experience helps the instructor explain certain topics in the curriculum. For the second time since Mrs. Dexter scared me with her grades briefing yesterday, I feel a little de-stressed, Atif's reassurance being the first. But the issue is still bothering me. I decide to ask Gail the next day about the way instructors mark the answer sheets.

The on-campus jobs section is actually a desk within the Employment Office on the second floor of the building. Ms. Jasper Hutton runs it. She is one of those people whose age cannot be guessed but I can easily see that a five-foot tailor's tape would fall short to measure her generous girth.

"Good morning. What can I do for you?" Her words come out as if she is gasping for breath. Her lungs seem inadequate to meet her body's oxygen needs while she is seated. I cannot imagine what would happen if she were to walk, much less run.

"I'm a new graduate student. I want to try for an on-campus job. What do I need to do?" She does not answer my question. Instead, she pushes the desk down with her hands to assist her legs in their effort to make her stand up. Once on her feet, she waddles the eight feet to the filing cabinet on her left, pulls out two application forms from one of the drawers and returns to her chair. The strain of the trip causes her to hyperventilate. She needs to sit quietly for several minutes to calm her breathing.

"Fill this one out to apply for an on-campus job. You can work twenty hours a week at minimum wage." She gives me one of the forms.

"Which is?" I ask.

"Two dollars and ninety cents. But it may go up in January."

"Good to know that."

"And since you said you're a graduate student, fill this one out too. You may qualify for assistantship." It is nice of her to volunteer the suggestion.

"Thank you so much." I really mean it.

It takes me ten minutes to fill out the forms and hand them back to Ms. Hutton. She asks me to check with her the next day about the two-bucks-ninety-an-hour job. It would be useful to start working again, even if part-time. I can surely do with some income.

Seven

Lunch is served at the dorm for two hours starting at noon. Not that I am looking forward to the bland food but I am hungry, having missed the breakfast to get to the class well in time.

The cafeteria covers the lower level of the dorm's west wing. It is the largest on the campus feeding around four hundred students thrice a day. The dining area is roughly the size of a tennis court and is furnished with several tables and chairs for four, some for six and a few for eight. The square island in the centre is mostly taken up by a large salad bowl containing different types of chopped lettuce: iceberg, romaine, red leaf, green leaf and bibb. It is surrounded by smaller bowls for cucumbers, tomatoes, beetroot, onions, carrots, mushrooms and olives, all sliced, as well as corn, peas and sunflower seeds. Next to the salad items are jars of dressings: French, Italian, Thousand Islands, ranch, bleu cheese, honey mustard and vinaigrette.

The wall separating the dining hall from the serving line fronting the kitchen has two doors about forty feet apart. The one on the left is to enter the serving area and that on the right to exit it. A long sideboard is placed against the wall spanning the two doors. It carries two soup kegs, a large toaster, a soda fountain and a basket filled with soup sticks and bread rolls. Further down from the door on the right, the loading end of a tunnel-type dishwasher projects from the wall to allow used tableware to be fed to its conveyor directly from the dining area. The other end of the long dishwasher is behind the wall, deep inside the kitchen.

Right by the entrance to the serving area are stacks of plastic trays and glasses. Next to them are containers carrying cutlery. I take a tray, a couple of glasses and a set of silverware before joining the line of students queuing up to be served. The unfamiliar odour of burnt lard is floating in from the kitchen behind the serving line. It causes a mild unease in my stomach. I ignore it and evaluate the three choices of main course on the day's menu. I pick the easy option of fried chicken, preferring not to venture into the unknown territory of lasagna or roast pork with apples.

"White meat or dark?" The student serving the chicken asks. I want a leg piece but do not know if it falls in white category or dark. Feeling shy to expose my ignorance, I decide to take a fifty-fifty bet.

"White, please." The student picks a plate from a stack by his side, places two breast pieces on it and passes it to his colleague serving boiled vegetables and mashed potatoes with brown gravy. I decide to ask for dark meat the next time.

I locate an unoccupied table in the corner and place my tray on it. Students are helping themselves from the soup kegs, the salad bar and the soda fountain but I cannot find water anywhere; nobody seems to drink it in this country. I ask a student refilling one of the milk dispensers. He directs me to a lonely spout by the serving line. A couple of students look at me in surprise as I fill a glass from it.

I notice the diners starting the meal with their salad, finishing it before proceeding to the main course. It is an unfamiliar practice for me. I am used to eating the salad along with the other items in the meal.

It occurs to me that the main course options do not include a vegetarian dish. Had I been a vegetarian, my diet would be restricted to salad, bread and dessert. I am glad I am not. Although the meat is pretty much tasteless, I try to develop a liking for it, sending the thoughts of delicious home cooked food back in India to the recesses of my mind. The dessert, however, more than compensates for the unappetizing chicken. The cheese cake is delicious, exactly the way I like.

Overall, my first meal at the cafeteria is a mixed bag.

The instructor for principles of marketing is Dr. Haas. He starts the lecture by warning students to take care in pronouncing his name, emphasizing not to miss the 'H' to avoid the obscene connotation. At first glance, I am not impressed by Dr. Haas. Having worked at McDonald's before taking up teaching, his anecdotal illustrations to support marketing theory are primarily from the fast food industry. To me, his understanding of other sectors of the economy appears limited. I hope he proves me wrong in the days and weeks to come.

My first two classes have been a welcome change. Almost all my college education till now covered sciences in which results are predictable. Engineering problems are solved with tools from mathematics, physics and chemistry. If the solution is not right, then it is wrong. It can never be partially right. I am, therefore, habituated to correct or incorrect outcomes, without the middle ground. But now I am studying human behaviour, where it may not be possible to slot choices in right or wrong categories and fallouts may often be unpredictable. I find this subjectivity refreshing and ambiguity engaging.

The statistics course is taught by Mr. Peter Numbers, an amusing coincidence. He is an energetic man in his mid-thirties with an animated style of teaching. I find his class a cakewalk. Some aspects of statistics were covered in the mathematics courses at the engineering college. Many of those are included in the syllabus here. My task is made even simpler by the system of open-book open-notes tests, eliminating the need to memorize formulae. The concept is new to me. I have never written an exam where one is allowed to access reference material.

After the class, I walk down to the post office to buy aerogrammes. I need to write to my family. On the way back to the dorm, I assess my first day of classes in an unfamiliar education system. I reckon that the curriculum in India was much harder to cope up with. But a definitive conclusion would be possible only after I understand the manner of grading the tests.

Tim is in the room when I get there. We are meeting for the first time since our short altercation the previous afternoon. He was gone for his football training when I woke up this morning and was somewhere else when I popped in for a bit before my marketing class.

"Goddammit, man." He gets up from the lower bunk, pressing an icepack to his right shoulder.

"What's wrong?" I ask, wondering who could hurt this pillar of strength.

"Got rammed into at training. It's hurting like crazy, man." He winces.

"But I thought that's part of the game, isn't it?" I had drawn that conclusion in the first five minutes of watching a game on Atif's TV.

"Not while I'm warming up." He complains.

"What position do you play, Tim?" I ask, knowing well that his reply is unlikely to make much sense to me.

"Wide receiver. I want to be in the offense. Defense sucks." I believe him.

It is approaching five thirty. The supper time at the cafeteria is between five and six. That is too early by Indian standards. Our normal dinner time at home is after eight. I am going to take some time getting used to this timetable.

Although I am not exactly hungry, I decide to join Tim for the meal. It is a pleasant surprise to find rice and pork stew on the evening's menu. I don't bother to look at the options thereafter.

"How can you eat that shit, man?" Tim asks even before he sits down, pointing at the rice. He has spaghetti and meat sauce on his plate.

"Back home, we eat rice every day. Love it."

"I don't remember the last time I ate rice. Hate it." He wrinkles his nose.

"Do you know rice's good for the brain? Those who eat rice regularly are found to have superior memory." I justify my diet.

"Really? I didn't know that." He rotates his fork to roll the spaghetti around it.

"Along the coasts of India, rice forms the staple diet, in addition to fish. The people in those regions are smart, especially in maths." I explain without the hope of changing his opinion.

"Fuck the memory, man. I won't eat it even if it makes me an Einstein." I expected that.

"Talking of Einstein, do you know he couldn't remember dates or phone numbers? And he once used a fifteen hundred dollars cheque as a bookmark and lost the book?"

"I can remember birthdays and phone numbers. And I haven't lost a cheque. Does that make me smarter than him?" He laughs, enjoying his own humour.

"What does your father do, Tim?" I change the subject.

"Farming." He answers after draining his glass of milk.

"What does he grow?"

"Corn and soybean." I remember my high school geography book mentioning Iowa as a leading state in corn production and not far behind in soybean. Now I am seeing someone whose family contributes to that distinction.

"How big's the farm?"

"Oh, about seven hundred acres." His casual response surprises me. Someone holding a farm of that size in India would be a big farmer.

"Wow, that's large. Need a lot of hands to till it?" I go by my Indian benchmark.

"Not really. There're farmers out there who own two thousand, three thousand acres. My dad needs only my mom, brother and his wife to work his farm." I am astounded. Four individuals farming seven hundred acres! I feel the need to start recalibrating my reference points.

Before going to bed, I write to my mother, not forgetting to mention that the dorm food is no problem. That would put her mind at ease.

Eight

The anxiety over the grading system does not allow me to sleep well on the second night in a row. I wake up in the middle of the night, startled by the nightmare of returning home in disgrace. I cannot wait to get the matter clarified.

In the morning, I reach the industrial sociology class early, hoping that Gail too turns up well before Dr. Donald. She disappoints me. Dr. Donald and Gail get in almost simultaneously. During the class, I am distracted by my thoughts on the grading system. But I manage to earn Dr. Donald's penny by being the only student to know what a wildcat strike is. I thank the trade union leader at the steel forge for concocting one during my tenure there.

As soon as the bell rings and Dr. Donald leaves the class, I raise the issue of grades with Gail.

"Are the teachers very liberal in grading tests?" I ask, framing the question to mask my fear.

"Why do you ask that?" She does not see where I am coming from.

"If a majority of students get A or B, which's more than eighty points, the grading must be liberal." Although my shot is in the dark, it must be true at least for graduate students. How else can most of those who enroll complete their degrees?

"I don't know if a majority get A or B. But I do know that the instructors take off points if the answer omits anything that they expect it to include."

"So, if you write everything that's expected, can you get full points even for a descriptive answer?" I ask for the sake of abundant clarity.

"Yes, that's right." Her reply is what I wanted to hear. I can feel relief spreading over my entire body. Back in India, it is well nigh impossible to get full marks for an essay; if you get eight out of ten, you deserve a pat on the back. The system here is simply different. I should be able to meet Mrs. Dexter's requirements.

"Thanks, Gail."

With the load of grades off my chest, I can feel a spring in my step as I walk to the Administration building to see what Ms. Hutton has to dish out for me.

"Good morning, ma'am. I'd filled out the form for on-campus employment yesterday. You'd asked me to check with you today." I remind her when she looks up from the paper she is writing on.

"Oh, yes. I remember. Let's see what we can offer you." She has to make the Herculean effort of rising from her seat and walking to the filing cabinet to pull out the folder of my documents. On returning to her desk, she waits to regain her breath before speaking again.

"They need a student manager at Seymours cafeteria. Can you fill that slot?"

"What would the timings be?" Working at my own dorm would save the icy trudge in the winter freeze. But I cannot commit unless the timing fits into my class schedule.

"Four to seven Monday through Friday, noon to two thirty on Saturday and Sunday."

"That'll work for me." My classes do not clash with the proposed schedule.

"Okey dokey. Elaine Maurer runs the Seymours cafeteria for the catering contractor. Meet her there at four o'clock today and she'll take this forward."

"Thanks a lot, ma'am."

I note down the manager's name in my note book and leave.

Sharp at four o'clock, I enter the cafeteria's kitchen and ask for Ms. Maurer. I am directed to a staff room adjoining the main cooking area where she is sitting at a desk in the corner, poring over a sheet. The room has another desk in the opposite corner but little else. Its bare walls are fitted with pegs to hang overcoats.

"Good afternoon, ma'am. I'm the new student manager. Ms. Hutton at the Employment Office asked me to meet with you." She looks up at me, taking off her reading glasses and letting them dangle on the neck cord. She is a middle aged lady who seems to succeed in her effort to look younger.

"Oh yes. Jasper did call about your meeting with her earlier today. I understand you'll be working evenings Monday through Friday and afternoons Saturday and Sunday."

"That's right." I confirm, noticing her use of 'through' between 'Monday' and 'Friday', rather than 'to' I am familiar with. Since the difference in the two is almost unnoticeable, I thought I had misheard Jasper Hutton's same expression earlier. But now I know better.

"Have you worked at a cafeteria before?" Elaine Maurer asks the logical first question.

"No." I hope she does not throw me out.

"In that case, let me start by showing you around the place so you understand the work involved." She is very considerate.

"That'd be helpful."

"Let's go." She stands up and starts walking to the kitchen. I fall in step.

"How many students work at a time?" I want to know the number of individuals I need to oversee.

"We'll come to that a little later. First up, you should know that except for the actual cooking, all the other work's done by the students." Her manner is very businesslike now.

"Does actual cooking include ready-to-cook items like hamburger patties, fries and onion rings?" At a Burger King in New Jersey, I had seen the staff drop these items directly from plastic bags into frying pans. I presume they come in the same condition here.

"Good question. The answer's no. The cooks do only those items that can't be done by students." She looks at me to assess if I have understood.

"Such as lasagna, stew or spaghetti sauce?" I hope she realizes I have caught on.

"Correct."

"Understood."

She leads me to the kitchen. It is equipped with modern gadgets to cook for a large number of diners: mixers, grinders, slicers, extruders, pulverizers, hot plates, ovens, fryers, pressure cookers, stoves. Two women, dressed in white chef's coats and aprons, are busy cooking. They are assisted by six students.

"Meet Claudia and Bernice." Ms. Maurer introduces me to the two women, one with amazing similarity to Jackie Kennedy. The other, Ms. Bernice, reminds me of Jean Stapleton from the TV sitcom I happened to see the previous night. Both of them say "Hello" and get back to their work; they need to be ready when the diners start arriving in another forty five minutes. Ms. Maurer does not bother to introduce me to the students. May be she is planning to do it when everyone is in. Apart from the six students assisting the chefs, one other is in the kitchen, chopping lettuce.

Once we are back at Ms. Maurer's desk, she hands me a list containing names of students.

"You've a crew of twenty four students for the supper service to cover everything from chopping and tossing the salad to leaving the kitchen spick-and-span after everyone's fed."

"Can you suggest the number of students required for each task?" I need a head start before I can run the group. I find the job similar to the one I did at the steel forge in Pune.

Ms. Maurer is kind enough to share her insight. I note down her comments.

The students I need to deploy start trooping in as Ms. Maurer finishes her briefing. I assign the first arrivals to fill milk, juice and soda pop in the dispensers. Those who follow set up the salad bar and ready the crockery and cutlery. The next lot mans the serving line. Thereafter, everything pretty much runs on autopilot. The peak time is between five fifteen and five forty five, when most of the diners walk in, putting pressure on the clean-up and replenishment group. Their work is increased by several diners leaving their plates and glasses on their tables instead of taking them to the dishwasher. I keep an eye on such bottlenecks and chip in to unclog them quickly. I also detect a few flaws in the system that can easily be fixed.

After the supper service is over and the kitchen is cleaned up, I assemble the entire group in the staff room. I need to talk to them.

"I've made a few observations today that I want to share and make the necessary changes." I begin. Kevin and Jonathan, the two guys who were deliberately slow in their work, are talking with each other. I politely but firmly ask them to pay attention.

"Sorry for the interruption but can you please hurry?" Gustavo asks impatiently. He is the only Hispanic in the team.

"Okay. One, not all tasks here require the same level of physical effort. For example, cleaning up is a heavier toil than serving food. We need to be more equitable in distribution of labour. From tomorrow, we'll rotate the work." I look around the group. Expectedly, the ones who had done the cleaning up look relieved while those who had served food look a little unhappy.

"What happens if someone on a harder slog doesn't want to trade it?" Kevin asks. The group laughs. I think they are trying to be ornery, wanting to undermine my position, not my effort to be fair.

"If both agree, it's fine. Otherwise, not." I reply confidently as if I had thought of this possibility, although I had not.

"What's the other observation?" Jonathan asks, again trying to be a nuisance.

"I'm coming to it. Two, I saw a few of us dragging their feet in whatever they were doing, in effect burdening their colleagues more. That's not fair. Again, we've to be equitable."

"Anything else?" Juliet asks, looking at her watch to show her impatience.

"One last point. All of us will elect the best worker every week. I'll award the elected worker one hour's extra wage. Any questions?" There are none. The students disperse.

Before leaving the cafeteria, I spend a few minutes to brief Ms. Maurer on my work redistribution plan. She looks concerned when I mention the idea of rewarding the best worker each week.

"The company doesn't allow any extra payments." She objects.

"That's expected but not a problem. I'll foot the bill. It's a small sacrifice to improve the team's performance." I try to put her mind at ease.

"That's surely a first in here. I guess you know what you're doing." She shrugs her shoulders and leaves the matter at that.

On the way up to my room, I decide to watch TV in the lounge by the dorm's entrance lobby. The access to the lounge is through a door in its back wall, with the TV placed at the far end. I enter and occupy a seat in the last row, spotting Kevin and Jonathan sitting with an African

American student in the row just in front of mine. They are engrossed in the popular fantasy sitcom *Mork & Mindy*, not noticing me in the subdued lighting.

After a few minutes, a student enters the lounge carrying a box of ring donuts for sale. He works from the front of the lounge to its rear, reaching the penultimate row a little later.

"Take it. That's the closest you'll get to a white hole." Kevin chides his African American friend, pointing at a donut topped with white frosting. Kevin and Jonathan laugh. The vulgar racist remark is shocking. But I am stung by what follows.

"Don't show off, sucker. Now you've to take shit from the Indian asshole running your cafeteria." The African American retaliates.

"Screw him, man. I'm taking no shit from that Cherokee." Kevin's tone is steeped in disdain.

I feel hurt, even angry, by the mindset that pigeonholes people purely on their appearance. I cannot change my skin but must deal with the moniker of 'Cherokee asshole'.

All my life I have lived in a seriously stratified society where discrimination, though illegal, is widespread. I believe in egalitarian ethos, not in hereditary entitlements. But many in India place me high up in the social hierarchy because of my pedigree. Consequently, I have never faced derision back home, although a large number of Indians are not so lucky. I am, however, a victim of reverse discrimination caused by affirmative action. For my engineering admission, for example, I had to compete for one of only a third of the total seats because the remaining two thirds were reserved for various categories including the historically deprived.

Yet I recognize the need to compensate for the injustice committed in the past and strongly support such measures.

The blatant bigotry I have accidentally tripped on tonight robs me of all my interest in watching the comedy being telecast. I quietly leave the lounge, exit the dorm and start running on the sidewalk. I need to release my pent-up anger. After running almost a mile, my feelings are still bursting my chest. I decide to race to the indoor sports facility at the multipurpose building a couple of blocks to the south. Once inside, I find a punching bag and let my fists pummel it till all my rage is spent.

With the steam out my system, I wander back to the dorm, trying to deal with the disappointment of the evening. My father taught me many years ago that disappointment is the gap between expectations and reality. It cannot be cured unless the two are matched. I expected a classless society here, but obviously it has yet to get there. Perhaps I should adjust my expectations. But I can also work on changing the reality the best I can.

On getting to my room, I prepare a grid chart showing the weekly schedule of each student's duty at the cafeteria. The work is divided in a way that evenly distributes the toil among the group. The schedule also provides room to incorporate any last-minute changes. The aim is to ensure that the job gets done without anyone getting the short end of the stick. I want my co-workers in the cafeteria to think of it as the best place on the campus to work at.

The next day, I run photocopies of the grid chart and give one to each team member. Of the twenty four, Gustavo is absent so I work in his place, making sure that the work does not suffer. By the end of the shift, my team's body language suggests that they are able to see the benefit in following my plan. If Kevin and Jonathan are still unhappy with me, they keep it to themselves.

I make sure that I am the last student to leave the cafeteria. While I am on my way out, I meet Ms. Maurer. She smiles and expresses her appreciation at the well-oiled functioning of the team.

"Thanks. I expect every member to eventually come around to liking my idea, but if one or two don't, can we let them go?" I want to know if she will back me in my endeavour.

"We'll cross the bridge if and when we get there." She is diplomatic.

My happiness at Ms. Maurer's complement is taken away from me when I enter my room. In place of Tim, I find an oriental man hanging his clothes in the closet. Although men from the Far East grow less facial hair and, therefore, look younger than their age, this individual looks far older than a normal college student. He has a round face and kind eyes behind a frameless pair of glasses. I am flummoxed.

"Hi, I'm Suh Jung Nam. From South Korea." His speech is gentle. We shake hands as I introduce myself.

"How come you're moving in now?" I ask a straightforward question.

"My roommate and your roommate want same room. So I moved." His English is heavily accented. But he speaks slowly. I can understand him without difficulty.

"Who was your roommate, Suh?" Tim had not mentioned his plan of changing rooms.

"Greg Hooks, a white American. And Suh is my last name." The first part of his reply does not surprise me but makes me wonder if this was just a case of birds of a feather flocking together or Tim's action has a racial motive. I try to push the thought out of my mind.

"So your first name is Jung?" I want to confirm.

"Jung Nam. In my country, I introduce myself Suh Jung Nam." He clarifies.

"Good to meet you, Jung Nam. Are you also a graduate student?"

"Yes. MBA. And you?" His manner is calm.

"Also MBA. How long have you been here?"

"My second term. I started in fall." I am glad he is more experienced on the campus than me. He should be able to solve some of my queries about the school and studies.

"How do you find the MBA programme?" It would be interesting to learn his opinion.

"Mathematical subjects easy, descriptive subjects and term papers very hard."

I can easily understand his situation. With a severe language handicap, it is amazing how the students from the orient manage to complete their American education with flying colours. Their dedication is more than exemplary.

"What were you doing before coming to the US?" I ask him. Actually, I am curious about his age but enquiring it directly may seem impolite. So I find a way around it. He looks too old to join graduate school either directly or soon after completing his bachelor's degree.

"Work in a bank. For thirteen years." That explains his mature looks. I figure he must be thirty five.

"Did the bank send you for the master's?" It is hard to imagine a man of his age, possibly having a family to support, simply quitting his job to study abroad for two years.

"Yes. Me and two more managers, one man and one woman. They're here too."

"And your family?"

"In Seoul. Wait." He takes out his wallet from his hip pocket and extracts a photograph of his wife flanked by two cute little kids, a girl not more than four and a boy about two.

"What a lovely family! Don't you miss them?" It must be emotionally tough for a father to be separated from his family, especially so young.

"Yes, very much. But they'll come in spring and stay with me till I complete my degree." The bright prospect of the family reunion is evident on his smiling face.

"Where're you going?" I ask him when I see him pick up his books and reach for the door.

"Have to study. Go to library with my Korean friends." He closes the door behind him.

Being alone in the room allows me the opportunity to think about my feelings towards the unprovoked change of my roommate. On the one hand, I cannot dispel the ache of Tim's rebuff, but on the other, Jung Nam seems more seasoned and sensitive than Tim.

My ambivalence over the episode continues to bother me well into the night.

Nine

New foreign students are introduced at the university's international club with a small party. It is a get-together generally held during the first week of every term. All overseas students are invited. The introductions are followed by an international potluck. New students from each country cook food representing their land. It is a great potpourri of cuisines from all continents.

I wish to use the opportunity to showcase my country's food but do not know where to start. In December 1979, Indians in America are few and far between in all states barring California, New York, New Jersey and a couple more. Grocery stores rarely stock Indian spices. Without knowing what is available, it is impossible to choose the dishes to cook. The simple way out is to go to Safeway, see what is available and decide the menu. The shop is located about half a mile from my dorm. In windy freezing conditions, it can seem like ten, especially if one has recently been plucked out of the tropics.

This is my first time in a large grocery. I am more used to the mom-and-pop stores that dot most residential areas in my homeland. At first I am lost, not knowing where to look. Once I find my bearings though, I focus on three areas: meats, spices and vegetables. My plan is to serve a meat dish and a vegetarian recipe. I choose the convenient option of minced meat because of the ease of cooking it right, neither scorched nor half-cooked. When sautéed with peas, chopped onions and condiments, it can be wrapped in egg roll shells and deep fried to make great samosas. Picking spices is not difficult because of the limited range available: cumin, mustard, turmeric and curry powder. That leaves vegetables.

Like samosas, I want my vegetarian dish also to be uncommon in this part of the world. To get there, I need to start with an uncommon vegetable. I look around but cannot locate it. Left with no option but to seek help, I approach a young woman in Safeway uniform.

"Can I help you?" She enquires. The name mentioned on her uniform is 'Megan'.

"Yes please. I can't find what I'm looking for."

"And what're you looking for?"

"Lady's fingers." I innocently name the vegetable.

"What?" Megan does not seem to believe what she heard.

"Lady's fingers." I repeat, slowly this time. Hopefully, she should understand.

"I don't get you, sir." She must be new to this store. Perhaps does not really know it well. I spot a grey haired lady in the store uniform.

"May be we should talk to her. She would know." I suggest to Megan, shifting my gaze in the elderly lady's direction.

"Sure. Ms. Stewart!" Megan calls out her senior colleague's name slightly louder than the 'sure' aimed at me. Ms. Stewart nods and walks the ten paces to reach us.

"What's the problem?" She asks Megan.

"I don't know where to find what this gentleman's asking for." Megan hands over her problem to Ms. Stewart, preferring not to state my need.

"What're you looking for, sir?" Ms. Stewart is politeness personified.

"Lady's fingers." I mention my requirement a third time. Ms. Stewart does not understand me either.

"And what do you do with them?" Perhaps the use will help her know what I am looking for.

"Cook and eat." I reply casually. Now it is Ms. Stewart's turn to be aghast.

"Pardon me?" She wants to be sure she heard me right.

"Cook and eat." I repeat, bringing the joined thumb and index finger of my right hand close to my mouth and miming a bite with my teeth. That should make them understand.

Their reaction is sudden and extreme.

Megan's pink complexion turns ashen; Ms. Stewart looks set to throw-up. The two women appear horrified. Ms. Stewart runs her nauseated stare from my top to toe as if I am Tarzan in a tattered loincloth, fresh out of the jungle. The look hits me like a bolt of lightening; the import of my answer dawning on me in a flash. I feel certain they think I am a man-eater from some unknown primitive tribe. I want to die. But I collect myself quickly.

"It's a vegetable. So naïve of me to sound like a cannibal!" I clarify with a laugh, remembering our motto to deal with cricket field errors: 'self-deprecation is the best cure for embarrassment'.

Both the women heave an audible sigh of relief. I am glad neither of them has fainted. But they have still not understood what I want. We need to try a different approach. So I describe the vegetable. Green, four to six inches long, slightly curved, half an inch thick at one end and tapering to a blunt point at the other.

"Chili peppers?" Megan is off the block first.

"No. Not them." I hope they zero in on the right answer.

"Jalapenos?" Ms. Stewart looks hopeful.

"Not jalapenos." Actually, I had not heard of them till I went to Tony's Pizzeria in New Jersey with Arun. But now I know they are not lady's fingers.

"String beans?"

"Too thin and long. Not what I need."

The two staffers have run out of vegetables that fit my description. I start feeling disappointed, wondering if I am asking for something that is not known here. As the last resort, I decide to try my hand at sketching a lady's finger. I am no artist but hopefully, my representation would be close enough to the vegetable's real appearance. I ask Megan for a sheet of paper. She whips one out of her pocket and hands it to me along with a ballpoint pen. I draw.

Suddenly the two women understand. Their faces light up like electric bulbs.

"Oh, you mean okra?" Ms. Stewart shrieks in glee. Archimedes' jubilant cry echoes in my mind. Funnily, his eureka and Ms. Stewart's okra almost rhyme.

"Is that what you call it?" I continue to learn Americanese.

Ms. Stewart walks to the frozen vegetables section and pulls out a packet of okra cut up in one inch pieces. That is exactly what I am looking for: lady's fingers. My day is made.

Regrettably though, the accidents caused by ignorance or misuse of local parlance do not end. Three days after the international club get-together, I walk out of my industrial sociology class at ten in the morning. I have no other class till two o'clock. I decide to go back to the dorm to do my laundry.

Mehmood joins me while I am crossing the quadrangle. A new undergrad from Bangladesh, he is short and skinny, with twinkling brown eyes and a flared nose. His parched black mop of hair is fashioned on a girl's bob that even a slight breeze blows on to his face. He has an irritating habit of frequently sweeping the unruly tresses back with his hand.

I barely know Mehmood. We met at last week's international dinner but did not go beyond introductions. I remember him because he had cooked fish curry and rice, a typical Bengali combination. It was delicious.

Mehmood and I rush side by side on one of the four concrete-paved walkways converging to the centre from the four corners of the otherwise grassy quad. The walkways are crowded with students hurrying to get to the warmth of heated buildings. Once we reach the middle of the quad, I continue on the way to my dorm. After a few paces, I realize

Mehmood is no longer by my side. I stop to look and spot him about twenty paces from me, walking away on another pathway.

To attract his attention, I call his name over the din of the milling students. He hears my voice and turns to face me. I shake my raised hand to enquire where he is going.

"Let's go find some fags at the students' union." He shouts, using the South Asian slang for cigarettes. All the students within his earshot turn to look at him and then at me, aghast. It takes both of us three seconds to realize his blunder.

We are in an age where most Americans have learned to be tolerant of many social sins but brazen hunt for homosexual partners is not one of them. The gay movement is yet to gather steam. Gays, branded faggots or fags in America, are widely frowned upon and prefer to remain very discreet about their sexual orientation. It is only in avant-garde San Francisco and perhaps New York City that they dare come out of the closet. Yet here is a foreigner loudly proclaiming his intention to find homosexuals on a university campus in conservative Midwest. By inviting me to go with him, Mehmood has made me an accomplice.

As we stand there sullied, he mimes smoking a cigarette by placing his two straightened fingers on his lips and inhaling. His valiant attempt to exonerate himself is in vain. The slip is a gigantic embarrassment. And this time I can think of no self-deprecating quip to cure it. The only comfort is our anonymity; no one in the crowd knows us. It is unlikely to help much though. Being in a minuscule minority on the campus, South Asians can easily stand out in the predominantly Caucasian or African American population. Most witnesses would remember the incident every time they saw us. Worse, the hatred my mistaken Iranian identity attracts may intensify further if I am besmirched with this new stigma. I wish the ground under my feet opens up and swallows me alive.

Although this is not my *faux pas*, I resolve to be careful in my choice of words.

Before opening my mouth, I stop to make sure that the utterance does not convey an unintended meaning. The precaution serves me well. I avoid further gaffes, at least for some time.

Ten

In just about three weeks after my first term at the B-school commences, it is holiday time. We are into Christmas season. I used to look forward to holidays in India, but not here in America. The dorm is closed during the three-week break so I need to find a place to stay during that period, without spending too much money. Dhani Chand offers some help.

Dhani is a Sikh but shaves his beard and trims the half-moon mop of hair left around his otherwise bald head. He flies cargo planes for the US Air Force, operating from the base located about fifteen miles from the campus. He has never been to India in his thirty five years, having come to the US over a decade and half ago from Jamaica where his grand parents shifted to from the Punjab many decades ago and parents continue to live. Yet he can speak broken Hindi with a Caribbean accent and has a soft corner for students from the land of his ancestors.

Dhani, his Caucasian wife Julia, six-year-old son Kuldeep and four-year-old daughter Kauser live in a small house on Hale Lake Road in the south-west corner of the town. They are going away for a short holiday to Chicago and would be happy if I could occupy the house in their absence. That would still leave two weeks over which I need an accommodation.

My problem gets sorted out in a strange turn of fate.

On the last day of school before the Christmas break, I go to Ed McGovern's office to wish him.

"Merry Christmas, Ed."

"Good you looked me up, Guru. I was going to call you at the dorm." His deep bass is enveloped in genuine warmth.

"What about?" I ask.

"We'd like to invite you over for Christmas dinner." He proposes with a smile.

"Thanks. It'd be great to celebrate your biggest festival with you folks. What time?" In my country, dinner is understood to be an evening meal. But I ask just so that I am not late.

"Noon would be good." His reply comes as a surprise. I thank myself for asking.

"Look forward to the occasion."

The season's first snow on the morning of the 25th makes it a traditional white Christmas. When I enter the McGovern home, Donna expresses her happiness at the snowfall. All of them are in a festive mood. One corner of their drawing room is occupied by a five feet tall Christmas tree, adorned with jingle bells, lights, garlands, ornaments and a star-shaped light at the top. The base of the tree is surrounded by boxes wrapped in shiny foil. The room is decorated with streamers and twinkling lights.

I have never celebrated Christmas in a Christian household; the event packs immense novelty value for me. And I enjoy every minute of it. Donna's personality is the exact opposite of Ed's. She is talkative, lively and entertaining. Anissa seems to have taken after her. The little child and I hit it off almost immediately. For a two year old, Anissa understands just about everything. She brings out her picture books, sits on my lap and shows me the animals and birds, correctly identifying all of them.

Ed has cooked a wonderful traditional Christmas meal of roast turkey with stuffing, cranberry sauce and green beans. He opens a bottle of Sauvignon Blanc with much fanfare and we raise a toast in celebration. Little Anissa joins in with her glass of apple juice. Ed seems to take a lot of pride in deftly slicing the turkey and serving large fillets to each of us. I consider myself fortunate to have such a lovely and young host family.

When we are rounding off the festive meal with Donna's delicious pumpkin pie, she asks me if I would like to join them on a shopping trip to Kansas City a couple of days later. I am perplexed.

"Why'd you want to shop now? I thought the shopping season's before Christmas." I cannot hide my bewilderment.

"Because after Christmas, prices fall like ninepins." Ed explains.

"Really?"

"The retail chains need to get rid of the unsold stock, don't they? Actually, the week after Christmas is the best time to shop." Donna adds. I cannot argue with her solid logic.

"I've not planned anything spectacular on Friday, so I will be happy to go along." I really look forward to the outing.

On Friday morning, Ed and Donna pick me up from Dhani's house.

"Where's Anissa?" I ask on getting into the car's empty back seat.

"She's spending the day with my parents." Donna informs.

"Well, I thought she would join in the fun."

"She isn't fun when shopping." Ed remarks, with a shake of his head.

The hour long drive ends at Crown Centre, one of the biggest shopping, dining and entertainment facilities in the area. The Centre is comparatively new, completed just a few years earlier. It is hard to believe that the site of the beautiful cluster of modern buildings was once a limestone hill covered with abandoned warehouses.

As Donna had predicted, most shops offer great discounts to dispose of the Christmas leftovers. Despite the bargains available, the mall is sparsely populated, probably because few people possess Donna's savvy. She shops for a variety of items: clothes, toys, linen, crockery and cutlery. Ed spends a significant amount of time in the book store. As for me, I find the prices of a portable Panasonic tape recorder and a digital calculator too tempting to ignore.

Taking a break in shopping, Ed decides to have Mexican food for lunch. Since I have never been to a Mexican restaurant, I do not know what to expect. But I like the fare because the flour tortillas are almost identical to the *roti* that forms an integral part of diet at my home, while the rice and red beans make the meal even more enjoyable.

Over lunch, Ed probes me about India.

"I've read that India's also a democracy like ours. Is that so?" He asks.

"Democracy? Yes. Like yours? No." My response confuses him more than it educates.

"What'd you mean?" He has a quizzical look on his face.

"We're a parliamentary democracy. And a young one at that, only thirty two years old. The prime minister's the head of the government. But you directly vote to elect your president; we don't do that for our prime minister."

"Then who does?"

"We elect the member of parliament from our area. The members of parliament elect the prime minister." I clarify.

"I get it now. It's the same as the British system." He hits the nail on the head.

"That's right."

"Do they also follow free-market capitalism in your country?"

"Not really. After winning independence from the British in 1947, the government embraced socialism and opted for a planned economy. It stopped short of the Orwellian Soviet model, allowing the private sector to operate, but with considerable restrictions." I doubt he will be able to imagine the landscape.

"Why?"

"To protect the infirm from the unforgiving market forces." I explain.

"That's a fair goal." It seems he is a liberal with left-of-centre leanings.

"Yes. But bureaucratic thinking hijacked the noble policy, choking innovation and enterprise."

"Why should protecting the underprivileged stifle innovation?" He does not see the connection.

"Because to ensure fair distribution of national resources, the government exercises a rigid control on which products are produced by how many producers in what quantities. And many industries - airline, power generation and insurance, for instance – are run exclusively by the government, mostly as monopolies."

"You mean there're only a few local players? But they'd still need to compete with the products coming in from overseas, wouldn't they?" He enquires.

"Not quite. Imports remain throttled by sky-high tariff and non-tariff barriers erected to shield the fledgling local industry from the predatory multinationals." For someone raised in this country, such measures will probably seem like xenophobia. But Ed's reaction is subdued.

"Well, competition keeps businesses honest. Lack of competition compromises the consumer's interest." He makes the point in favour of the free-market system.

"Exactly. As the undesired upshot of limited competition, the local industries have become complacent; secure in the knowledge that the public has few choices, if any." I hope he is able to get the picture, although he is unlikely to have witnessed it.

"Don't you have anti-trust laws to prevent private monopolies?" His question catches me off-guard. I am ignorant of the legal framework for ensuring fair competition.

"If the laws exist, many industries must be exempt from coming under their purview." I cannot think of a more specific response.

Just then the waiter brings the cheque. The discussion gets terminated as we go back to shopping.

It is almost dark when Donna finishes her bargain-hunt. I am still getting used to the short winter days at these higher latitudes, sometimes finding the evenings a little depressing. Today is not one of them.

We get into the car in high spirits. Once we are on the way, I narrate the hilarious story of how my brother and I conspired to frighten the daylights out of a visiting family friend by enacting ghosts.

"Ghosts?" Donna is curious.

"We live in a huge one-hundred-year-old house. It has three floors and several attics, nooks and crannies." I describe the setting.

"Wow! That sounds right out of an Enid Blyton book." Ed sounds excited.

"When we were kids, we used to play hide-and-seek at night in total darkness. Turning on lights was not allowed."

"That's creepy." Donna turns her head to look at me, her eyes wide.

"Not for us. But fifteen-year-old Nitin, visiting from Bombay, actually a few years older than us, insisted on keeping at least one light burning. We guessed that he was scared." For effect, I turn my voice hoarse while saying 'scared'.

"I'd be petrified even now." Donna admits.

"So we fabricated a story that the previous owner of the house was murdered and his ghost roams at night. Nitin swallowed the lie hook, line and sinker."

"You must be a real Devil." Donna looks at me in mock anger.

"Nitin shared our bedroom with us. In the middle of the night, my brother or I would quietly step out, put the burning end of an incense stick in our mouth and re-enter the bedroom, exhaling through bare teeth." I mime the action with clenched teeth.

"Why?" Donna probably finds it hard to visualize the scene.

"Because the stick's smouldering tip inside the mouth lights the teeth up in a red glow like embers. Nitin got petrified to death believing they were of an oncoming ghost."

"That sounds really eerie. I'd like to try it myself with a joss stick." Ed seems genuinely interested in the prank.

"But Nitin then thwarted our move by tightly pulling a comforter over his head, to hide from the glowing teeth."

"Smart." Ed laughs.

"We were smarter. We had *ghungaroo*s at home, small spherical brass bells mounted on a cloth band or string. The band or the string is wrapped around ankles while performing Indian classical dance forms." I show the size of each bell to Donna by holding my index finger and thumb half an inch apart.

"What's dance got to do with ghosts?" She cannot connect the two.

"We told Nitin that the murdered owner was a dancer and his ghost danced too."

"And?" Her eyes widen.

"On the second night, my brother wore *ghungaroo*s and ran down the wooden staircase next to our bedroom. Nitin couldn't avoid hearing the bells jingle." I smile, recalling Nitin's reaction to the sound.

"That's mean, Guru." Donna smiles too.

"On the third night, we wanted to grab Nitin's face with hands chilled in ice-cold water, as if the ghost was pawing him."

"Then?" Donna's eyes widen in anticipation.

"By evening, Nitin looked so terrified of the looming night that we feared he'll drop dead if we went ahead with the prank."

"Did he?" Donna grabs my hand. The suspense is getting unbearable for her.

"No. We abandoned the plan and let him in on the secret."

"Thank heavens. How'd he react?" Donna seems almost as relieved as Nitin was.

"He was planning to ask his father to come and take him home the next day."

"I'm sure you didn't want that." Ed looks at me in the rear view mirror.

"We didn't. It was fun to have him around. And our father would have shot us for ill-treating a guest." All of us enjoy a hearty laugh.

Then Donna notices me riding without fastening the seat belt.

"I think you should wear the seat belt, Guru." She suggests.

"It's not mandatory, is it? And rather than living with a crippling injury, I'd much rather die." I joke, brushing aside her advice.

Ed decides to shun the dual carriageway if favour of slightly shorter but mostly undivided Route 50. In spite of the fatigue of the day-long shop-crawling, Donna is in a chirpy mood, probably buoyed by the basement bargains she managed to secure.

"Is life in India very different from what we've here?" She enquires.

"Yes. Humans live under the sea and fish occupy the land." I pretend to be serious.

"Very funny." Donna glares at me.

"Jokes aside, quite a bit, actually." I add.

"In what way?"

"You won't believe this Donna, but my standard of living's actually plummeted after coming here." I claim in mock honesty.

"Really?" She asks without picking out the lighter vein of my statement.

"Yes. Here, you've automated your household chores. But you still need to operate the washers, dryers, food processors, dishwashers, vacuum cleaners and such." I continue, pretending to be serious.

"So? Isn't it efficient?" Her question suggests she has still not seen through my ruse.

"My home in India has most of these gadgets and also people to run them. So, we get all the comforts delivered: laundered clothes, cooked food, washed utensils and tidied-up rooms, not to mention groceries. And my father employs a chauffeur." I declare with a smile.

"Wow! And we think thirty-minute pizza delivery is the ultimate convenience." She laughs, turning her head to look at me.

I want to tell her that I was just joking, but never make it. Between the raised backs of the two bucket seats in front, threatening headlights of a fast oncoming vehicle blind me. Donna notices the horror in my eyes, realizes I am looking at something dreadful, returns her gaze to the road and screams "Edwin". My body jerks violently as Ed hits the brakes hard. Then the tyres lose traction, the car abruptly skids on to the soft shoulder and overturns. Without the seat belt to pin me down, I levitate for a brief moment as the car rolls over, then my head viciously bangs against its hard-top.

The last thought to cross my mind before I black out is 'what a place and time to die'.

Eleven

When I come to, my mind is completely blank. I cannot remember who or where I am. I try to open my eyes but cannot find the strength to do so. My limbs feel as if they weigh a ton. Slowly, although I cannot decide how slowly, I become aware of my breathing. It is noisy. I sense pressure on my face but cannot figure out what is actually causing it. Then I hear muffled voices without understanding what they are saying.

A wave of pain rolls from my neck down to the left calf. As it subsides, a finger pokes under my right eyebrow and pulls up the eyelid. I can see the blur of a moustache and a pair of spectacles facing me from two feet or so. When the finger is withdrawn from my eyelid, it droops. Then I hear a few words and feel the pressure coming off my face. I try to open my eyes but need to apply all my strength to retract the eyelids a tiny bit. I recognize the moustache and the spectacles as part of a human face. In the distance behind it is a white surface. My eyes close again.

I become aware of someone caressing my hand, trying to raise it.

"Do you feel my hand?" I hear a gravelly voice ask, although I am not certain if that is actually what is said.

Slowly, ever so slowly, I labour to lift my eyelids one more time. Grudgingly, they oblige. It takes me a while longer to get used to the bright artificial light. The moustached face is joined by another one. My mind begins to kick in, but only in fits and starts. I am able to infer that the moustached face is that of a man while the other has feminine features. I cannot place either of them. They do not seem familiar. Then the feminine face moves away bringing into view a white light at a distance of about ten feet. It is fitted on a surface that I think is a ceiling. I see shiny chrome tubes coming out of the man's ears. The tubes, held apart by a U-shaped stainless steel strip, converge into a single rubber pipe below the metal strip.

I recognize the contraption as a stethoscope but cannot recall what it is used for. While I rack my brain to reach the answer, one side of my rib cage feels the pressure of the stethoscope's chest-piece, then the other. I suddenly gain awareness that the person using the stethoscope is a doctor. But I cannot understand why he is leaning over me.

When his face disappears from my range of vision, I see an inverted glass bottle hung from a tall stand in chrome finish. A thin transparent hose runs down from its stopper. About a foot or so down from the stopper, the tube is swollen into a two-inch-long cylindrical bulb, half filled with a colourless liquid. The lower end of the bulb is shrunk back to the size of the tube that then runs down to my arm. Every second, a drop of the colourless liquid falls from the top of the bulb into its accumulated pool. It takes me time to deduce that I am on an intravenous drip. That means I am in a hospital. What am I doing in a hospital? My eyes close again.

The next time I surface, I do not need to strain so much to open my eyes. I also manage to focus my vision, albeit with some effort. My mind appears to regain a part of its skill to connect the dots. I am able to make out that the pressure on my face is caused by a mask and feel the air pumped through it. That means I am on assisted ventilation. The intravenous drip is still on too. If I am hospitalized on life support, I must be seriously ill. The conclusion confuses my weakened intellect. I do not remember feeling unwell, but if indeed I am in such a bad condition, why is no one from my family with me?

"Good you've woken up. I was wondering why you're sleeping so long." I hear a feminine voice and this time I am able to make out the meaning of the words. A woman's face smiles at me. The moustached doctor joins it.

"Let's take out the obstacle to your speech." He says and reaches out for my head. I feel the pressure easing from my face as the mask is removed.

"Can you feel my touch?" The woman asks. Soft fingers stroke the back of my hand. I open my mouth to answer but my throat cannot generate the sound.

I suddenly realize that the man and the woman are Caucasian and that they are not speaking in any Indian language. That means I am not in my native place. I must be away from my family. Perhaps that explains their absence. Even in that half-conscious haze, I long for my mother. My eyes moisten. The woman tending me dabs them with a tissue. I wonder if she can make out I am crying and, if so, why.

My mind continues to play see-saw with consciousness, although I cannot estimate how long. Every time I wake up, not knowing where I am or why, burdens my ego. But till such time as I am able to speak, I am unlikely to find out. And absence of my family members remains a source of great grief. It intensifies further as the periods of wakefulness get longer.

And then, while I am emerging from one more spell of soporific sleep, my dormant memory suddenly reactivates itself in a series of short staccato bursts. The graduate school, the Christmas celebration, the day spent shopping with Ed and Donna, followed by the car crash, all appear in my mind's eye like a night scene under bright strobe lights. I have no way of knowing how long I have been in the hospital but regaining the lost bearing is a mental boost that may help hasten my physical recovery. I dearly cling to that flashback as if my life depends on it, afraid of losing it to another bout of amnesia. Mercifully, my wounded mental faculty co-operates.

"Good morning. How're you today?" A young nurse asks while I am awake, sometime after I reclaim my memory. She is accompanied by an energetic man in a white coat. I look at them and try to smile.

The nurse checks my temperature and leaves. The man continues to stand by the bed.

"My name's Johan. I'm here to conduct your physiotherapy session." He goes on to make me flex my arms and then lift my feet off the bed, one at a time. It is painfully hard but I manage to raise each foot just a tiny bit. The maneuver is exhausting. I want him to stop.

"Enough." The sound of my own words jolts me. Then I feel the elation at retrieving my voice. We take the ability to speak for granted, till we lose it. Only then do we realize how precious a gift speech is.

"Just one more time. I know you can do it." The physiotherapist eggs me on, oblivious of my delight. The conquest energizes me. I submit to Johan's exhortation.

The young nurse returns a few minutes after Johan departs. I am dying to show off my new-found ability to speak.

"Good morning." I wish her. The words come out softly but she hears them. Her face lights up in a dazzling smile.

"My word, young man. You're surely getting better in leaps and bounds." Her joy is reflected in her tone.

"How long was I unconscious?" I wish to know.

"Let's not worry about that for now." Obviously, she does not want to tell me.

"Can I sit?" I ask.

"We don't want to go overboard, do we? Why don't I call Dr. Hirsch to take a look? He can make the determination." She is cautious, not willing to exceed her brief. Rightly so, I decide.

She returns with the moustached man, who I now know is Dr. Hirsch. The medico examines me with his stethoscope, then holds his three fingers in front of my face and asks me to tell him the number. I seem to pass the test.

"I'm happy with your progress. We'll move you out of the ICU and into a standard room." His manner is assuring.

"Thanks." I feel really grateful for his decision.

Twelve

As soon as I am rolled out of the ICU, I see Ed, smiling. The sight of someone I know makes me feel human again. He accompanies the gurney to the private room and sits on the chair by the window until the hospital staff leaves. I am desperately waiting for someone to fill me in on what happened on the fateful night of the crash.

"You look fresh, Guru." He says cheerfully, standing by my bed, his hand gently placed on mine.

"Good to see you, Ed." My voice is still rough. It does not have the finesse to convey my true feelings. But even if it did, I am not sure Ed will ever understand what his presence means to me. My eyes well up but I cannot judge if it is due to the relief and joy of seeing him again or the grief of my family's absence.

"Donna and I've been waiting for you to be out of the ICU. They wouldn't let us in there."

"What happened, Ed?" The tiredness in my voice hides my impatience in knowing the sequence of the fateful night's events.

"Remember we were returning from Kansas City?" He asks.

"Yes."

"In trying to avoid an oncoming truck, I skidded on to the shoulder and the car overturned." He pauses.

"I know."

"Unfortunately, we'd just topped a small hill, so the car rolled over and went down a knoll, ending belly up." He acts out the car's trajectory by rotating his index finger in air and stopping with his palm facing upwards.

"Bad."

"Not for Donna and me. The seat belts kept us strapped to our seats. We didn't get as much as a bruise but you got thrown about like a pebble in a rolling can."

"Hmmm."

"A trooper saw the accident and called the emergency service. They sent a chopper. You must've been on the hospital bed within fifteen minutes. That was crucial."

"Lucky." Ed cannot read my thoughts but I know I am alive because of the prompt attention available in an affluent nation. In my own country, it would have taken hours to get me to a hospital bed. I would not have survived the delay.

"We were scared for you. If you remember, you hadn't taken off your seal-skin winter coat. That might've prevented any superficial injuries. But the unconsciousness was worrisome."

"I can imagine."

"When the brain scan report came in, we were somewhat relieved."

"Why?"

"It showed injury only to the brain stem, not the entire brain. That's a very rare occurrence." His face is calm as ever.

"Hmmm."

"Recovery from brain stem injuries is rapid and nearly complete once the person wakes up." He makes out from my tired eyes that I have had enough exertion for now. He promises to return in the evening with Donna and leaves.

After he is gone, I blame myself for not asking him how long I was comatose. My thinking is not sharp yet, I conclude. And then a far more troubling omission hits me. Does my family know of the accident and my coma? If they do, they must be worried sick, more so because they cannot see me for themselves. I need to know as soon as I can, but have to wait for Ed to return.

The hours till the evening seem like years. I find my anxiety difficult to bear, hoping to fall asleep again and wake up when Ed is back. But my restlessness does not let sleep take hold. I try to divert my mind to my childhood friends, jogging my memory to see how fast it can run. It is no help. My thoughts, although not well synchronised, keep returning to my parents; how concerned and agonised they must be. My already brittle mental frame weakens further with the new vexation. Hard as I try to control my feelings, my eyes repeatedly moisten.

Finally, Ed arrives with Donna. They are accompanied by Anissa.

"I'm glad you're awake. You look good, Guru." Donna is obviously trying to pep me up.

"What's wrong with him?" Anissa is confused. Her parents must not have told her much, if anything, about my condition.

"He fell down and broke his crown." Donna sings the improvised nursery rhyme for the little girl.

"How long was I gone, Ed?" I cannot hold myself back any longer, coming straight to the point.

"Six days, almost." He says it as if it is no big deal but his eyes reflect his concern over the duration of my unconsciousness. The news stuns me. I expected his answer to be in minutes, perhaps hours, surely not days. But I am dying to know the other vital piece of information.

"Have you told my family?" I ask with bated breath, almost willing him to reply in the negative.

"We wanted to but your contact information's in Jim Copperthwaite's office. He's away for Christmas, as is Jane." I can feel relief cascading down my whole body.

"Thank God." I am also grateful to the foreign students' adviser for keeping out of my life.

"As the days went by, we got more and more worried, not really knowing what to do." Donna butts in.

"I can understand." I express my hope, not knowing if I really do. It is impossible to imagine what the McGoverns must have gone through while I precariously hung on to life on a slender thread.

"Anyway, all that's behind us now. Anissa, you're happy to see Guru, aren't you?" Ed tries to get Anissa into the conversation.

"When's he coming home to stay with us?" She asks her father. Her question forces my mind to switch from the past to the future. Frankly, my thoughts had not progressed beyond the hospital bed.

"As soon as the doctor lets him." Donna promises the child.

"I think he needs to rest now. Anissa, let's say bye to him. We'll come again tomorrow." Ed persuades his daughter to leave.

I know they have their own lives to run, yet I yearn to hold them back. It is a huge relief that my family back home is blissfully unaware of my dalliance with death. But it has not reduced my longing for my near and dear ones. And in this distant land, the McGoverns can partially fill that void.

In India, a close family member remains with the hospitalized patient all the time. I now understand the value and importance of that practice. The psychological support it provides is priceless. I badly miss it here. To get over the melancholy shrouding me, I invent a game of imagining that my mother is sitting at my bedside and holding a conversation with me. It helps lift my sagging morale till the sleep takes over.

The next morning brings bright sunshine.

"You've progressed very well in the four days since regaining consciousness." Dr. Hirsch is cheerful in declaring his verdict as he makes me sit on the bed to test my reflexes.

"Thanks, doctor." I feel truly indebted to him.

"We expected it, once your injury was known to be restricted to the brain stem. But it's good to see it actually happen."

"What's next, doctor?"

"I'll try and let you go this evening. But you must to be careful while the residual effects of your injury fade." His tone turns serious.

"Like what?"

"The difficulty with your movements and swallowing will continue for some more time. You may not have a clear vision at times and may experience lack of eye-hand coordination." He is clear.

"Understood."

"Refrain from climbing stairs and don't watch TV for more than fifteen minutes at a stretch. Continue with the prescribed exercises and slowly increase normal walks from three minutes to twenty minutes over a week."

"How long will the restrictions remain in force?"

"That's hard to say right now. We'll make that determination when you come back for the follow-up in a week." He is forthright.

The reprieve promised by Dr. Hirsch provides a reason to look forward to the evening. I feel increasingly expectant as the hours pass by. Finally, it is five o'clock.

"Dr. Hirsch's already signed your discharge papers." Ed announces cheerfully as he walks into my room. His comment stirs my mind into thinking about the cost of my treatment. The monetary angle of the mishap had not occurred to me. And I do not have the foggiest idea as to how much the amount is.

"Ed, I guess I need to pay before leaving the hospital. But I don't have my cheque book." I am not sure how the problem can be solved. Ed though is unperturbed.

"Don't worry. The insurance company shall take care of that. Jim Copperthwaite returned last night. His office's already filed the insurance claim." The information is puzzling. I do not recall buying health insurance.

"I wonder if I'm covered." I express my doubt.

"You probably don't remember. All foreign students are insured when they enroll." I find no point in taxing my already bruised brain. I let the discussion pass.

Expectedly, Ed is driving a rented car, not the Citation involved in the wreck. Yet I feel shaky to get aboard. I see the wisdom in flying out a pilot immediately after surviving a plane accident to prevent fear of flying from setting in. Ed notices my hesitation and promises to drive as slowly as the law permits. I do not forget to fasten the seat belt this time. It is a relief to leave the hospital but I would have preferred to go home to my biological family, the assurance of McGoverns' gentle attention notwithstanding.

Donna and Anissa greet me as if I am Neil Armstrong returning from the moon. There is a colourful welcome sign hung on the door. As I enter the house, Anissa hands me a delightful bouquet of pink, purple and yellow carnations. Clearly they are trying their best to make me feel as comfortable as they possibly can and I am grateful to be looked after by such caring hosts in this distant country. But not having my mother around to fuss over me makes my already vagrant emotions impossible to control. I have no choice but to let my tears flow in the privacy of the bathroom. Once the deluge subsides and eventually stops, my heartache drops to a tolerable level.

Thankfully, the move from the hospital's detached care to a home's affectionate warmth speeds up my recovery. And the McGoverns spare no effort to nurse my body and spirit back to health. When I visit the hospital a week later, Dr.

Hirsch is extremely satisfied with my progress. I perform the drill he asks me to with little difficulty.

"I'd like to lean towards caution and ask you to continue with the restrictions for another week. Hopefully, we'll be able to start tapering them off when you come again next Wednesday. And carry on with your physiotherapy and walks."

"Can I resume reading and writing?" I have not held a book or a pen for over two weeks now.

"Yes, but only fifteen minutes to begin with. You can increase it gradually by five minutes every day." I am happy with the concession. I decide to write to my mother about the accident, omitting the gory details of my brush with death.

A week later, I anticipate an all clear from Dr. Hirsch.

"My school starts tomorrow. Can I return to my dorm tonight?" I come straight to the point.

"Yes. You can also get back to your normal routine with the caveat that you'll call me immediately on sensing anything unusual." His voice is stern, almost like a school master.

"I'll do that." I have no intention of disobeying him.

"I suggest you ask those around you to promptly point out your abnormal or atypical behaviour if they spot it."

"Like what?" I want to be clear.

"Like slurred speech, lack of coordination in movements, memory loss or irregular sleep patterns." He explains.

"Okay, doctor. Thanks."

"Please come down a month from now so we can monitor your progress." His tone returns to its usual softness.

"Sure."

Anissa does not understand why I have to leave her home and return to the dorm. She has started thinking of me as a family member who is always around. I too have got accustomed to being with the McGoverns during my two weeks' stay. I wistfully admit that I will need to readjust to the dorm all over again.

Jung Nam is happy to see me when I get to my room. He obviously has no idea of my ordeal during the break. I decide to narrate the episode to him the next day. I just want to soak in the relief of returning to the campus alive and in one piece.

Thirteen

After the comforts of the McGovern household, getting back to the dorm's austerity does seem a little hard. I liked having Ed, Donna and Anissa attend to my needs without ado. We also played scrabble and cards, saw old photographs or simply chatted over cups of decaf coffee. Their companionship helped alleviate my homesickness at least to some extent. And on the eve of my return to the dorm, I felt fit enough to cook an Indian meal of yoghurt-cucumber salad, grilled chicken and saffron rice. They called it 'exotic' but I suspect it was a euphemism for 'strange'.

The dorm appears lonely in comparison, making me miss my family even more. Jung Nam is rarely in the room, mostly away studying with his Korean bank colleagues. During the three weeks before the Christmas break and the accident, I had adjusted to not having anyone around. Now I have to learn to be with myself once again.

As soon as the classes resume, the results of the tests we had written before the break are announced. I am thrilled to score A grades in all the subjects. My initial fear of getting thrown out of the master's programme appears such a false alarm. Dr. Donald is especially pleased with my performance, making it a point to mention my name in the class. Although I feel proud to get recognized, I assign the real credit to my tenure at the steel forge back in India.

The busy schedule of classes, studies and the cafeteria duty helps me get back into the groove within a week. When I mention the accident to my team at the cafeteria, they want to know its details and the treatment thereafter. They ask if such an experience is any different India. I cannot really provide an answer because, luckily, I never had to stay at a medical facility before coming to this country. But I do cite the quick response of the emergency apparatus as the primary reason of my survival. I refrain from disclosing that in my own country, I would not have been flown to a hospital in a matter of minutes.

By end-January, I have almost forgotten the hospitalization except for the next appointment with Dr. Hirsch. The increase in my workload to meet the approaching deadlines for submitting term papers leaves no time to think about much else. I am also required to work hard to retain my unblemished grades.

And then, quite unannounced, another surprise comes my way.

It is a Thursday like any other. The snowfall has been heavy in the last twenty four hours, a customary occurrence in late January, I am told. I scamper to the dorm's heated interiors at about four in the afternoon after attending classes. The incoming letters are generally dropped in each student's pigeonhole by then, so I normally check my mail box at this time. Today, I hope to see my friend's update on India's ongoing cricket series with Pakistan.

Instead, I find a sealed cover from Jasper Hutton.

My first reaction is surprise. She is the last person I expected to get a note from. Once I overcome the feeling, I try to guess the reason for her missive. She probably wants me to take up another assignment. Perhaps someone in my team cribbed about my high handedness in denuding the unfettered distribution of work to even out the toil. I open the envelope with rising apprehension.

The small folded sheet taken from a yellow legal pad carries a very brief message written in a steady hand:

Please see me ASAP in connection with your application for assistantship. – Jasper Hutton.

My guess of a change in job is correct; the fear though, of a team-member prompting it, appears unfounded. I heave a sigh of relief but my curiosity at what exactly does Ms. Hutton have on offer prevents me from delaying the meeting. I decide to brave the blizzard and trod to the Administration building straightaway.

Ms. Hutton is standing in front of her filing cabinet. Her feet, wrapped in grey canvas loafers, appear too small to support her considerable mass. But I feel glad she does not have to undergo the hardship of rising from her seat.

"I got your note asking me to see you regarding my application for assistantship." I hand over the yellow sheet to her when she walks back to her desk, hoping for her own sake that she reads it before sitting down on her chair. Much to my relief, and hers, she does.

"It seems you got lucky." She smiles her tired smile and slowly retrieves a folder from the filing cabinet.

"I can definitely do with some luck." After making the remark, I realize she would not know about my accident and would probably not understand my comment.

"Let's see…Dr. Fingleton at the Applied Technology Department needs a teaching assistant for materials science. It'd be good if you can see him." She says, looking at a sheet in the folder.

"I'd be happy to, whenever he wants. Do I need to seek his appointment?"

"Well, he said he needs a TA rather badly. Let me ask him if he's available right now." She dials a number on the phone in front of her.

"I'd appreciate it." I actually feel grateful.

She asks the person at the other end if she can send me, waits for the reply and hangs up.

"You can go see him now on the third floor of McPherson building." She hands the note back before I leave her section.

McPherson building is located across the central quad, now completely covered in foot-deep snow, except for the concrete walkways. My sense of anticipation tempts me to sprint all the way there but the icy pavement makes it a risky bait. Yet I find myself in a brisk walk, reaching the building in less than three minutes. Once inside, I cannot hold down the urge to run up the staircase, three steps at a time. I stop to catch my breath outside the closed door with Dr. Derek Fingleton's nameplate nailed to it. A white sheet of paper is pasted below the name. A quote is printed on it in prominent black letters:

An optimist will tell you a glass is half-full; a pessimist, half-empty; and the engineer will tell you the glass is twice the size it needs to be. - Chauncey Depew

I recall reading the quip sometime during my undergraduate years but did not know it came from Mr. Depew. To me, the US senator from New York at the turn of the nineteenth century is known for his fiendish claim: 'I get my exercise acting as a pallbearer to my friends who exercise'. Waiting for Dr. Fingleton to respond to my knock, I hope he has Mr. Depew's sense of humour.

"Come on in." a booming voice orders me to enter. I obey the command.

Dr. Fingleton appears to be in his fifties, grey hair at the temples adding to his distinguished bearing. The military uniform of a general would better suit his crew cut, handlebar moustache, sharp nose and piercing blue eyes. He is seated at a desk placed along the wall of his small cubicle. The enclosure also has a shelf overflowing with books of various sizes, small and large. But the desk is bare, apart from a telephone, a slide-rule and a folder.

"Ms. Hutton asked me to meet with you. She said it's regarding a teaching assistantship." I make the introduction when he looks at me.

"Oh yes. She did call to ask if she should send you." He opens the folder on his desk.

"She mentioned materials science." I am eager to close this without delay.

"She's right. Sandesh Thapa, the TA who taught materials science, had to return to Nepal because of some family emergency. He can't return till the end of the term." Dr. Fingleton is no army general. He has a friendly, welcoming manner.

"I did material science as part of my engineering curriculum." I do not want to leave the important part unsaid.

"I see that. You've also done strength of materials." He looks up from my transcript in the folder.

"Yes, sir."

"Good. I want you to start tomorrow and make up for the four days Sandesh has missed. The class is held at seven every morning in room two fourteen downstairs." He points his index finger to the tiled floor to articulate 'downstairs'.

"I'll be there." I assure him.

He takes out a file from the top drawer of his desk and places it in front of himself.

"This contains all the information about the course and how far Sandesh had covered it till his departure last Saturday." He taps his finger on the dossier and then hands it to me.

"Thanks. I'll get started tomorrow." I suspect my voice betrays my excitement.

"Fine. Just let Ms. Hutton know that your assistantship commences tomorrow."

I fly with the file to the Administration building, ecstatic about my new assignment. It may last only till the end of the term but that possibility fails to dampen my spirit. I am thrilled to get the opportunity even for a short duration. Ms. Hutton cannot miss my panting when I reach her desk.

"That was the shortest job interview of the century and the fastest dash ever, wasn't it?" She smiles. I presume she empathizes with my gasping for breath.

"Well, Dr. Fingleton seemed to have screened my background before I met with him. And your call to him helped too." I reply between deep breaths.

"You seem excited about the new job." She observes.

"Absolutely. It's a promotion, in a sense." I see no harm in being open about my feelings.

"Good for you. But now I need to find someone for the Seymours cafeteria." She pretends to be burdened by the responsibility.

"It shouldn't be hard."

"No, it shouldn't. I suggest you come back tomorrow afternoon to complete the paperwork for your assistantship. But be sure you take the material science class tomorrow. Otherwise, Dr. Fingleton'll kill both of us." She play-acts slashing her own throat with her index finger and laughs.

"I will."

"And don't forget to do your shift at the cafeteria tonight." She shouts after me as I leave her desk and head for the staircase.

Fourteen

Once I am alone, I perceive the need to prepare for starting my new job. It has been a while since I studied materials science; five years to be precise. In all likelihood, my knowledge of the subject is rusty. Given the limited time on hand to de-rust, I decide to start working on it without wasting a minute and take a detour to the library to collect all the recommended reference books. They are more than a handful but I manage to haul them to the dorm to ready myself for the morrow.

Sandesh Thapa's record keeping is meticulous. His date-wise teaching plan and its implementation log simplify my job of continuing from where he left off. He has already covered almost sixty percent of the curriculum but the four classes he has missed since his departure have created a backlog. I need to re-draw the teaching plan to complete the course in the remaining days.

The exhilaration of suddenly landing the assistantship subsides once the news sinks in. It is quickly replaced by jitters of teaching for the first time ever, either in India or here. However, the prospect of taking over from someone out of the Indian subcontinent provides a bit of comfort. The students must already be used to Sandesh's diction; they should not face difficulty with mine. But the lingering memory of Kevin's racially motivated comment in the TV lounge a few weeks earlier does not allow my mind to purge the anxiety completely.

In an effort to smoothen my jangling nerves, I try to focus on the task at hand. I begin by making a fresh teaching plan to accommodate the topics that Sandesh would have covered had he not missed four classes. Then I go through the books borrowed from the library to whip up my hibernating knowledge of ceramics, the material on the next day's roster. I take down copious notes not only to ensure rigorous coverage of the topic but also to act as back up for any memory lapses during the class. Finally, I squeeze these notes into a one-page decoction of bullet points to act as navigating beacons during the course of my lecture.

The preparation makes me feel confident of my proficiency in the subject. But unless I can effectively impart this insight, it is of no value. I have never stood in front of forty college students to deliver a lecture. It is a daunting task, made harder by the need to be the expert. While I am trying to figure out a way to deal with it, I suddenly remember the training I had undergone at the steel forge in India.

Twenty four of us young recruits were assigned to a two-day workshop on public speaking, held at a local starred hotel. Mr. Raman, the trainer, was an experienced professional who knew our pulse.

"You consider this program redundant because you're engineers, not politicians. You don't see yourselves giving speeches. So you want to treat the training as a two-day break from the heat and dust of your factory, with breaks for coffee and lunch thrown in." He began, correctly echoing the thoughts in our minds.

"In air-conditioned comfort." An obnoxious participant amongst us interjected.

"But please understand that any time you speak to more than one person, it's public speaking. And unless you're able to effectively articulate the ideas in your head, they're worth nothing." He continued, oblivious to the interjection.

"We can communicate through engineering drawings and specification sheets." At least one participant still refused to take Mr. Raman seriously.

"True. But more often than not, you need to explain your views orally. If you can't do that cogently, you'll be consigned to the lower rungs of the corporate hierarchy." It was evident he had encountered skeptics before and knew exactly how to sidestep their interruptions.

"Do you think a two-day programme can turn us into great orators?" The trainer had made us appreciate the value of public speaking.

"You'll decide that, not me. In a few moments from now, we'll start with each of you getting thirty seconds to stand here and talk about the subject you know the best." He paused for effect.

"Which is?" An impatient participant could not hold back the question.

"Your own selves. And we'll close this workshop tomorrow evening with extempore debates in which each of you'll speak for five minutes. You be the judge of how you progress between now and tomorrow." The chorus of 'wow' from the captivated trainees showed Mr. Raman had taken a firm grip on his audience.

The next two days turned out to be an amazing transformational experience. Mr. Raman made us understand and internalize the nuances of speaking to an audience, embedding the dos and don'ts of oratory in all of us. Over this short period, we morphed from tongue-tied mumblers unable to fill half a minute with the highlights of our twenty two years into fluent speakers who could hold a gathering in a thrall.

Fortunately, I have carried to America the notes taken down during that programme. I use them as cues and rehearse in front of the mirror for dusting my lecturing skills. The fifteen-minute workout helps me get rid of the earlier nervousness. I feel relaxed when I walk down to the cafeteria for my last day this term as the student manager.

"I guess assistantship is better for you but I'm sorry you won't be coming in from tomorrow. We'll miss you." I am not sure Ms. Maurer means it.

"Ms. Hutton promised to send my replacement immediately." I assure her nonetheless.

When I return to my room, I remember that teachers are required to wear a necktie and, therefore, a dress shirt. They are in my suitcase stashed under the bed. As I finish taking them out and stowing the suitcase away, there is a knock on the door. Kevin, Jonathan and Tim enter when I open it. I am taken aback.

"I didn't think you knew each other." I refrain from adding that I did not expect Kevin and Jonathan to ever come looking for me.

"Goddamit man, I heard you won assistantship." Tim slaps my back with his usual gusto and guffaw. I had not looked at the assignment in terms of winning and losing. But Tim is right; Sandesh had to lose it before I could have got it.

"No big deal, really. I just got lucky the original TA left midway." I downplay the appointment with a shrug.

"Bullshit, man. Five hundred bucks a month and out of state tuition waiver is no small deal."

"Well, that's a help."

"We should celebrate, shouldn't we guys?" Tim looks to his friends for support.

"You bet. Calls for a party." Kevin seconds Tim.

"Where'd you guys want to go?" I realize they are unlikely to budge. Besides, I would not mind a celebration myself.

"We're thinking of Godfather's Pizza." Jonathan proposes.

"Godfather's it is. Let's go." I concede.

Tim is full of raucous fun but I am not sure about Kevin and Jonathan. They do not know I overheard Kevin's petulant comment in the TV lounge. Since then, I have been civil with them but do not foresee having a great time in their company. Tonight, I plan to avoid an altercation for everyone's sake.

We first drive to a house on Franklin Avenue where Samantha and Doris, both sophomores from Iowa, join us. All of them seem to know one another. I welcome the presence of two more members in the party; it would reduce my interaction with Kevin and Jonathan.

But I am in for another surprise. Both of them display a wry sense of humour and are out-and-out party animals. Kevin does great mimicry, too. He keeps us thoroughly entertained by speaking like Jimmy Carter, Ronald Reagan and, best of all, Clint Eastwood. When I tell them about my encounter with Ronny Parton, he acts Parton the stand-up comedian.

"A friend of mine returned to LA last week after spending a couple of years in Europe. He couldn't find a parking slot on Sunset Boulevard. All of them were taken by camels." He sounds exactly like Parton.

"Are the Arabs really buying the whole world?" Doris wonders.

We are in splits.

None of them has traveled much. They know little beyond the geography lessons taken at school. India is an unknown entity.

"We still have many joint families." I am sure they would not know that.

"What's that, Guru? Some kind of commune?" Tim is puzzled.

"No. Three generations, sometimes four, living in the same house."

"Really? You mean boys and girls don't move out when they grow into men and women?" Samantha finds it hard to imagine the scene. I consider her way of putting the question interesting.

"That's right. The children, their parents and grand parents, all live together." I am amused by the surprise on their faces.

"You mean they share one house?" Kevin appears shocked.

"Yes. Actually, it works out very well for everyone. The children benefit from their grandparents' wisdom and the company of their cousins, their parents can work without sending the kids to a crèche and the grandparents don't face loneliness in their infirm years."

"You make it sound like a win-win. But we're too individualistic in this country." Tim explains the reason behind nuclear families.

"I might actually enjoy having my grandpa around all the time. I love listening to his stories from the World War he fought in Europe." Doris is honest.

I want to return to the dorm and go to bed at a decent hour; the teaching commitment at seven in the morning is weighing on my mind. But the five of them ambush my attempts to wind down the evening. Finally, the restaurant manager virtually throws us out. By the time we drop Samantha and Doris on Franklin, Kevin and Jonathan at their apartment further south and return to the dorm, it is well past midnight.

My plan to kick off my treasured new assignment with a focused mind in a relaxed body is sunk in the sea of benumbing somnolence. I sleep through my alarm; when I eventually wake up, it is six thirty five. I jump out of the bed and scamper through my morning routine, losing precious minutes in knotting the mandatory necktie. Reaching late for any appointment is a sin here; on the very first day it would be sacrilege. Desperate to avoid it, I sprint across the campus to McPherson, barely managing to stay up on the icy walkways.

I enter the class on the run, beating the bell by a couple of seconds. The books and the folder of notes are resting on my left shoulder, clasped between the thumb and fingers of my left hand. As I approach the table in front of the blackboard, I trip. Although I somehow manage to avoid the fall, my fingers lose their grip on the books and the folder. The bunch flies forward, landing in the waste paper basket by the leg of the table. I miss a heartbeat. What an embarrassment! But I quickly spot an opportunity in the mishap.

"In my class, that's where the books belong." I pretend the book-drop was deliberate.

"Wow." The students cheer in chorus. A few clap.

"Let me clarify. I expect you to read the books before the class. We'll devote the time in here to learn the application of what you've read." They should not conclude that I do not care for the books.

"Mr. Thapa followed a different practice." A student in the first row volunteers the information.

"Unfortunately, Mr. Thapa can't return till the end of the term. We'll follow the practice I just mentioned." I neither know how Sandesh taught nor wish to discard my method.

"Can you introduce yourself?" The question comes from the last row.

I briefly outline my background. A few nods of approval suggest respect for my engineering education and industrial work experience. The response heightens my self-assurance. I hoist myself to sit on the table facing the class, feet dangling, to show informality and foster rapport with my students.

"Those of you suffering withdrawal symptoms are excused." I make an oblique reference to the police raid two days ago on the cache of a drug peddler not far from the campus.

The whole class erupts in uproarious laughter. From then on, I blossom as a teacher, not needing to retrieve the bullet points lodged in the dustbin until the hour gets over. At the end of the session, the studious of the lot surround me. They want to know if the tests will be descriptive or multiple choice. I am not a fan of the multiple choice format and tell them so. While speaking to the group, my attention is drawn to a student on my right intently staring at me through her lovely clear blue eyes. The notebook held flat against her front by her folded arm has 'Sarah Walker' written in bold black marker near its top edge. She has an oval face and Chris Evert nose. I find her very attractive, if not beautiful. I ignore the distraction.

On leaving the class, I reflect on my debut performance. I feel satisfied and ask God to bless Mr. Raman, wherever he is, for grooming me to speak in front of an assembly.

Fifteen

My life is now settled in the routine of a graduate student on teaching assistantship. I am as busy as I have ever been. And I enjoy it. But the cold weather continues to be a source of bother. The locals are complaining about the severity of this winter compared to several previous ones. With a body acclimatized to warmer climes, I would be uncomfortable even in milder temperatures. This iciness is frost-biting my bones, try as I may to cope up.

It is a Tuesday morning in the first week of February, as frozen as many before it. I exit the dorm on my way to teach material science, all wrapped up to keep myself warm. While I descend the steps of the building, an oriental student approaches from the opposite direction. He stops me.

"You from India?" He asks straight up front; no pleasantries. I do not mind the discourtesy; he has not asked if I am Iranian.

"Yes."

"Me from Taiwan. Are you Hindu?" I am stumped. That is the last question I expected.

"Yes. Why?" His line of questioning is curious.

"Your room?" He asks instead of answering.

"Two forty nine."

"You okay me come eight evening." His English is frugal. I decipher it without difficulty.

"Okay."

All through the day I rack my brain to figure out why this guy wants to come to my room. I cannot come up with a plausible reason. Although I have been here barely three months, I know that students from the Far East possess excellent numerical skills but need help in writing term papers. English is their weak link. I would understand if he wants me to draft his term papers. But why would he want to know if I am a Hindu? My religion has nothing to do with my English writing ability.

For no other reason but to solve the mystery, I await the appointed time. I need to work on my marketing term paper but find it difficult to concentrate. At long last, the watch shows eight. The knock comes a minute later.

"Me come in?" Mr. Taiwan asks with a smile. I wave him in. He is carrying a thick red hardbound book. His white canvas Reeboks are laden with frozen slush. It melts into a dirty puddle on the floor. He is embarrassed and profusely apologizes, saying sorry, or rather 'solly', a million times. He acts out the mopping action and enquires by raising his eyebrows. I point at the mop standing in the corner. He asks me to keep the red book on the desk, tiptoes to the mop and wipes the mess on the floor.

The hardbound book looks like a dictionary. Most oriental students carry their compact editions around the campus but this is a much bigger volume.

I take a closer look at Mr. Taiwan. The young man is of medium height and build, probably around five feet seven weighing less than a hundred and thirty pounds. He has a round face, small nose and straight black hair falling into a fringe on his forehead. His eyebrows are shielded by the large tortoiseshell frame of Christian Dior glasses. Inside his quilt-lined leather winter coat, he is wearing a white half-sleeved T-shirt tucked in white cotton trousers. The stainless steel Rolex Oyster on a loose strap appears too big for his wrist.

"Me Cheng Jian from Taiwan. MA economics class. And you?" He shakes my hand and initiates the dialogue in his no-frills English. I introduce myself and bid him to take the chair. He is more interested in persisting with his inquisition.

"You student which class?" I have heard this question many times before. For reasons best known to them, most oriental students think one's course of study is an intrinsic part of one's identity.

"MBA." I want to ask him the purpose of his visit but he gives me no opportunity. He pops his next question even before I finish my answer.

"You learn Sanskrit?" His pronunciation of 'Sanskrit' is more like 'Sanklit'. But the morning's reference to Hinduism helps me interpret his query.

I want him to know straight off the bat that I am no Sanskrit pundit, lest his expectations rise too high. But neither am I completely illiterate in the ancient language.

The unexpected question I am confronted with takes me back more than a decade and a half.

As children, my brother and I had to learn Sanskrit mantras or verses from Hindu scriptures. This was a highly demanding pursuit, an extra-curricular activity forced into our carefree lives when my brother was nine and I seven. Our school was secular; it preached no religion. Scriptures were taught at home, at the cost of our week-end fun. From Monday to Friday, the school ran right through the day, leaving no time for much else. On Saturday, we had morning school finishing before lunch time. Sunday was the weekly off, a holdover from the British rule. Hinduism has no concept of Sabbath. Prayer is prescribed daily; not on one designated day of the week.

Although the school set us free at noon on Saturday, our teachers buried us under a mountain of homework. Completing it devoured much of the week-end. The only time left for outdoor sports like cricket and soccer was the afternoons on Saturday and Sunday.

Our house has a large front yard. It is circumscribed by a high brick wall fitted with a wide two-paned gate made from thick panels of seasoned timber. It completely screens the courtyard from the street outside. The gate is bolted shut except to let oversized objects through. A small spring-loaded door encased in one panel of the gate allows access to pedestrians. The spring holds the door closed unless someone pushes it open. The enclosed yard provides ample space to play without fear of losing the ball to neighbours.

The priest appointed to teach us the mantras did not keep a fixed time. 'Week-end afternoons' was the description of his schedule. He arrived any time between four and five to incarcerate us for one hour, sometimes stretching the punishment by an additional half hour. Sadly, we had no way to plan our game without his unannounced interruption. On a good day, he would not turn up at all, presumably because of some ailment. Much to our chagrin though, he rarely fell ill despite his advancing age.

Our friends from the neighbourhood would regularly turn up to play at around three. We would split the group into two teams and start the game. But invariably, just when it reached its most interesting phase, the priest would walk in through the spring-loaded door to throw a wet blanket on our keenly fought match. Negotiating some grace period before the lock-up was out of the question. We had to stop the game in its tracks and start the tuition. Our friends would wait impatiently outside our room for the lesson to end. With two out of six players grounded, they could not continue the game.

The tutor was an old man. No one seemed to know his exact age but he looked well beyond sixty five. He was thin and short, not much taller than five feet. His face was wrinkled, eyes deep set, sunken cheeks emphasizing high cheek bones. He had lost most of his teeth, choosing not to replace them with dentures. We had to show absolute respect to him for he was a learned man. Privately though, we made fun of his small size, imagining a gust of wind blowing him away. We rarely saw him smile and at times debated if he had ever laughed. His usual visage was strange; angry and sad at the same time, prompting us to describe it as 'Hitler in mourning'. Other than the mantras, he spoke little.

The routine of the lesson was simple: the tutor chanted a verse from the scriptures; we heard it carefully and tried to emulate him. He would repeat the verse till we could recite it exactly the way he did. When we felt terribly peeved, we would deliberately make mistakes, inviting several repetitions. That was our rebellion against the tyranny. We hoped that the waggery would force early termination of the irksome incarceration. Regrettably though, it bore no fruit. The mischief would annoy him, but it only prompted a razor sharp glare. The wake-up call almost always worked. We could not risk his complaining to Dad. That would attract serious trouble.

Halfway into the tuition, the maid would serve the tutor a cup of tea and some sweets. He would pour the tea into the saucer to cool it quickly, then gulp it down before taking his own time to enjoy the sweets. We had to wait in silence till he finished his snack. Sometimes we suspected he intentionally took long to stretch our agony. The prolonged confinement would test our patience but we had to grin and bear the hardship.

Eventually, he would take pity on us and call it a day. But more often than not, the release would be after dusk, preempting resumption of our unfinished game. If that happened on a Saturday, we would resolve to finish the match on Sunday before he turned up. When a game had to be paused on a Sunday, we would just abandon it. Cricket matches the world over are known to be interrupted by rain or bad light, acts of God. Ours did due to His agent's.

The relentless torment hurt even more because of two reasons. One, we considered this training pointless. Neither my brother nor I wanted a career in priesthood. We saw no future use of the ability to rattle off mantras. Two, our sister was exempt from this punishment. She was free to enjoy her week-ends the way she pleased. It was another matter that she inadvertently memorized the mantras by simply overhearing us.

The painful coaching went on right through our primary and high school years. Despite our reluctance, our receptive young minds picked up and retained the Sanskrit verses. On some religious festival or another, we would be asked to recite them. The credit for our progress, whatever that meant, was always claimed by the tutor. He no doubt considered it his divine duty to sabotage most of our keenly fought games. We often wondered why God displayed such little sportsman spirit.

The practice eventually came to an end when my brother finished high school and joined a college in Bombay. Coincidently, the tutor also aged while we were growing up. He became too frail to leave his home. By then I had stopped playing in the front yard, so the free time available could not be spent in making up the aborted games.

As the days went by, I lost touch with the scriptures and my recitation skill gathered rust. After a few years, I pretty much forgot most of what I had committed to memory as a child. But the grounding received during those years was good enough to let me pick it up again without difficulty.

Sixteen

"You learn Sanskrit?" Cheng repeats his question, bringing me back from my trip down the memory lane.

"I did as a child. I stopped over a decade ago." I consider it wise to be completely transparent.

"Good. Good." He grins, nods with a violent up-and-down shake of his head and pushes the thick red hardback towards me. I open it to see the contents. It is no dictionary.

Cheng's book contains Sanskrit mantras written in Latin alphabets. Sanskrit grammar has an intricate verbal system, rich nominal inflection and widespread use of compound nouns. The language uses different plurals for referring to two and more than two objects or living beings. It has several vowels that exist in no other language. Scholars are divided on the difficulty levels of Greek and Sanskrit but most believe Sanskrit is more difficult.

Sanskrit mantras consist of phonetically complex and often long composite words strung in verses. An unwritten code of placing accent or stress on certain letters is practised.

Without the correct stress, the rendition is treated ineffective. Most westerners are unable to pronounce simple Sanskrit words; even Indians need years of coaching and regular rehearsals to reel them off without mistakes.

Sanskrit is traditionally written in Devanagari, a phonetic script. Being a phonetic language, Sanskrit can be precisely expressed in Devanagari. Latin script being non-phonetic, requires improvisation to correctly convey Sanskrit phonology. Copious notation is, therefore, employed to articulate Sanskrit pronunciations through Latin characters. Sometimes, the available notation is inadequate. For example, Sanskrit includes two slightly different pronunciations of 'sh', each with its own nuance. Devanagari provides different alphabets for these two different sounds. Latin script has nothing that can help separate the two. And in spite of elaborate phonetic notation, proper Sanskrit pronunciation may not be possible without knowing the unwritten code of placing accent and stress on certain letters in a word.

I have never seen Sanskrit text written in Latin script, much less read it. The task poses a formidable challenge. My attention span does not last beyond two minutes. I am still not sure what Cheng wants from me.

"This book contains Sanskrit scriptures describing and praising different incarnations or avatars of God as conceived in Hinduism. But what do you want from me?"

"I know. I know. Wait. Wait." He exhibits another oriental trait of repeating short answers. He dips into his trouser pocket and takes out an audio cassette.

"Your tape deck?" The cassette in his hand and the question mark on his face suggest that he is asking for my tape recorder. I pull out the Panasonic from the closet and place it in front of him on the desk. He inserts the tape in the slot and hits the 'play' button.

The recording is not a divine acoustic experience. The audio is faint, diminished further by heavy static. I try to listen with my ear close to the speaker. It appears to be a rendition of a Sanskrit verse. But the pronunciations are incorrect; the accent on various syllables is either missing or not to the code. I am relieved my tutor is not around to hear this slaughter. He would have either died of shock or killed the culprit for such a serious felony.

I hit the 'stop' button in indignation. After going through the torture, I am none the wiser. It is past eight thirty now. I have a test tomorrow. I need to study. I decide to repeat my question.

"I've heard the tape. It's terrible. What do you want from me?"

"You can read book?" He asks, pointing at the red volume. His habit of countering a question with his own question is getting under my skin.

"Yes, but not now. I've a test tomorrow morning." I want to get out of this boring encounter. Fast.

"Okay. Okay. I go now. Tomorrow eight?" He ejects the tape, pockets it, picks up the book and leaves. I deliberately do not answer his question in the hope that he will not turn up tomorrow.

I have a busy schedule on Wednesday. Apart from the test, I have to attend two classes and teach one. I also spend a couple of hours in the library collecting reference material for my marketing term paper. I am back in my room just before eight in the evening, planning to write a letter to my mother. She must be wondering why I have not written for a month.

My plan is scotched by a knock on the door. When I open it, Cheng is unbuttoning his heavy coat with his left hand. The red volume of Sanskrit mantras is held in the crook of his flexed right arm, flush with his chest. His shoes have no muck on them.

"Me come in?" He smiles. I stand aside and let him enter. After keeping the book on the desk, he takes his coat off and from its inside breast pocket takes out a folded polythene bag.

"For you." He proudly proffers the packet as if he is gifting a bottle of vintage Dom Pérignon. Inside the translucent packet is a black sheet the size of my palm. I take it out, curious. It resembles a crude variety of paper, hand-made from parched melanoid strands, but is not. The look of it scares me; is this some kind of banned substance? I have seen marijuana; it does not look like Cheng's papyrus, although both are dried plants. But then this could easily be a narcotic native to Taiwan. Is this guy into drug peddling?

"What's this?" I almost shout at him, revealing my anxiety in handling the suspicious wild swath. Cheng does not understand my unease.

"Eat." He says, plucks a flake from the membrane and puts it in his mouth. I cringe.

"What're you doing?" I cannot stop myself from screaming.

"Very good." He attempts to assure me. His face reflects ultimate pleasure.

"Not for me, unless I know what it is." I do not want to try anything suspicious.

"Seaweed. Good for you." He acts out the clenched-fists outstretched-arms-bent-at-elbows pose of musclemen in a body-building competition to highlight the health benefits of his precious present. I am still doubtful but my curiosity eggs me to try out the weed. I take a morsel of the stuff and gingerly place it on the tip of my tongue. It has no particular taste except a little saltiness. I do not understand how Cheng can find it delicious. I wait to experience its effect. There is none. No double vision, no hallucinations, no grogginess. I remain stone sober. Cheng is no drug peddler. I have nothing to fear.

"It's not great; nothing really to write home about." I wonder if he understands me.

"Special for you. From my country." I try to pretend I am very impressed. It is hard.

"All right Cheng, what'd you want from me?" I come to the point. The letter to Mom is still very much my priority. He pulls out a cassette tape from the hip pocket of his Calvin Klein jeans, inserts it in the tape deck on the desk and hits 'play'. It is the same rendition I had heard yesterday. I cannot stand it. I punch the 'stop' button without seeking Cheng's permission.

"That's a terrible way to recite the mantras. Where'd you get it?"

"In Taipei. One Indian man I know. He read from book." He taps on the red volume on the desk.

"It's no good." I hate criticising my own compatriot. But I do not want to lie.

"You read more better?" My emphatic condemnation of the recording makes him expectant. His hope is written in his eyes. I ignore Cheng's grammar and focus on the meaning.

"Absolutely. Your Indian friend mustn't have learnt Sanskrit. Not every Indian knows how to recite the mantras. But I trained for it as a boy." I reply confidently. The agony of losing all those week-ends to the grim tutor has dulled. Now I am proud to spread the refined spirituality of my ancient civilization.

"You tape for me?"

"Yes."

He pulls the red tome towards himself with a flourish, flips several leaves and stops on page 273 about halfway through the book. Then he pushes the open volume towards me, his breath bated in anticipation. I read silently. It is a verse in praise of the much revered Hindu Goddess Durga, the invincible, all powerful deity that is believed to have exterminated demons to free the mankind from harassment and subjugation.

Cheng ejects the cassette tape in the deck and replaces it with another one whipped out of his shirt pocket. He hits the 'record' button and shoves the tape recorder close to me.

"Okay. Ready." He nudges me in a hushed voice to avoid recording his own words. I start to read out loud. It is harder than I had imagined. I expected the unfamiliar Latin notation to pose a challenge but I have grossly underestimated its severity. I struggle to achieve even the basic level of fluency. I am forced to stop after a minute of halting rendition. Cheng is perplexed. I wonder if he has started doubting my claim to Sanskrit knowledge. It is sensible to come clean.

"Cheng, I'm not used to reading Sanskrit written in Latin script. The script I trained in is Devanagari. If the verses are written in Devanagari, I can read them correctly and fluently. Do you have a book that has the mantras in Devanagari?" I realize the needlessness of the question as soon as I finish asking it.

"This only book." He looks disappointed. I too feel bad for the let down.

"I wish you did. I can have one sent from India but it'll take at least three weeks, possibly four. And there's no guarantee it'll include these verses." I want to solve the problem but can only do so much.

"Last term. Go back Taiwan. You understand?" He sweeps his right arm in an upward arc and whistles the sound of an airplane.

The term ends in three weeks. Getting a book from India is out of the question. We need another way out. Cheng has an idea.

"You write?" He asks, hope evident in his eyes. My interactions with friends from East Asia have taught me to unravel thrifty oriental English. Cheng wants to know if I can write in Devanagari.

"Of course I can write in Devanagari. But I'm out of practice. I'll be slow." I caution him.

"No problem, no problem." Obviously, it is not a problem for him. It will be for me if I am required to rewrite a lengthy text.

"How many pages do you want me to record?" He pulls the book towards him and turns a few pages to come to the end of the set of verses about Goddess Durga.

"Fifteen pages." He works backwards after looking at the bottom of the page. I follow his gaze to the page number: 287.

"Rewriting fifteen pages of Latin fine print in Devanagari is a lot of work. It must be done carefully; a tedious job. I'll take hours; thirty, forty, may be more. It's hard to guess." I am not looking forward to the prospect.

"Taiwan no many Indian. Very hard to make good tape. You understand?" His difficulty in getting decent Sanskrit recording done in Taiwan is mirrored on his contorted face. I can empathize with him. It would be equally hard to find someone in India to read Chinese scriptures.

"Since there's no other way, I'll write the mantras in Devanagari and then we can record. But I need a few days." I realize we do not have much time but I would like to buy as much of it as I can.

"Okay. Okay. I come Sunday." He goes away leaving the thick book behind.

Seventeen

With the end of the term approaching, I have much to do. In addition to preparing for the upcoming exams, I need to complete the term papers in all the courses I have opted for. Writing the term papers is not hard but typing them is time consuming. I have never learnt typing; my speed using only two fingers is slow. I also make mistakes that require careful correcting. Expectedly, I land up spending a lot of time in the typing room of the university's library.

The back-end chores of teaching assistantship increase my workload further. Not only do I need to compile notes for lectures but also frame quizzes and grade them. And my efficiency is hit by Sarah Walker's distraction. I am most certainly attracted to her. She too seems to quietly stare at me right through the class and comes up with some pretext or another to talk with me after the bell. But I am unable to decide if she has a soft corner for me or I am misinterpreting her behaviour. After all, I am not fully familiar with the American culture.

Although Sarah keeps popping in my thoughts even when I am occupied with other work, I do not want to increase my interaction with her. I warn myself to maintain the neutrality mandated by our student-teacher relationship every time I am tempted to seek her company beyond the classroom.

In the midst of all the hectic activity, Cheng's scriptures get sidelined. When he turns up on Sunday evening, I have yet to put pen to paper. I must bargain for more time.

"I'm very sorry, Cheng. I couldn't even start rewriting the mantras in Devanagari. There were too many assignments to complete."

"Ohhhh. No much time. Me go Taiwan soon." He touches his heart with his palm and waves the other hand in a bye-bye to suggest his imminent departure. He stands in the middle of the room not knowing what to do next. I want to use his visit to know his motivation for listening to Hindu religious verses.

"I know. But it's a lot of work. And I need to concentrate to do a good job. As I said, it'll take many hours." I justify the delay.

"I know. I know. But no time. You understand?" He is getting worried.

"If I don't finish before you leave, I can send the tape to Taiwan by post." I suggest a plan to reduce my burden.

"Can't trust. Must carry tape." He sounds desperate. I am not sure if he doubts my commitment or has no faith in the postal service. Whatever the case, he is not ready to grant me more time. Perhaps he thinks the assignment is easy.

"I understand. But you've got to appreciate it's a highly skilled job. You won't be able to find anyone else to do it here." I boast and laugh to lighten the mood.

"Okay. Okay. No problem. No problem. I pay twenty dollar for one hour." He does not see the humour in my statement. Worse, he seems to have misunderstood me, thinking I am hankering for my pound of flesh.

"No, Cheng. I was only joking. I don't want any money. I'll do the writing and recording before you leave for Taiwan." I assure him of my sincerity.

"My father very rich. Make tennis, badminton, squash rackets. Big factory in Taipei." That explains the fancy designer labels on his personal effects.

"Good for you but I'm not looking for money. Please, Cheng, I was just joking."

"No problem." I do not understand his implication. I decide to change the track to focus on his motivation.

"Tell me, Cheng, why do you want to record and listen to these Sanskrit scriptures?"

"Me Buddhist. Very religious. Pray many time. Buddhist and Hindu same same." He goes on to utter several words that make no sense. I purse lips and shake head to convey my inability to understand. He reaches for my notebook lying on the desk, opens a blank page and writes down *kamma, dhamma, saustika, nibbana* and *dhamma chakka*.

I quickly get what he wants to convey. *Kamma* is *karma* in Sanskrit, literally meaning 'action' or 'deed' but understood as 'that which causes the entire cycle of cause and effect'. *Dhamma,* or *dharma* in Sanskrit, literally means 'religion' but implies 'duty' or, in a more profound context, 'the way of life to eternal truth'. *Saustika*, originally *swastika*, is a sacred symbol of Hindus. *Nibbana*, or *nirvana* in many languages, is the ultimate peace with oneself, attained through liberation from earthly desires and aversions. *Dhamma chakka*, or *dharma chakra* in Sanskrit, literally means 'wheel of *dharma*'. It is a symbol representing the 'path of enlightenment'. It appears at the centre of the Indian flag as 24-spoke 'Ashok c*hakra*', named after the great ancient Indian king who converted to Buddhism around 250 BC. The c*hakra* also appears in different forms as a seal or coat of arms in Mongolia, Sikkim, Sri Lanka and Thailand. It is not yet a part of the US military chaplain insignia but would be inducted a decade later.

Cheng Jian is interested in Sanskrit scriptures because of the similarities in his religion and Hinduism. It sounds reasonable, even logical. Perhaps he believes Buddha was born a Hindu, although the claim stands contested by many scholars.

He reaches into his hip pocket and draws out his leather wallet, probably Gucci. His action scares me; I do not want him to pay me anything, now or later. But before I can stop him, he reaches in the dollar bills compartment and withdraws a small piece of folded paper. He unfolds it and hands to me. It carries a neatly typed philosophy:

We are not human beings having a spiritual experience, but we are spiritual beings having a human experience. – Pierre Teilhard de Chardin.

"You think?" Cheng wants my opinion on the quote of the French paleontologist-philosopher, more famous for his controversial book *Le Phénomène Humain*, or

The Phenomenon of Man. I am clearly not qualified to comment but find irony in devout Cheng preserving the quote of a man initially scorned upon by men of religion.

"I don't know." I reply in all honesty.

"Me become monk in Taiwan." He shares his intent. It does not add up.

"Why are you doing economics? You should study theology." I try my hand at counseling.

"Theology?" Obviously he has not heard the word. I need to rephrase my question.

"Why don't you study religion?"

"My father. Businessman. He want economics. Me, no." I get the picture now. Cheng is his father's retirement plan; someone to handover the business to. The Taiwanese culture forbids Cheng from revolting; he must walk the path his parents choose. Along with the parental support comes the parental diktat. I can appreciate Cheng's circumstances; many in India also endure them.

"Hopefully you'll manage to convince your father when you go back." There is nothing else to say.

"Hope." In Chinglish, it means 'hope so'. He rises to leave.

The next two weeks are awfully busy, yet I am determined to find time to rewrite the scriptures. It takes longer than my estimate. Every night I start the exercise after supper and don't stop till the small hours. I virtually re-live the long nights devoted to completing the engineering drawings during my undergraduate years, except that the rewriting process is slower. At the end of each session, I find I have covered a page and a half, sometimes less. But eleven back-breaking nights later the Devanagari text is ready. Now it is a matter of a couple of hours for recording my recitation on Cheng's tape. That is the easy part. I feel relieved. Cheng can visit any time.

He turns up on Saturday evening. This would be his last week-end at school.

"Finish?" He enquires as soon as I open the door.

"No. I couldn't find any time at all. I'm really sorry." I pull a fast one.

"Ohhh. Very bad. Term end Wednesday. I go Taipei Thursday morning." He remains rooted in the hallway, too dejected to enter the room. I fear he will start crying any moment.

"Come in, please. Don't worry. I'm done." I call off my bluff.

"Really? Good. Good. Good." He cannot hide his ecstasy.

For the next two hours, we record my rendition. The ease with which I read from Devanagari script convinces Cheng of the need for re-writing the fifteen pages. He re-plays a few segments to verify the recording quality. His face attains the tranquility of nirvana.

While leaving the room, he walks backwards facing me. In India, the gesture conveys ultimate deference. Either it carries the same import in Taiwan as well or he has bothered to find out the Indian way. Whatever the reality, I feel gratified. I suspect he considers the new audio cassettes more precious than the master's degree he is poised to receive on Wednesday.

The next few days whiz past in a blur as they are wont to do at the end of a term. Cheng Jian, his red hardback of Sanskrit mantras and the long nights of slow Devanagari scribble seem distant history. My happiness at getting good grades eclipses everything else. On Thursday, I have to leave the dorm for the week-long term-break. I am going to Chicago to spend the free time with friends.

Just before leaving, I remember to check my mail box in the dorm's entrance lobby. I hope to get a letter from my family before going away for a week. I unlock the pigeonhole and take out the packet inside. It is not the familiar bluish grey aerogramme from India but a square-flap #10 envelope. Since the place earmarked for a postage stamp is blank, it must have been hand-delivered. My name and room number seem to be written by an individual who normally writes one of the oriental scripts. More surprisingly, the sender's name is missing. Rather than guessing it, I decide to check the contents and find out.

Neatly wrapped in Cheng's 'thank you' note are ten crisp new $100 bills.

Eighteen

Come March, the new term begins. I audit a course in basic economics. This is a great way to informally catch up on background knowledge without increasing the number of credit hours towards the degree. Auditing a class is new to me. The concept does not exist in India. One cannot choose to attend a class but not get a grade or credit for it. I enjoy auditing Dr. Dolecke's economics course.

The class is held in a room furnished with tables, each accommodating two students sitting side by side. I occupy the second row from the front, third from the back. I split my table with Kieron Washington, an African American majoring in economics. Kieron is tall and muscular, sporting an oval face, bright eyes and Arthur Ashe mane. His swagger reminds me of Viv Richards, the famous Caribbean cricketer. Kieron has a studious look about him. His voice is gravelly, laugh boisterous.

At the beginning of the first lecture, we introduce ourselves but before we can go further, Dr. Dolecke walks in to shut us up. I look forward to talking with Kieron. I know no other African American on the campus. Despite civil rights and affirmative action, few of them go to college, fewer still reach graduate school.

During the first week, we do not get time to go beyond "Hello", "Good morning" or "How're you doing?" On Thursday of the second week, I oversleep and miss breakfast. I decide to go to the union cafeteria to grab a bite after the class. Kieron joins me. Once we are seated, he with a coffee and I with donuts, we get an opportunity to chat. He is easy to talk with, except for my difficulty in following his accent.

I ask him about his family, a safe topic to begin with, I reckon. I do not want any mishaps.

"My dad picked cotton in Arkansas. We're from Blytheville."

"Do you've any siblings, Kieron?"

"Ya, we're eleven, five girls and six boys. I'm the youngest."

"Big family."

"My mother died when I was eight months old. Otherwise we may've been more." He chuckles. It does not bother him that he barely knows me. Back home, such a comment on parents is blasphemy.

"Does your father still pick cotton?"

"Nah. Quit long ago. Retired. He's wasted on moonshine all day long." Another heresy. His candour is shocking.

"Must've retired early, then."

"Can't blame him, can we? Got framed in a theft charge and went to prison. Couldn't work on getting out." He is startlingly blasé. His story reminds me of

To Kill A Mocking Bird , Harper Lee's literary masterpiece I had read years ago as a teenager.

"How'd you manage when he was locked up?" I cannot stop myself from asking.

"Scavenged, pretty much. Jokes apart, my brothers and sisters fended for us. Brothers worked the cotton gin. Two sisters turned hookers in Memphis. They're pretty, you know." I am dumbstruck by his astonishing disclosure and need to search for an appropriate comment.

"Must've been tough." I eventually say, knowing the inanity of the remark.

"I hate poverty ma'an. It's hard growing up in a hood. We never saw Benjamin."

"What's a hood? And who's Benjamin?"

"Neighbourhood, ma'an. An inner-city neighbourhood. And haven't you seen a hundred-dollar bill with Benjamin Franklin's face on it, Guru? That's a Benjamin."

"But you've done well to get to college." I want him to change track to middle-class topics.

"Was tough, ma'an. No one finished high school in my whole family. I shined shoes in the evenings." He is entering plebeian territory again.

"Are you on scholarship here, Kieron?" I try to bring him back to white-collar ground.

"Nah. I ain't that smart, ma'an." He laughs his bubbly laughter.

"Does your family support you, then?"

"They ain't that well off. I work nights at QuikTrip."

Kieron spots a couple of his African American friends entering the cafeteria. He calls for them. I have had my dose of jolts for the day. Any more and I will get dizzy. I finish my donut and leave. But the rustic exchange helps to develop bonhomie between us. Kieron praises my handwriting and makes fun of my diction. I complement him for his determination and joke about his vernacular slang. He becomes a friend, asking me to explain some principles in trigonometry.

The day before the Easter break commences, I ask him his plans for the holidays.

"No plans, ma'an. Gotta work my butt off. Can't afford a break." He is matter of fact about his fate.

"Too bad." I don't wish to allow the discussion to wander to his family. God knows what he will have to say about his other siblings.

"Not really. They pay double time on public holidays. I'll also get to moonlight at the mall. They need extra hands in the season." He actually sounds upbeat. From the context, I make out the meaning of 'moonlight' as working a second job. I add another word to my repertoire of Americanese.

About a month after our trip to the union cafeteria, both of us happen to get to the class early. Dr. Dolecke would not appear for another ten minutes. A few other students are scattered around the room. Kieron and I get a chance to talk.

"It's cold, ma'an, not normal April weather." He complains about the lingering winter, rubbing his palms against each other.

"I know. Hate it." I join in as he sits down.

"You're lucky, ma'an. Don't have to worry over tests and grades." He refers to my auditing the course.

"I like that. But I've other classes to worry about." I explain.

Kieron brings up the upcoming Super Bowl. He is an Oakland Raiders fan and thinks they have the best chance of winning the championship. I don't understand rugby, much less American football. I hold no opinion on the subject.

Then suddenly Kieron shifts to another topic.

"Hey Guru, are your ears pierced?" I find him looking at my earlobe. This is the first time anyone has asked me the question. It takes me by surprise.

Ear piercing is an ancient Hindu tradition. In my community, ear lobes of both male and female infants are pierced when they are twelve days old. *Karnavedha*, as it is called in Sanskrit, is ceremoniously carried out by a goldsmith with a fine gold wire. Gold earrings adorn the infant from that day on. No one really knows when the practice was introduced or why it is followed. A number of theories have filtered through the centuries.

Many attribute scientific reasons for the rite. They claim that earlobes carry several vital acupuncture and acupressure points. Piercing and pressing the middle of the lobe where the baby's ears are pricked is purported to prevent breathing ailments. That is why ancient Hindu men and women wore earrings, a practice that is still common in many parts of rural India.

Some others consider *Karnavedha* a Vedic rite of passage. It is supposed to open the child's senses for receiving holy reverberations. The ritual is assumed to have profound spiritual importance. Simply hearing holy sounds is believed to cleanse sins and nurture the soul.

Several Hindus from Tamilnadu, a state on the south-east coast of India, believe piercing a hole in the ear completes the shape of symbol *om* in Tamil script. According to the *Vedas*, the ancient Hindu scriptures, *om* represents the life energy of the whole universe including the Supreme Being or God. Some scholars believe that *om* is the sound of the infinite expanding energy of the cosmos that can be heard by those who achieve absolute mental stillness or focus. Chanting *om* is said to be therapeutic for one's body as well as soul. As a holy symbol, it is as important to Hindus as the cross is to Christians.

And still others, although in a small minority, consider it a simple trick employed by Hindus to distinguish their men from Moslems during the Mughal invasions of the Indian subcontinent.

Whatever the reason, the bottom line is, my ears are pierced. And I see no reason to be shy of the fact.

"Yes, they are." I reply to Kieron's query.

"Oh, I didn't know you followed the practice." His tone reflects his surprise.

"You're not alone. Few in this country know about life in India." The disappointment buried in my mind re-surfaces.

"Good to know that, ma'an." His tone turns cheerful.

"Well, you're a bit wiser now, aren't you?" I feel proud to help reduce ignorance of my country.

"Have you been to parties here?" I find the question odd. Why would I not go to parties if I am invited?

"Of course I've been. It's fun to have a good time." I want to announce my gregarious character.

"Great. I'll take you with me this week-end." He promises, taking my hand into his.

Before I can respond, Dr. Dolecke walks in and starts taking attendance. I turn my attention to him and withdraw my hand from Kieron's. The topic for today's class is free-market economy. My experience with this model is recent, only since I got to America. In my country, the government drives most aspects of the financial system. I am engrossed in the lecture, realizing the hour is over only when the bell rings.

While I am going down the stairwell, Janette Helmuth joins me. She sits behind Keiron and me in the economics class. Janette is a short and plump blonde with a freckled round face. Her chubby cheeks pinch her piercing blue eyes into thin wedges and also make her normal sized nose look smaller. It is a mystery how she can speak without much moving her slender lips. Janette has a habit of wearing tight blouses and tighter skirts or slacks, probably in the hope of looking less portly. Unfortunately, she seems to spill out of them and look flabbier. Nobody has dared tell her that.

Behind her substantial façade hides a very sharp mind and highly perceptible senses. She is a straight-A student. All teachers respect her; students often mob her to get their doubts cleared. She is far more aware of the world outside America than most Americans and, in fact, has told me a few facts about India that I did not know. It is always enlightening to speak with her.

"I didn't know you were queer, Guru." She starts the conversation.

"What do you mean?" I really do not understand her remark.

"Are you telling me you don't know what queer is?" She is testing me. I am not too happy about my English proficiency being questioned.

"Of course I know what queer is. But why'd you want to call me that?" I suspect I say it more forcefully than is necessary.

"What else to call you after overhearing your exchange with Kieron?" She asks. I do not know what she is talking about.

"What's odd in what we talked, Janette?" I am getting perplexed. Janette is not known to pull anyone's leg.

"There's nothing odd, Guru. It shows you're queer." She expects me to understand. I do not.

We are out of the building now. She turns towards the library. I stop her. She has pierced my ego. That is a lot harder to bear than a pierced ear.

"Look Janette, I've no clue what you're trying to suggest. You need to explain." I accept defeat.

"So you admit you don't know what queer is. That shows your ignorance. It doesn't change the reality." She still has not told me what I want to know.

"What'd you mean?" I am getting impatient now.

"What I mean is I didn't know you're gay." I reel as if Nolan Ryan's fast ball has hit me in the groin. Then I look around, trying to gauge if anyone has overheard her. Fortunately, no one is near enough.

"Why do you say that?" I ask after gathering myself.

"Don't tell me you didn't understand what Kieron asked."

"And what do you reckon he asked?" I am getting more and more confused now.

"I don't need to reckon. I heard." She wants every word to be precise.

"Come on Janette, let's not pick on semantics. Just tell me what you heard Kieron ask." I want to bring this discussion to its end. Quickly.

"He asked you if your ears are pierced." I expect her to continue. She does not.

"Okay, so that's what he asked. And I told him my ears are pierced. How does it make me gay?" I hear my voice getting agitated.

"You're either ignorant or naïve or both. In this country, gay men pierce their ears to wear earrings. Your ear lobe shows a jab. Kieron asked you the question to verify your orientation. And you answered in the affirmative. Now he wants you to join him in his gay parties." She rattles off the clarification I was pleading her for. I am not sure if my explanation is too little too late but I go ahead and outline the significance of pierced ears in my country. And I beg of her to stop thinking I am gay.

"I couldn't care less what you thought if I were indeed gay. But I'm not." I add to seal my argument. As I finish, I realize my voice has climbed more than a few decibels.

"Okay Guru, I accept your explanation. I need to go now." She turns and starts walking.

I hate looking stupid in front of Janette but I am grateful to her for alerting me, albeit inadvertently. I shudder to think what would have happened had I gone to one of Kieron's parties. The thought makes me feel nauseated; I am relieved to enter my room, knowing it has an attached bathroom if I need to throw-up.

I am reluctant to meet Kieron again but have no choice. The task of clearing the misunderstanding is a great burden. I struggle to come up with a plan to handle it. While entering the class the next day, an idea strikes me. I am happy to see Janette at her desk behind mine. She looks at me with a knowing smile. I quickly get to her; it is important we talk before Kieron gets in.

"Can you do me a favour, Janette?" I do not wait for her answer before continuing, "I want someone to provide credibility to my explanation. You're the right person for the job. Will you back me up when I speak to Kieron?" I express my requirement in one breath.

Janette agrees just before Kierron walks in. He has a grin on his face. I look at him with a serious expression. I want to wipe the misunderstanding before the class begins.

"Kieron, I think you're terribly mistaken about my pierced ears. I'm grateful to Janette for pointing it out after yesterday's class." I turn around and look at Janette. So does Kieron. She nods to corroborate my claim.

It takes me a couple of minutes to expand on my point. Janette supports me when I look for her endorsement. Kieron hears me out and breaks into his trademark animated laughter.

"No problem, ma'an. Gay or straight, we can still be friends."

A ton of load is lifted off my chest before Dr. Dolecke walks in.

Nineteen

Missing the fall term for one dollar was undoubtedly a disappointment. But now I see its silver lining. The time to summer break is shorter if you join a new school in winter. I find welcome comfort in that realization.

Between an alien's initial weeks of wide-eyed amazement and subsequent adaptation to the new ways that may take months, lies a miserable phase of what I christen 'domusphilia'. This is a zone where the newness of the experience has waned but the moulding of one's body and mind to the foreign setting is still work-in-progress. The symptoms of domusphilia include chronic hunger for home environment coupled with acute intolerance of present conditions. Even small lifestyle differences between home and abroad, that otherwise would go unnoticed, start getting under the afflicted's skin. Five months on, I find myself suffering from this disorder. It is caused by prolonged withdrawal from deeply ingrained habits. Except for breathing and sleeping, every other facet of my life here has been different to what it was during the previous twenty five years.

Back in India, we do not have to keep doors and windows closed; they are always left open to let the fresh air in. The tropical climate in our part of the world makes heavy clothing unnecessary. I rarely needed to wear a cardigan; never an overcoat. The warm temperatures ensure perpetual blossom of a stunning range of flora. One can always enjoy the splendour of nature's kaleidoscopic pageant: lively greens, brilliant yellows, vivacious pinks, vibrant reds, exciting crimsons, energetic mauves, bubbly violets and earthy browns. A sizzling motorbike ride on colourful country roads in friendly breeze can enhance the pleasure of appreciating this gorgeous landscape. It was a permanent fixture of my week-end afternoons since I earned a license at eighteen. The spin was relaxing and, at the same time, energizing.

On the food front, the difference between America and India is like the proverbial chalk and cheese. Unlike the emphasis on meats here, my diet at home is heavy on plants. In addition to rice, wheat and cereals, the daily menu includes a wide variety of vegetables: leafy, tubers, bulbs, roots, pods, stalks, legumes. And Indian food is spiced with a judicious combination of delicate and strong seasonings. Refined subtlety of saffron, cardamom, cloves, nutmeg and cinnamon is deftly blended with hardy twang of coriander, cumin, paprika, turmeric, garlic, ginger and asafetida to create mouth-watering recipes.

In comparison, I have found everything here strange. The sliding window of my room has remained tightly shut to guard me from the monochromatic freeze outside. The white icicles hanging on its other side and the thick blanket of snow beyond make me feel colour-blind, not to mention sad; back home, the dead and the mourning are clad in white. If I want to step out even for a minute, I must endure the burden of heavy, unwieldy clothing for fear of risking pneumonia. A spin on a motorbike is out of the question in these icy temperatures; my only option to go anywhere in or around the campus is to walk. My diet here includes large portions of meat but few vegetables, fewer still spices. The food I have been eating can be termed bland at best and tasteless at worst.

I feel like an Arabian camel paradropped in the north of Siberia.

There are other parts of my current routine that I did not follow before coming here. After my graduation in India, I neither had to attend classes nor prepare for tests. And as an undergrad, my life was very different. At the engineering college, I enjoyed the concession in class attendance available to sportspersons. The evaluation pattern was different too. We did not face a barrage of exams, they were few: one mid-term quiz covering twenty percent credit followed by an end-of-the-term test for the balance eighty percent. And we wrote one dissertation in the final year. Other than that, submissions comprised only engineering drawings and the results of the experiments we conducted in various labs.

In contrast, my routine here is crowded by classes, study, more study, work and more work. Attendance is mandatory in B-school, tests frequent and term papers a constant nag.

It is an unfamiliar world, any which way I choose to view it. But I remind myself of the primary reason for my enlisting in this adventure: opportunity to gain a wider experience not possible in the cocoon of my home. I also know that given some more time, my body and mind will adapt to this place. Yet right now I am craving for ventilated rooms, colourful landscapes, light clothing, larks in warm breeze, spicy vegetarian food, reprieve from classes, freedom from exams and escape from term papers.

Simply put, I am looking for a piece of home.

The rising mercury in the thermometer promises relief from my domusphilia, at least partly. The approaching summer can provide almost everything I need, short of family and old friends. The thought warms my heart. The change in weather will allow me to mothball heavy clothing and re-open sealed windows. The thaw has started melting the snow; the emerging new green shoots will soon grow into resplendent beauties. And I am excited at the prospect of leaving the dorm and moving to a place where I can cook my own food. My culinary skills have not won me any Michelin stars but those who taste my cooking often ask for second helpings.

Three months of break from school will also provide a much needed breather from classes, study, tests and term papers. I look forward to it. Most of the students plan to use the free time to take up temporary employment of one type or another: manning a convenience store cash register, counting people for the census bureau, pumping gas, waiting tables, restocking supermarket shelves or tending bars. None of these interest me. I am a marketing student at school and would like to make a career in that profession. An important part of marketing is sales; I would like a sales job in summer. I am wondering where to find one.

The opportunity springs out of nowhere. Atif and I are at a fast food joint one Sunday evening just before the summer break. We order and wait to collect our meal. My eyes wander to the pin-up board on one side of the delivery counter. A notice attracts my attention. Midwest Bible Sales out of Chicago are looking for Bible salespersons. I consider it a great opportunity to get some hard-core sales experience. I note down the phone number in the ad before leaving the eatery.

While we are getting into Atif's car, Tom Weber parks right next to us. Tom was in my marketing class last term. I mention to him the idea of selling Bibles. He jumps on it and immediately decides to apply.

On Monday, I call the number I have noted. The conversation is brief. The female voice at the other end of the line tells me to mail an application with my photograph to an address in Chicago. I do as I am told. So does Tom. On Friday, we receive a letter each from Midwest Bible Sales asking us to attend their one week sales training starting on 9th June at a Saint Louis Holiday Inn. We are required to reach the hotel the night before and register. The letter also states the terms of the contract. I find them reasonable and fair. But I doubt if my mother would back my idea of selling religion. Any religion. I decide to go ahead with my plan regardless.

On 8th June, Tom and I report at the Holiday Inn on Wilson Avenue. Midwest Bible Sales have set up a registration desk in the lounge. A thin elderly lady is sitting behind it. The name plate on the desk identifies her as Audrey Manning. She must have been a brunette many years ago but currently sports a snow-white mane of ruffled Marilyn

Monroe curls. Ms. Manning exudes the disposition of a no-nonsense grandmother. But she sounds sweet when she asks our names.

We introduce ourselves. Ms. Manning finds the two of us on the list of trainees in front of her and ticks both. Then she browses through a stack of papers on her right and takes out two sheets from it. One has Tom's photograph stapled at the right top corner. The other has mine.

"Will you sign at the bottom for me please?" She slides the sheets toward us. We do as asked and push the papers back to her.

"Thanks." She sounds cheerful now. On the desk is a sheaf of ruled paper slips held together by a rubber band. Ms. Manning reaches for it, pulls out a slip, writes our names on it, signs at the bottom and hands it to Tom.

"Give this to the reception staff and they'll check you in."

"Thanks, ma'am." We say in unison as if on cue.

"The training starts at nine o'clock tomorrow morning in the conference room at the end of the hall. Don't be late."

"We'll be there." Tom assures her.

"Have a good evening, gentlemen."

"You too, ma'am." Again we are in unplanned unison.

The young man at the reception counter is super-efficient. As soon as Tom presents the slip Ms. Manning has given, he pulls out a key from one of the pigeonholes on the wall behind him and hands it to Tom.

"You're in room two fourteen, sir. You will find the elevators on the right. Complimentary breakfast is served between six thirty and nine thirty every morning. Enjoy your stay." He points in the direction of the elevators.

"Thanks." We take our bags and head for the room.

I pick up a newspaper from a stand in the lobby. Chris Evert has won the French Open title, defeating Romanian Virginia Ruzici in straight sets. Bjorn Borg is to play Vitas Gerulaitis in the men's final today. The hostage crisis in Iran shows no signs of resolution.

When we enter the room, Tom switches the TV on. One channel is discussing Ronald Reagan's chances in November, now that he is assured of the Republican presidential nomination. The other is debating various options before the Carter Administration on the Iran hostage situation after the failure of the rescue mission six weeks back.

I have hardly watched the idiot box since landing in the US. So Tom brings me up on the attempts of TV channels to keep the Iran hostage crisis in focus: Walter Cronkite ending the nightly news with a count on hostages' days in captivity and ABC starting a late night show named *Nightline* with Ted Koppel to cover the latest developments in Tehran. The public anger against Iran is, understandably, growing. It continues to be mistakenly targeted at me. My defense is a baseball cap with the Indian flag and 'INDIA' boldly embroidered on it. The cumbersome needlework took me hours to complete but Tom thinks it is a brilliant move and calls the cap 'hard hat' for the protection it provides.

The training starts sharp at nine on Monday morning. We are thirty six trainees seated classroom style in rows of six. Four sessions are scheduled for each day, two before lunch and two after. Fifteen-minute coffee breaks are inserted after the first and third sessions to ensure that the participants are not required to focus for more than two hours at a stretch.

The first two days are devoted to product training. We are made to learn different types of Bibles the company has on offer. Although I am from a different faith, I know that the Old Testament of the Catholic Bible contains seven more books than that of the Protestant Bible. But I am amazed by the variety of sizes and formats to suit specific people and special occasions. The list is impressive: family, devotional, children's, teen, student, one year, topical, specialty, compact, pocket, large print, giant print, wide margin and so on. Some contain supplementary material for study and prayer. There are even seconds, or slightly imperfect ones, available at a hefty discount. And, of course, there are audio versions in the form of cassette tapes. We are taught the features of each type and the profile of the reader it is meant for.

The next three days are assigned for role-plays and screening of films to illustrate various situations faced by salespersons. Simulations help us deal with them. After each role-play, the trainers point out our mistakes and explain ways to avoid them. It is a comprehensive program. I am sure it will be of use even after the summer is over. I feel glad to have chosen this option over manning a convenience store cash register.

In our spare time, we visit a few Saint Louis tourist attractions along with some of the trainees: the Gateway Arch, the Botanical Garden, the Zoo and the Soulard. There is no opportunity to do more. The week quickly flies off and before we know it, the training is over. We need to choose our sales territory. Tom and I consider various options but finally agree on Chattanooga in Tennessee for compelling reasons. Chattanooga is in the Bible Belt. Its population has grown by almost thirty percent in the last two years. The two factors combined promise a large and fertile catchment area of potential customers. Chattanooga sits on Tennessee's border with Georgia. It is a good place to make inroads into the neighbouring state. And by all accounts, the landscape around the area is nothing but beautiful. Midwest Bible Sales has a depot near the city. That is a bonus. We can collect copies of Bibles from the depot before stalking the streets.

On Sunday morning, we are mandated to attend a service at one of the selected churches. Tom and I choose the Lutheran Church off Grand Avenue. I have been inside a church in India but have never attended a service. I am not sure what to expect but look forward to the experience for its novelty.

The church is housed in an imposing old building constructed in grey stone. The sanctuary has high sloping timber ceiling and teak wood pews. The tall arched windows in the chancel, the apse, the transept, the nave and the narthex are paned in stained or painted glass. They depict major events from the Bible such as Ascension of Christ, Six Days of Creation and The Holy Communion.

The central aisle between the rows of pews on either side is covered by a red carpet running up the steps to the chancel. The knee-high wooden communion rail fitted on the first step to the chancel separates it from the nave. A gap in the centre of the rail allows the pastor and the acolytes to walk up to the altar adorned in green satin. A tabernacle and two tall candles occupy it. The altar is flanked by a pulpit on the right and a lectern on the left.

As we enter the nave, an enthusiastic young usher gives Tom and me copies of the bulletin. It lists how each service is scheduled to run along with the accompanying hymns to be sung. We can hear strains of pre-service music as we take the pews. Tom informs me that we will participate in a liturgical service.

"What's that?" I am hearing the term for the first time.

"To put simply, a worship that includes elaborate traditional ceremonies and rituals. Every church does not follow the practice. Actually, I don't know much more than that." He shrugs his shoulders.

"If that's so, I'm glad we picked this church over a non-liturgical one. Might as well go the whole hog."

Before long, we are required to stand and turn around to face a white robed acolyte walking on the red carpet towards the chancel, holding high a cross with the statue of Christ nailed on it. The acolyte is closely followed by Pastor William Bell in a flowing knee-length satin chasuble over an alb. The congregation sings the designated hymn during their walk through the aisle. On reaching the chancel, the acolyte positions the cross in a hole in the floor next to the pulpit, like the flag on a golf putting green.

Pastor Bell is a tall fatherly figure; large blue eyes, straight nose and thick thatch of silver hair adding to his imposing presence. His shiny green mantle with its six inches wide lightening arrester shaped gold stripes makes his already broad shoulders look broader. In my opinion, his serene demeanour contributes significantly to the solemnity of the occasion.

The pastor begins the service with a welcome. Then he makes a few announcements and shares prayer requests. His voice is resonant and speech dignified. A gathering song is then sung. It is followed by Confession and Forgiveness, a greeting and the kyrie from the hymnals. A Hymn of Praise is sung, followed by the Prayer of the Day and the day's lessons in the form of Bible reading. All the children are called upon to go to the front of the nave for the Children's Message. After the children return to their pews, message for the grown ups is conveyed, and the Hymn of the Day sung. The Christians in the congregation affirm their faith using one of three main Creeds. It is succeeded by the Prayers of the Church.

God's peace is shared among the congregation by hand shakes and wishes for peace to be with all. The ushers collect the offerings and carry them forward while an offertory hymn is sung. Then the devotees also say a short offertory prayer.

As the music for the prayer fades, the pastor, a communion assistant and a few helpers guide the Great Thanksgiving. After the Words of Institution and bread-breaking, an usher bids us, pew-by-pew, to the front of the nave to receive the bread. Then another helper at the steps guides us to the acolyte to receive a cup each. We kneel at the communion rail with cups in hand to accept the wine. On receiving the bread and wine sacrament, we return to our pews using the aisles along the nave's walls. Music During Distribution continues right through the dispensing of the communion.

Not being a Christian, I am unsure if I should partake in the sacrament. But the embarrassment of standing out like a sore thumb makes me follow the congregation. I am reminded of the stories of nineteenth and early twentieth century Christian missionaries converting Indian villagers by surreptitiously dropping a loaf of bread in the village well and letting the villagers unknowingly drink that water. I feel glad that the world has moved on from those dogmatic days.

After the partaking of the sacrament, all the recipients are blessed, followed by singing of the Post Communion Canticle for the day, a prayer and blessing. The pastor dismisses the congregation and a sending song is sung. Bells toll as we rise to leave. The post-service music resonates when the devotees begin to disperse.

While Tom and I are moving with the group towards the exit, Audrey Manning spots us. She had registered us for the training programme when we arrived at the Holiday Inn the previous Sunday. We are meeting her for the first time since then. She is dressed for the occasion in a pleatless knee length sky blue skirt and a white chiffon blouse with a lace jabot under a navy jacket. Her Marilyn Monroe curls are hidden under a dressy blue sinamay church hat. The attire makes her look younger than her years.

"How're you, gentlemen?" She seems to remember us, either because she has a sharp memory or I am the only Bible sales trainee from the Indian subcontinent.

"We're good, Ms. Manning." Tom replies on our behalf. But she is interested in speaking with me.

"Is the Sunday service in your country like ours too?" She has correctly deduced my foreign background. I am unable to decide if it is due to my skin's color or my accent she heard a week ago or just a shot in the dark.

"I'm not sure. Actually, this is the first time I've attended a service." I see no harm in being frank.

"How come?" She asks with a smile, not able to understand my reply.

"Because I'm not a Christian." She is stunned. Her face looks as if I have hit her in the solar plexus. But she manages to recover quickly.

"Oh, really? I thought you enrolled to sell Bibles because you wanted to spread the gospel. What's your faith then, if you don't mind my asking?"

"I'm a Hindu." She tries to take my reply without changing her plain expression but her eyes give away her thoughts. She has surely demoted me to the status of a lesser mortal. Then she smiles again, perhaps recognizing an opportunity.

"How'd you find today's service?" She pops the question I see coming from her desire to continue the conversation.

"Interesting, although I mustn't have understood everything that went on." I cannot think of a better answer although I suspect she expects superlatives.

"Well, I'm glad you observed all the rites. Why don't we go and meet Pastor Bell?" I have no problems with her proposition expect that we want to leave for Chattanooga.

"Provided it doesn't take much time." Tom speaks my mind.

Most of the attendees have exited the nave by now. A few elderly and disabled are still making their way out. When Ms. Manning approaches Pastor Bell, he is about fifteen feet from us, speaking to a very old man in a wheelchair. She waits till they finish their conversation and then engages in a tête-à-tête with him for a couple of minutes. They walk towards us and Ms. Manning introduces Tom and me to the pastor.

"Why don't we go to my office? We'll be able to talk there without getting disturbed." He leads us through the commons to a hallway punctuated with doors signed 'Kitchen', 'Church Office', Conference Room' and 'Nursery'. He walks past all of them and stops in front of the door marked 'Pastor's Office'. He waits till we enter his chamber, then follows us and closes the door behind him.

We step into the spacious room, our feet sinking in the lush white rug on the floor. The office's two walls on the left and the right are fitted with book shelves holding several leather bound volumes, presumably on theology. The wall across from the door is fitted with a large sliding window, hidden partially behind half-drawn drapes. The pastor's desk is placed below it against the wall. A reading lamp, a Bible and a small bronze sculpture of crucified Jesus are the only items on the desk. The middle of the room is occupied by a circular table with three chairs around it. Pastor Bell asks us to be seated on them and joins the table himself by dragging the high backed chair near his desk.

"I'm happy you could attend our service today." He begins pleasantly.

"It was a revelation. I'm glad I participated." As soon as I complete my sentence, I realize that 'revelation' may be an exaggeration of my experience. But the pastor and Ms. Manning seem gratified to hear my feedback.

"And I understand you're a Hindu. From India?

'Yes, that's right." I am not sure why we are here and am not keen to stay long.

"We don't see many worshippers from India in our church. In fact, I don't recall the last time we had one." Ms. Manning's comment does not surprise me.

"Very few Indians live around here to begin with. And the Christians among them would be an even smaller fraction. Less than two and a half percent of Indians are Christians." I explain the reason for her observation.

"Do you believe in God?" The pastor asks; his eyes turn intense.

"Well, I believe in the Supreme Being." I reply honestly. In spite of being a student and practitioner of science, I recognize man's inadequacy to scientifically explain the occurrence of certain events. We rationalize them through concepts of luck, misfortune, destiny, fate and providence.

"I'm sure Jesus loves you. Do you believe in Jesus?" His question baffles me. I am not sure what I should reply. The simple fact of the matter is that my religion believes in presence of divinity in every entity in the universe. I have no reason to doubt Jesus.

"Yes, I do." I answer, wondering what he is going to make out of my affirmation.

"That's good. Did you partake in the sacraments today?"

"Yes, I did." His eyes light up and face breaks into a satisfied grin. He swivels his chair, takes out a Bible from the drawer of his desk, swivels back and keeps the Bible on the table in front of me.

"That's for you." He clarifies, in case I had any doubt about who it was for.

I am in a quandary. I want to tell him that I am out to sell Bibles for the next twelve weeks and can get a copy of my own any time of my choosing. But I am afraid that would be construed as rudeness. At the same time, accepting his copy is also problematic. It would indicate a desire to imbibe it, an uncomfortable lie.

"Thank you." I choose to worry about the lie later.

"Well, you believe in God, you accept Jesus Christ and you've received the sacrament of Holy Communion." He pauses. But before he can continue, Ms. Manning interjects.

"And he's going to spread the gospel by promoting Bible sales."

"In that case, you've already walked a considerable distance down the road to being saved. You should continue your spiritual journey in the same direction to reach its logical destination." Pastor Bell concludes.

His contention hits me like a bombshell. This is no friendly small talk. So naïve of me to think it to be! The pastor and Ms. Manning are trying to convert me to Christianity. And everything I have unsuspectingly said or done suggests my openness to the idea. I'm not a religious fanatic, nor do I wear religion on my sleeve. But I happen to have inherited one of the most enlightened and tolerant religions. It is an integral part of my identity. Giving it up is nothing short of abandoning my persona.

I would not mind Pastor Bell saving me if I were indeed hurtling down a precipice. But I feel offended by his implication that I am, simply because I do not belong to his faith. Actually, I need to save myself from him by getting out of this conversation. And do it fast, before I say something I would regret later. While I try to think of the best way to accomplish that goal, Tom comes to my rescue.

He knocks his knee on mine under the table. When I look at him, he almost imperceptibly tilts his head, implying we should leave.

"Thank you, Pastor Bell." He says and rises from his chair. I follow suit.

"Please do come back sometime soon. God bless you." The pastor sanctifies us as we exit his office.

"Don't tell me you didn't understand what they tried to do." Tom says as soon as we get into the car.

"Not in the beginning. But I caught on when the pastor offered to save me." I admit, feeling a little stupid.

"How could they do that?" He sounds indignant.

"They thought I needed help. Besides, that's a part of a pastor's job, I guess." I sound generous when, in fact, I do not wish to.

"Don't be so damn magnanimous. I don't practise my religion; never did. But that doesn't give anybody the right to convert me." He says, throwing a sharp sideways glance at me.

"I'm just looking at it from the pastor's angle. And I agree with you a hundred percent. So cool down now, will you?"

"Okay, if that's what you say. But you'd better be careful from now on." He laughs. We close the topic at that.

Twenty

We return to the hotel, check out and set off for Chattanooga. I notice more and more anti-Iranian bumper stickers, from innocuous 'Ayatollah Assahollah' or 'Down with Iran' to more virulent 'Kill Iranians in America'. The public mood is getting troublesome for me.

A little over three hundred miles into the drive, we pull into a Mobil gas station near the town of Kuttawa on Lake Barkley in Kentucky. Being a truckers' stop, the station also houses a convenience store. While Tom is filling up, I enter the store to look for a map of Chattanooga. As I search for it at the revolving map-stand, two burly truckers resembling WWF wrestlers accost me thinking I am Iranian. They start asking me questions on the American hostage crisis unfolding in Tehran. I try to tell them I am an Indian, not an Iranian. But they seem unconvinced. Tom walks in as the exchange is turning nasty. He sees me without my 'hard hat', quickly understands the problem and runs out to get my India cap. His intervention prevents an ugly altercation.

When we hit the road again, I narrate my previous year's episode with the airline staff and the subsequent chance encounter with Ronny Parton.

"Don't you hate us for targeting you as an Iranian, not to mention attempting to convert?" Tom wants to know.

"Not really, to be fair. But for the hostages, no one will bother me. And to look at the brighter side, I got to meet Ronny Parton because the airline staff thought I was Iranian." I explain, knowing Tom will brand me crazy to be so darn philosophical.

"Clearly, you're from the land of Mahatma Gandhi."

We take turns driving. The four hundred miles take almost eight hours, thanks to President Carter's fifty five miles per hour speed restriction. But we do not complain; much of the road winds through picturesque verdant countryside.

On reaching Chattanooga, our first objective is to look for inexpensive accommodation. Yellow Pages throw up several options. We zero in on Armstrong Trailer Park off Lee Highway. The trailer we choose has a small sitting room cum kitchenette, flanked on either side by small bedrooms with attached baths. The kitchenette has some utensils. They are good enough for us.

As soon as we move into the trailer, Tom and I spread the map of Chattanooga on the small dining table and list the neighbourhoods to comb through for selling as many Bibles as we can in the coming weeks. To begin with, we want to focus on thickly populated areas, to meet as many prospective customers as possible. We decide to start with Bushtown and Ridgedale. The next to rake through would be East Lake and Mission Oaks. Once we are done with these, we would trawl others.

Out first task the next morning is to go to collect copies of Bible from the depot of Midwest Bible Sales located at Chickamauga across the state border with Georgia. It is a forty-minute drive through beautiful scenic countryside. The depot's paneled main office is rectangular, furnished with three desks placed one behind the other along its length. A young Hispanic woman is seated at the first and a middle-aged Caucasian man at the third. The one in the middle is unoccupied. The wall at the far end has a door marked 'Allayne Gibbs, Manager'.

Tom introduces himself to the Hispanic lady and asks if we can see the manager. She points to the door behind her without a word. We get the message. Tom knocks on the door to Allayne Gibbs' office. A high pitched "Come in" pierces through the panel. When we enter, Allayne Gibbs is standing behind her desk. She is a tall African American in her early forties possessing an oval face, dark eyes under finely tweezed eyebrows, a sculpted nose and full lips. Her perfect complexion has the sheen of polished granite. She is smartly clad in a white V-neck blouse and a grey skirt. Appropriately for her profession, a large silver cross on a matching chain dangles from her neck.

"Good morning, gentlemen. What can I do for you today?" She extends her right arm. Her smile easily reaches her eyes, making them twinkle. I find her enthusiasm infectious. Tom shakes her hand. I follow.

"We intend to sell Bibles during summer. We're ready to start." Tom explains the purpose of our presence after we introduce ourselves.

"Oh, yes. I've received a telex from our HO. You completed the training last week, didn't you, gentlemen?" Her tone makes us feel welcome.

"Yes, we did. In Saint Louis."

"Excellent. How'd you like to start then?"

"We'd like to take a few copies of the various types. We'll come back for replenishments as we sell them." I lay out the plan.

"That'd be perfect. I'll have Juliet arrange it for you." She calls the Hispanic girl in and instructs her to issue the copies to us. Juliet is impervious to Allayne's enthusiasm. She nods in silence and starts to leave.

"Why don't you follow her?" Allayne suggests.

Juliet may not be very expressive but is helpful. Her recommendation of how many copies of each type of Bible we should carry is based on experience. We go by her advice.

"Thanks for your valuable input." I say while leaving the warehouse laden with two back-packs of scriptures. The appreciation evokes a smile on her otherwise serious face.

We start our house calls on Tuesday morning. The plan is simple: we drive up to the decided neighborhood at nine o'clock each morning, Tom drops me at a residential locality and proceeds to another similar area nearby. I walk from house to house with my inventory of Bibles to sell. Tom does the same in his domain. We meet at one o'clock to lunch on sandwiches brown-bagged before leaving the trailer, relax in a shopping mall in the vicinity for an hour or so and resume door-to-door gospel selling. Our workday ends every evening at six. After that, we take turns cooking dinner.

It is a hard toil, made harder by the heavy load of Bibles in the back-pack. Most of the time, I walk three miles in the morning and another two in the afternoon, seven days a week. But the work is rewarding. On a good day, the sales can hit $300, earning me a decent $100. The first week fetches a margin of $550 on sales of $1,800. Tom has done slightly better. We congratulate ourselves for choosing the right summer work.

Before long, we get a fair idea of which Bibles sell fast, which at a moderate clip and which rarely. The experience makes Juliet's advice redundant when we go to the warehouse for replenishing the sold stock. Allayne makes it a point to ask us our sales numbers. Her response is encouraging. We are happy to deal with a manager like her.

Our sales routine works well for eight weeks. During this time, Tom and I cover neighbourhoods close to each other. Tom does not spend much unproductive time driving long distances to drop and collect me. But by the ninth week, we have run out of densely populated areas. We need to now approach far flung suburbs. Tom is forced to lose valuable sales time to chauffeur me around. He does not crib about it but I feel embarrassed. And things are going to get worse from here on in. We still have a few more weeks to go.

The solution lands in my lap out of nowhere one Wednesday afternoon.

I am hawking gospel in Jasper, a community off Interstate 24 about twenty five miles west of Chattanooga. I spend the morning going through every house on both sides of Victoria Avenue. By afternoon, I am on Hudson Street. Sales are not great today. It is approaching four o'clock but I have yet to hit the $150 mark. I feel tired.

The fifth house on the east side of the road is an ash-grey single storey Ranch type L-shaped wood structure with an attached two-car garage. A car covered in a liberal layer of dust is parked on the driveway in front of the garage. The name on the stake-mounted mail box at the edge of the pavement reads 'Maynard'. The house has a large covered veranda in front with two timber posts supporting its rafters and sloping roof.

I climb the two steps to the veranda, cross it to reach the door and ring the bell. The movement inside vibrates the wooden deck under my feet. The door slowly opens a wee bit. Through the crack, a lady peers at me. I identify myself as a Bible salesman and show the identity card issued by Midwest Bible Sales. The lady feels secure enough to open the door and let me enter a spacious drawing room furnished with bulky sofas upholstered in blue and white tapestry. The thick azure rug on the floor appears new. The large glossy art paper book on the coffee table has a picture of a red pagoda on the cover with 'Japan' printed across it in big thick font. The lady asks me to take a seat.

She is short, not more than five feet, slightly built, presumably of Japanese extraction. Her complexion is smooth, free of any lines. That makes it hard to guess her age; I would put it at forty, take or give five years. Her face is triangular, nose flat and lips thin. A frilly wine red band holds her long silky black locks in a pony tail. She is casually dressed in beige sweat pants and a black round neck T-shirt.

The name on the mail box had promised a potential customer inside. But now I am not so sure. My training and experience of selling Bibles have not prepared me for this eventuality. I search for an icebreaker. After mentally rating a couple of openers, I discard them and go for a safe bet.

"I suppose you're Mrs. Maynard, ma'am." I desperately hope for her affirmative reply.

"Yes. Raymond's my husband." I wonder if my expression betrays the wave of relief washing away my doubts. There is no trace of oriental accent in her speech. Clearly, she is raised and perhaps born in the states.

"I presume your family is from Japan." It is a safe bet if the book on the coffee table is any indication.

"Yes. My parents migrated when I was two." That explains her American accent.

"I believe Japan has a small number of Christians in addition to the Buddhist majority?" I want to find out if she is a potential customer.

"Yes. I belong to that minority. We have, for generations, according to my parents." I am surprised by her openness. And grateful for it. I can proceed with my sales pitch now.

But despite my best effort for the better part of half an hour, Mrs. Maynard refuses to buy a Bible. Eventually, I concede defeat and decide to search for a more acquiescent household in the neighbourhood. But that is not to be. As I exit the room and step on the veranda, it starts to rain. My umbrella is in Tom's car. I kick myself for forgetting to take it although the conditions have been overcast since morning. The rain is quite light but I cannot risk the collection of sacred books in my back-pack. I am stuck. Mrs. Maynard is kind enough to let me hang around on her covered front deck.

I wait for the rain to stop, trying to think of a reason for Mrs. Maynard to let me inside her house even though she did not want to buy a Bible in the first place. Just when I am ready to assign it to her Japanese courtesy, I notice the

'For Sale' sticker on the rear window of the car parked on the driveway. The drops of rain are turning the dust into mud, covering the car in dirty blotches. Underneath, it is a moss green Buick LeSabre with vinyl top, probably of early 1970s vintage. The whitewall tyres look new. I would not mind owning the vehicle. In any case, I cannot go anywhere while the rain continues. No harm in finding out the car's asking price.

I cross the veranda and ring the door bell again. Mrs. Maynard's face contorts into a harassed look on seeing me back. I can understand her feelings. I have wasted her time. She does not want to prolong the agony. I decide to come straight to the point.

"Ma'am, sorry to bother you again but I was wondering if I could buy the Buick parked outside." I want her to consider me a serious bidder. I am not sure I succeed.

"We're asking four hundred bucks for it." Her demeanour suggests she does not believe I can afford it. She is not wrong. But I am glad she is willing to talk. Hopefully, no one has showed interest in the car yet.

"Isn't that a bit high for a car that's at least seven years old?" Actually, the price seems quite reasonable. But I must lowball given my shallow pockets.

"Well, it's only got fifty thousand miles on it. And no one other than my husband's driven it." She is trying to extol the virtues of her used wheels. Just a few minutes back, I was the salesperson. I am amused by our role reversal.

"I understand, ma'am. But it's a gas guzzler. That's a minus at today's fuel prices." I want her to drop the price substantially.

"Accepted. Why don't we settle for three fifty?" The ease with which she shaves off $50 makes me wonder if she has padded up the original quote. She is willing to negotiate. I decide to press further.

"That's still way too high for a really thirsty old vehicle."

"It has automatic transmission, radio, power steering and power brakes, not to mention the AC and heater."

"Look, ma'am, I'm genuinely interested in buying that beast. But not at the price you're asking."

"My husband's very particular on the maintenance. He's kept it in pristine condition." I am willing to accord Raymond Maynard his due, yet treat her comment more a hyperbole than fact.

"Granted. But he can't charge such a high premium for his effort."

Outside, the rain is heavier now. I cannot leave this shelter till it relents.

"The shower must've washed it clean by now. Let's go outside so you can take a re-look. Don't go by the dust you saw on the way in." The mention of dust triggers a new ploy in my mind.

"The thick layer of dust shows that the car's on sale for some time now, yet no one's bought it. The obvious reason's the price." I argue while we get up and step on the veranda. The rain has rinsed the LeSabre clean. The vinyl top looks as good as new. The sheet metal of the body has no rust anywhere. Raymond Maynard has indeed coddled his pet with loving care. I must have it.

"See how good it looks now?" She is not very crafty in her sales pitch.

"May be. But better used cars flood the market each summer as students graduate from colleges, get jobs, buy brand new vehicles and get rid of the old ones. Surely you know that." I try to exploit the annual feature to my benefit.

"Probably. But we have a very good product on offer." She has a point. Unfortunately, I cannot grant it.

"Ma'am, let me make an offer. I'll hand over all the money on me save a couple of dollars for gas. If you're okay with it, I'll not bother with an inspection of the car. We'll go straight to your bank and get the title notarised. You can keep your license plates and I can drive away with the car." She looks interested but seems sceptical.

"I've no idea how much money you have on you."

"Me neither. Yet I'm making the offer because I'm serious." I hope she bites.

"Let's go inside and find out how much money you have." She has bitten.

I take out all the money from my wallet and dump it on the coffee table. There are several bills of twenty, ten, five and one dollar. In addition, there is a fistful of change. I collate the bills in descending order and count. They add up to $138. Then I turn to the coins, making four separate groups of quarters, dimes, nickels and pennies. They total up to $4.39. I turn to Mrs. Maynard.

"Ma'am, that's all the money I've got. One hundred and forty two dollars and thirty nine cents. If I keep a couple for gas, I can pay you one forty bucks and thirty nine cents. If we go ahead with the transaction, you'll have the monster off your back and I can save the Bibles on mine from the rain."

"That's too low. My husband will kill me." Her fear implies she is okay with the deal but her husband may not be. I catch on that thread.

"Apart from the cash, I also have something else of value. Bibles. May be Mr. Maynard will find the deal fair if I throw in a Bible of your choice?"

"I can't make the decision on my own. I've to speak with Ray." I have no reason to believe she is referring to anyone other than her husband. She leaves the room and goes inside. After a minute, I can hear her voice but cannot make out the words. The conversation takes about ten minutes. I never expected Mr. Maynard to accept the deal without a debate anyway. Eventually, she hangs up and returns to the drawing room.

"He was reluctant to begin with but after I explained the points you mentioned, he agreed."

Relief flows down my whole body. Silently, I apologize to Mrs. Maynard for calling the Buick 'the beast' and 'the monster'. It suddenly becomes my beauty. I feel like the prince charming that turned the frog into a gorgeous princess.

"That sounds great. Why don't you choose the Bible from my collection? We'll have to hurry if we want to get to your bank before it closes for the day." I propose while picking up two dollars from the coffee table, leaving the remaining cash behind. I have no intention to give the Maynards a chance to reconsider their decision. I hurriedly take out different Bibles from my back-pack.

"We'll make it. The bank's only five minutes away." She chooses a hardbound family Bible from the display. I know it is priced at $24.50, but the cost to me is $17.00.

As soon as we return from the bank, Mrs. Maynard hands me the keys to the LeSabre. I place my back-pack on the rear seat and get behind the wheel. The engine kicks in the moment I turn the key in the ignition. Raymond Maynard has truly kept the machine in top condition. I am delighted to own it for all of $157.39.

I remember Tom's Oldsmobile of similar vintage cost him $450.

Twenty One

I return from Chattanooga two weeks before the summer break ends, leaving the tidying up to Tom. I need the free time to take possession of the studio apartment on Madison, shift my few belongings left with the McGoverns, organize cooking gas and telephone connections, buy a few household items that were not necessary in the dorm and enroll in the classes for the fall term.

A couple of days before the new term is scheduled to commence, I run into Hamzeh at the shopping mall. His full name is Hamzeh Hamzeh. It sounded odd until I learnt that the practice is not uncommon in his part of the world. Hamzeh cannot call the country of his birth his own. So he is forced to travel on a Jordanian passport. Much of Palestine, Hamzeh's homeland, is under Israeli control. The long festering geopolitical turmoil is a human tragedy that has snatched innocence from children, liberty from adults and dignity from both. Hamzeh has every reason to be bitter about the injustice he and his fellow Palestinians have suffered for years but he bears it with equanimity that much older people would find hard to emulate.

Hamzeh is huge; over six feet tall in his socks and tipping two hundred pounds on an empty stomach. I often joke that he was born so big that his parents had to repeat his name to fit his size. He is fair with black curly hair, a snub nose and thick eyebrows shading twinkling dark eyes. But his extra-large physical appearance is deceptive. At nineteen, Hamzeh may be mistaken for a minor league Sumo wrestler, but inside his sizeable bulk resides a very gentle and caring soul. His face mostly wears an infectious smile and often breaks into bubbly laughter that radiates childlike freshness. We have yet to hear his velvety voice climb beyond the minimum audible decibels, let alone reach cacophonic levels. An excellent student, Hamzeh is politically aware and speaks with quiet conviction. It is always a great pleasure to discuss any topic with him, especially the Middle East politics.

"Good to see you, Hamzeh. How was your break?" I ask him. We exchange stories of our summer jobs. Then Hamzeh turns serious.

"Don't know why I didn't think of you till now but I've a problem you can help solve." He begins.

"Your dream is my command." I quote an Egyptian saying.

"Actually, I bought a car two days ago from a Thai student. But now I've to rush to Amman to see my sick granny." He looks worried.

"So?"

"Can I leave the car with you?"

"Sure. As long as you want. When're you leaving?" Taking care of the car is hardly a problem.

"Tomorrow afternoon. I'll drop the car and proceed."

"Fine. You know my new place?" I doubt he does.

"How would I? You can show it to me now?" Good idea.

In the parking lot, I get into my car and he into a sky blue Chevy Nova. It is a nice vehicle. He follows me to my apartment.

"After you bring the car tomorrow, I'll take you to the airport."

"That would be great. Thanks."

By the time I return from the airport the next day, it is nine thirty in the evening. I am hungry. But my fridge is empty. I berate myself for the poor planning, make a list of items I need and decide to go to Safeway, taking Hamzeh's Nova.

It is a warm late-August night. The thought of not needing thick winter clothing for another ten weeks is pleasing. I cannot forget the drudgery of stomping the knee-deep snow under the weight of bulky sub-zero outfit. Despite enduring a severe winter, I am still uncomfortable in freezing weather.

Hamzeh's car is in good condition. I enjoy the two-mile drive to the grocery. The store is deserted. As I park the car in the lot, the memory of my embarrassment over lady's fingers comes back. I have called the vegetable okra ever since. That was my first week here almost nine months ago.

The shopping does not take much time. As a student, I cannot afford anything above subsistence-level existence. In this stratum, buying the least expensive food on the rack is the norm. I know the shelves it is stocked on. There is no point in looking elsewhere. I am back in the car in fifteen minutes. It is past ten o'clock.

Safeway sits on the east side of Maguire Street, which is a stretch on Route 13, a state highway, running north-south. I exit the store's parking lot, heading south on Maguire. Within a hundred yards is the intersection with Gay Street running east-west. The traffic light is green when I see it. There is nothing to help me know how long it will remain so. The hunger in my stomach pushes me to go through the intersection before the light turns red. I accelerate.

When I am about twenty yards from the intersection, the traffic light turns amber. I need to make the split second decision that drivers in my position must make: go or stop. Having opened the throttle, I reckon it is too late to stop safely. Trying to remember the thumb rule for point-of-no-return in such a situation, I elect to go through and press the pedal further. The light is still amber when I last see it. There is a small chance that it may turn red while I am under it. I take the risk in the absence of any other option.

I do not like such close calls; they always jerk my heart into palpitation. Generally, a few deep breaths bring it back to its normal beat. But before it does so this time, my rear view mirror lights up in the psychedelic flashers of a police car. The unmistakable siren wails in my ears. I am caught.

"Shitty luck," I mutter to myself, hit the right turn signal, find a convenient spot to pull over and stop. Switching the engine off, I roll the window down, place my hands on the steering wheel and wait. The police car parks behind mine, killing the hunger in my stomach. The siren dies. I only hope the cop does not think I started speeding on seeing his car.

Apart from the flashers, the car in my rear view mirror shows no signs of life. But after several annoying minutes, its passenger door opens and an officer slowly emerges. He walks to my window and asks me to step out of the car. We walk up to the sidewalk and stand there facing each other.

Jason Greene, as the tag on his chest names him, is a young officer, not more than 25. He looks sharp in his uniform of light grey shirt, dark grey trousers and matching tie. Although the sun must have set over an hour back, he continues to wear his grey felt Stetson. I cannot miss the firearm in the holster hanging from his belt. If I feel daunted standing in front of someone with a gun, Jason Greene dispels my concern. He is a chatty soul.

"Officer McCarthy should ask you to join him soon. But till then we can talk." He begins.

"Okay." I cannot think of anything else to say.

"You go to school here?" He asks. An easy guess.

"Yes. Graduate school." I give him more information than necessary for no particular reason.

"And where do you come from?" His manner is casual.

"India. A long way away."

"Half way around the world, isn't it? That's far." I wonder if he can imagine how far. Not unless he has ever crossed the Atlantic or the Pacific, I decide.

Jason Greene walks back to the police Pontiac, bends over the passenger side window and speaks to McCarthy for a couple of minutes. Then he opens the door and asks me to get into the passenger seat. I appreciate his courtesy.

Officer McCarthy is older, probably 30. He is a grim man, not given to wasting time on pleasantries. I don't mind him hurrying though; my hunger is returning.

"Can I see your driver's license, sir?" He asks.

That is an expected question. I take out the license from my wallet and hand it to him. Then I get jittery.

The photograph on the license, taken soon after my arrival on the campus, shows a clean shaven face. But now I sport a full beard, a change prompted by my rebellion against the unwarranted anger and abuse inflicted by people mistaking my nationality. If they thought I was Iranian, I might as well fool them even more, until they learnt the truth. My friends considered the step audacious. Yet I had refused to reverse it.

Apart from the beard, there is another difference between the photograph and my current appearance. The heavy mop of long hair hiding most of the forehead in the photograph is close cropped now for comfort in the summer heat. The man in the photograph and the man sitting next to the police officer look anything but the same person.

McCarthy looks closely at the photograph and then at me. He has every reason to suspect I am masquerading as the license holder.

"Are you sure you're the holder of this license?" He asks finally.

"Yes, officer." The truth is that the license is mine. I have no hesitation in confirming the fact. His face is immobile, not giving away any emotion. It is not possible to know what he is thinking. I start wondering if I have another photo ID on me that can corroborate my claim. McCarthy does not think it necessary.

He switches his walkie-talkie on, reads out my license number in its mouthpiece and waits. After a couple of minutes, a female voice responds. The heavy crackle in the wireless communication makes it hard to understand. I cannot make out the words. But the officer does.

"This license's reported lost." He says, turning his face to look at me, doubt and perplexity evident in his eyes. His pronouncement wakes up my memory.

Last week, I had gone to Hustle, the disco on Pine Street. After showing the license to the bouncer at the entrance as proof of age, I just dropped it in my shirt pocket rather than keeping it back in the wallet. That was careless at best and stupid at worst. It must have popped out unnoticed while I danced. When I looked for it on going home, it was gone.

The next day, I reported the loss to the license bureau. The platinum blonde with a seductive pout sitting behind the counter clicked my photograph, gave me the slip of paper as the temporary license and promised to mail the plastic replacement within four weeks. That evening, I thought of checking at the disco if anyone had found the license and deposited it with the staff. That indeed turned out to be case. I was happy to collect the license but I should have either destroyed it or informed the license bureau of the recovery. I did neither. The omission has come to haunt me now.

"I'm very sorry, officer. The license was lost but after I reported the loss to the bureau, an establishment I had been to found and returned it to me. It was careless of me not to inform the license bureau." McCarthy's weak doubt is now a strong suspicion.

My clarification would sound hollow even to someone who knew me, more so to a stranger unable to verify its validity. I need to back my story with a proof the officer will buy. I think of the slip of paper the license bureau issued as a temporary license. It is still in my wallet. I withdraw it and proffer to McCarthy. He tallies the information on the slip with that on the license. He seems satisfied. So far so good.

"Is that your car?" He asks, a little pointedly for my liking. I am really on slippery ground now. I neither know if Hamzeh has transferred the Nova's title nor the name of the person he bought it from. And I do not have the car's papers.

"I need to explain, officer. A friend of mine from Jordan bought this car a couple of days back and left for his home earlier today. I'm not sure if he's transferred it in his name." Each of my responses to McCarthy is dodgy. I try to imagine what I would have thought had I been in his position. From every angle, I seem a felon.

My jumping the traffic light looks an instinctive move to flee from the police car; the cops do not know I saw them only after they pulled me over. I produce a driver's license that is reported lost; the police may not accept it as my carelessness. The photograph on the driver's license looks like someone else's; the officer cannot verify the reason for my changed appearance. I cannot say who the car I drove belongs to; McCarthy can doubt my story of what transpired between Hamzeh and me. The only point in my favour is the temporary license. Even then my case does not stack up.

As I assess my questionable position in McCarthy's eyes, I suddenly remember Hamzeh's mention of buying the Chevy from a Thai student. Surely the cop will make out the name of an alien. The small detail offers me a ray of hope.

"If it's of any help, officer, I know that my friend bought the car from a Thai student. So the car's either in the name of Hamzeh Hamzeh, and that's the correct name, or in the name of a Thai individual.

"We'll find out." I cannot decide if his tone is really menacing or my imagination is playing tricks.

He reads out to the microphone the number on Nova's license plate. I fail to understand the reply in the crackle. McCarthy takes down the information on a notepad. I wait with bated breath for the officer to decipher the feedback for me.

"Your friend transferred the title to his name all right. It was earlier registered in the name of Athikom Booranakij. That sounds like an Asian name." The Thai name is a real tongue-twister for him. I ignore his hardship. The information coming in on the wireless has helped my credibility. I want to heave a deep sigh of relief but resist the urge.

Without speaking another word, McCarthy starts writing a citation. When he is finished, he tears the sheet from the pad and hands it to me along with my temporary driver's license. I pocket them and reach for the door handle, looking forward to going home and satiating the hunger in my belly.

"Follow me." McCarthy orders before I open the door to get out. I am not sure why he wants me to follow. I pretend not to understand his instruction.

"Pardon me?" I seek his reconfirmation, hoping he will drop the plan.

"Follow me." He repeats, this time a little more emphatically.

"Where to?" I ask, a little confused.

"Sheriff's Office. Not very far." He says, pointing a finger in the south-east direction. I have no option but to obey the order. It is 10:45 p.m.

Both of us park in the forecourt of a single-storey office block. The two officers enter the building with me in tow. The entrance lobby is small, furnished with three cushioned chairs placed along two adjacent walls and a desolate coat stand in the corner. The third wall has a glass door leading into the main office. McCarthy asks me to occupy one of the chairs and goes inside through the door. Jason Greene takes one of the two remaining seats. He looks at his watch and assures me that the remaining procedure will not take long.

After five minutes, McCarthy opens the door and beckons Greene and me to join him. The main office is deserted and dark except for the diffused light filtering through an obscured glass partition at the opposite end. McCarthy perfunctorily knocks on the door in the partition and enters the cabin behind it. Greene and I follow. While entering, I notice the board on the door marked 'Joseph Randall, Deputy Sheriff'.

Mr. Randall is seated behind an L-shaped Logan desk polished to a beautiful gold-maple hue. He stands up when we enter, yet has to look up to the two troopers. He has a round ruddy face, sagging double chin, wide mouth and blue eyes behind a rimless pair of glasses. His thick silver mustache completely hides his upper lip.

"Good evening, gentlemen. Please be seated." He welcomes us, extending his short stubby arm to shake hands.

"We gotta run. But we'd like to leave this gentleman with you to initiate the necessary action. I've already issued him a citation." McCarthy cuts short the deputy sheriff's welcome and starts to leave with Greene.

"Okey dokey." The two officers are out of the door and gone before the deputy sheriff finishes his response. Joe

Randall turns his attention to me with a smile. He looks a genial man. I produce McCarthy's citation from my pocket and hold it for him to take. I hear him cite my Miranda rights.

"You've the right to remain silent, anything you say or do may be used against you in a court of law, you've the right to consult an attorney before speaking to the police and you've the right to make a telephone call. Can I proceed?" I nod my consent. If my memory serves me right, Miranda rights apply to individuals in police custody. Being a detainee, although only technically, makes my bourgeoisie character feel violated. I do not want to remain here even a second longer than absolutely necessary.

"Hope we can be done with this soon." I comment as he unfolds the paper, pushes his glasses up on to his barren scalp and peers at the citation.

"You jumped a traffic light on Route 13, didn't you?" He says very casually.

"Well, it was touch and go. Had I hit the brakes, I'd have stopped in the middle of the intersection." I offer my defense.

"Doesn't matter young man, the damage's thirty dollars." He sounds jovial, probably trying to lessen my hurt.

"In whose name should I write the cheque?" I pull out the cheque book from my pocket. To be relieved of thirty dollars is never a nice feeling; on a student's budget, it stings.

"No cheques, I'm afraid. The troopers are highway patrol, not the city cops. They don't accept cheques. Only cash." I am stumped. This is the first time in my American stay so far that I am asked to pay cash and nothing but cash.

I do not have thirty dollars on me. I need to call for help. Mercifully, the law allows me the privilege.

Ed McGovern answers the phone just when I am ready to hang up thinking he is not home. His deep bass is comforting. I briefly narrate the events of the last forty five minutes and ask him to come and get me out.

"I've a small problem. Donna's gone to her parents. I'm alone with Anissa and she's asleep. So I can't leave home right now. But I'll ask George to go and help." He sounds reassuring.

Ed obviously has a genuine parental responsibility he cannot shirk. George is Dr. George Pettengill, a professor at the B-school who taught my quantitative methods class in spring. Dr. Pettengill knows me well because he is also the faculty adviser to the international students' club. I expect him to take about fifteen minutes to get to the sheriff's office. The time can be used to speak with the deputy sheriff.

"Quite a difficult condition, this insistence on cash." I express my grievance.

"You're not the only one to feel that way. But the trooper was very clear, no release without the cash." He deflects the blame to McCarthy.

"I know. He suspects I'll flee without paying the fine." I express my impression.

"Where'll that be?"

"I'm from India but I'm not going anywhere just yet. Need a little under one year to finish school."

"Oh, India. Been to Bombay about twenty years ago. I was a sailor then. Our ship docked there for a week. We roamed the streets drinking beer to counter the heat." Going by his pot belly, he must have continued the indulgence.

"I'm from Pune about a hundred miles east south-east of Bombay. But my family owns a condo in Bombay so we go there quite often."

"Let me try and recall what the long curved promenade on the sea is called. Someone's necklace?" He scratches his memory. His eyes narrow; forehead furrows.

"Well, it's sometimes referred to as the Queen's Necklace but the official name is Marine Drive." I help him remember.

"Ah, that's right. We wandered on the wide sidewalk in the sea breeze." He seems refreshed by the memory.

The knock on the door announces Dr. Pettengill's arrival. He enters on hearing the deputy sheriff's "Come in". Dr. Pettengill is a tall, slim man in his early forties. He has a narrow oval face thatched with silky golden hair falling on his forehead. He underwent a cardiac surgery a couple of years back and seems to feel its effects even now. The short walk from the car park makes him breathe heavily. He is in his summer attire of denim Bermuda shorts, T-shirt and sneakers with no socks. The mud stains on his clothes indicate a day spent in the garden.

Dr. Pettengill introduces himself and offers his tired hand to Joseph Randall. While taking the chair beside me, he pulls out a cheque book from his hip pocket, opens it and looks around for a pen. I realize my mistake.

"I'm terribly sorry Dr. Pettengill, for not asking Ed to tell you that we need to pay cash. I needed someone else to bail me out precisely for that reason." I feel awfully guilty of extending Dr. Pettengill's misery by at least another half an hour. But he is most gracious. Without ado, he stands up and starts to leave. The deputy sheriff feels for him too. He is almost apologetic.

"If the troopers had been from the city police, a cheque would've done the job. Unfortunately, our overseas guest was stopped by highway patrol." I hope his explanation makes Dr. Pettengill feel better.

"I don't mind the trip to my home and back but I'm not sure I'll find thirty dollars in cash there." He says and leaves. His doubt makes the deputy sheriff pensive.

"I hope for your sake that he manages to find the money. Otherwise, I'll have to lock you up for the night, much as I hate doing it. And I can tell you it's a wretched little dungeon back there." He points his thumb behind him in the direction of the detention room.

My heart sinks. Spending a night in lock-up would be a terrible prospect at any time. It is dreadful on an empty stomach. The grim situation hangs heavy in the room, choking my genial conversation with the deputy sheriff. He picks up the copy of *Popular Mechanics* on his desk and starts browsing through it. I stare at the calendar on the wall behind him, trying to enjoy the panoramic view of the Grand Canyon.

About half an hour later, Dr. Pettengill returns. As soon as he enters the deputy sheriff's office, his exhausted face lights up in a bright smile. I feel taut muscles relaxing in my whole body.

"I managed it. But I needed to break a bank. My daughter's piggy bank!" He appears energized by the heist. I have never met his daughter but decide to send her a new piggy bank as soon as I can.

Dr. Pettengill empties his pockets on Joseph Randall's desk: crumpled dollar bills and coins. I straighten the bills to make a wad and stack coins separately for each denomination. Once the tidying up is done, the only job left is to count the money. I am more than happy to tot up. Dr. Pettengill's arithmetic is sound. I borrow a sheet from the deputy sheriff's yellow legal pad and write down the count. It adds up exactly to $30.

Joseph Randall accepts the fistful of cash and drops it into the drawer of his desk. He writes a receipt and hands it to me. I am saved the blues of a night in the hole behind him. I cannot thank Dr. Pettengill enough.

By the time I reach home, it is past midnight. The inordinate delay has robbed my appetite.

Twenty Two

A little less than one year after leaving India, I do not mind being alone. I no longer feel like a stranger in this distant land. Of course, I still miss my family and friends back home, but the mind-wrenching domusphilia I earlier used to suffer from has all but disappeared. The move to my studio apartment after returning from Chattanooga has certainly contributed to the settled feeling. I was lucky to find it with ease. Debbie Smith, a close friend, occupied it till summer but wanted to move in fall. She introduced me to the landlord, who was happy to rent out the place to me.

I have got back into the groove of classes, studies, teaching and parties. The tests and term papers somehow seem less tiresome to handle now. I have also picked my favourite TV programs. The evening news with Walter Cronkite tops the list although I am seldom home to watch it. But I try and make sure not to miss Ted Koppel on *Nightline*. And I am addicted to the late night sitcoms: *Barney Miller, Bob Newhart Show* and *M*A*S*H*. Much of the credit for this acclimatization goes to the great friends I have made since coming here. They have made my life interesting. We have a simple motto: work hard, play harder.

Unless we are celebrating a special occasion such as someone's birthday, we rarely need to plan a party. Many of us live in apartments, allowing unencumbered freedom to cook and entertain guests. A few phone calls on a weekend evening and we have the quorum to meet at someone's home or to go to the disco. On such occasions, partying till late is the norm.

Yet there are a few times when most of us have tests to prepare for or assignments to complete. When that happens, those who are free need to find others who can join in. Today is one such Saturday. The fall term is well underway. All my friends are tied up for one reason or another. By afternoon, I am done with my studies and the visit to the library to trawl reference books for writing the term papers. I need to find some friends to have good time with. But before that, I decide to make the regulation trip to the grocery. My fridge is hungry for its weekly replenishments.

Shopping for the groceries does not take long; I know the shelves that stock the stuff I need. I drive out of the store's parking lot heading south and stop at the traffic light as it turns red. I can see in the mirror a grey car stop right behind mine. There are two girls in the front seat, a blonde with flowing locks at the wheel and a brunette with a short crop next to her. They are giggling. While I am trying to imagine what could have tickled them so much, I see the sign of Gay Street and suddenly remember Debbie Smith.

I first met Debbie when both of us attended personnel management class in spring. After one such class early in that term, I was walking down to my bank. The road became deserted after I left the campus behind. It was then that I noticed the young woman of medium height and build walking about twenty feet ahead of me.

My first observation was about her gait. She swayed. The next observation was about her clothes. She wore a snug pair of jeans and a shiny mauve winter jacket, a rather uncommon colour. Perhaps we shared telepathy because even before I could decide if I liked her jacket, she spun around. In front of me was a squarish face, narrow bluish-grey eyes, Cupid's bow over a thin lower lip and a broad chin. The breeze had middle-parted the blonde fringe on her forehead. I remembered seeing her in the class.

"Hi, I'm Debbie Smith. Where're you from?" She asked with a bright smile.

"India."

"Do you live off-campus?"

"No, no. I'm going to the bank on Washington, by the railroad station."

"Oh, that's pretty much where I'm going too."

"Good. It's nice to have company."

We chatted about the course we were taking until she parted to go west on Madison while I continued on Washington. We have been friends ever since. Debbie is great for fellowship. She has a flair for writing on various life experiences and, in fact, edits the university's alumni magazine. She likes Indian food and does not complain about my cooking. We have several common friends, so Debbie can barge in anytime we group to party. Even otherwise, we get together whenever both of us are free, drink beer, talk and generally have fun.

Debbie has a habit of disappearing every once in a while. We meet often for a couple of weeks and then suddenly she goes out of circulation for a few days. I never ask her the reason for what I call the 'vanishing act' but my guess is she gets enamoured by new friends, quickly gets bored with them and returns to the old gang when she feels disenchanted. The best part about our friendship is that we can pick-up the threads as if the hiatus was nothing more than a mirage. Most of our friends envy Debbie for her jaunty red-and-while Ford Mustang. But I rarely get to ride in it because she struggles to afford the gas. Every time I propose to take a spin in her car, Debbie declines, citing her standard reason of 'running on vapour'.

I bumped into Debbie on campus last week. We had not met for almost a month. She mentioned her move to a house on Gay Street. The connotation of the name reminded me of my near-mishap with Kieron Washington earlier in the year and the name stuck in my memory. But the house number slipped my mind.

On seeing the Gay Street sign, I impulsively decide to look Debbie up and perhaps invite her over. It is an abrupt thought. Just as the traffic light turns green, I hit the right turn indicator, spin the wheel and enter Gay, heading west. The grey car behind me also turns. The girls' giggle has now turned bouncy.

My sneaky hunch suggests they are tailing me. But I am not sure; I have never seen them before. Although I am not exactly petrified, I sense nervousness whittle down my confidence. Being stalked is an eerie feeling, even when the stalkers are beautiful young women. I need to verify my doubt. Without slowing down much, I make four right turns around a block, signaling the turn just before rotating the steering. By the time I am back on Gay, I am certain they are following me. Girls have made advances, even passes, at me but I have never been chased. Frankly, I do not know what to do.

While I am planning my next move, I suddenly spot Debbie's unmistakable Mustang, the signature stuffed poodle dangling from its rear view mirror. It is parked on the gravel driveway of a maroon two-story house on the right. I spin the steering to turn into the driveway, barely managing to avoid overshooting the property. I park on the side of the house and get down. The grey car slows down but cannot emulate my maneuver. It misses the driveway and disappears behind the building on the next plot.

As I walk around the house to get to what I presume to be Debbie's front door, the grey car reappears and stops on the other side of the street. It is an Audi 80, a rare brand in a university town. The fender above its left front wheel-well is brown primer coated, hopefully waiting for a paint job. Ostensibly, the girls have made a quick U-turn and found me before I am gone inside.

The glass on its driver's window rolls down. The girl at the wheel turns her gaze to me, her giggle under control.

"Hi." She smiles mischievously, showcasing a row of straight white teeth. Her perfectly round face, large blue eyes and chiseled nose would be considered enchanting by most. I find her simply gorgeous.

"Hi." I respond as I walk up to the Audi across the road.

"I'm Daphne." She introduces herself in a husky voice when I am six feet from her.

"Nice to meet you." I hope my apprehensive excitement does not percolate down to my tone. I want to sound cool.

"Are you from Iran?" Daphne asks when I reach the Audi. Déjà vu! A big disappointment too. But I notice no hostility in her question. Still, I wish I were wearing my India cap.

"No. India." They giggle again, throwing sly glances at each other as if hiding a secret. I cannot resist the urge to ask what is so funny in my being an Indian. But before I frame the question, the pretty bespectacled brunette clarifies, pointing at Daphne.

"She dated a guy from Iran. We nicknamed her 'Foreign Affairs'. She seems to like immigrants." So it is Daphne's idea to stalk me. I feel a slight relief at not being called an alien.

I doubt if any girl in India would dare do what Daphne and her friend are doing. I am reminded of an incident at the engineering college. A young lady from my neighbourhood, on a stroll with another girl, bravely approached me on the street to ask the time of the day. She hastened to add that the incursion would win her ten rupees she had bet with her accompanying friend. Back then, I had found her pluck scandalous. But that seems like a chaste overture compared to this wanton advance.

"Want to go to a party tonight?" Daphne comes to the point. Her question brings back the grisly memory of Keiron Washington's similar invitation last spring. I shove the unpleasant thought aside, feeling secure in the fact that the questioner this time is from the opposite gender.

"Sure. Where?" I could not have asked for a better evening.

"One fifty six Larkin." She reads from a scrap of paper on the dashboard.

"Where's that?" I have not even heard of the street.

"I don't know. I'm visiting from Saint Jo. She's a freshman at college here." Daphne points at her passenger.

"I know where it is but I won't be able to give directions. Why don't you meet us at my dorm? We'll go from there." The passenger responds. Her suggestion makes sense.

"Sounds good. Which dorm?"

"Fitzgerald. Room four sixty eight."

"What time?" I don't want to miss the party.

"Eight o'clock?" Daphne proposes. That works well for me.

"Perfect. See you at eight then."

I walk back to the maroon house across the road and ring the bell. When the door opens, I am relieved to see Debbie and not someone else. She is surprised to find me in the doorway. I apologize for arriving unannounced but she smilingly accepts my intrusion even though she has guests.

"Hi. I'm Nancy and this is Richard, my fiancé." The visiting lady beats Debbie to the introduction. The lovey-dovey couple is cuddled up on the sofa, often stealing affectionate glances from each other, sipping coffee from a single mug.

"Sorry, I didn't mean to intrude."

"Not at all. We're not hatching a plot here. Where're you from?" Nancy asks the customary question.

"Currently going to graduate school here but originally from India."

"Would love to go there sometime." Richard expresses his wish. I have heard the hollow remark before and stopped taking it seriously months ago.

"It's different." I respond automatically.

Nancy, Richard and I talk about weather, school and politics, in that order, before running out of topics of mutual interest. I notice Debbie's uncharacteristic silence. May be she does not want me to hang on. I get up to leave but decide to poke some fun on the way out.

"Debbie, you just lost out on a wonderful evening." I tickle her curiosity.

"Why? What happened?"

"Actually, I was planning to cook for you at home but found something more interesting just outside your house." I tease.

"Really? Do I live in such an interesting neighbourhood?"

"The interesting offer came from Saint Jo." I go on to tell her what exactly happened from the time I drove out of the grocery store till I reached her door.

"Have fun." If she is disappointed, she does not show it.

Twenty Three

Although I have seen hand-painted posters around the campus advertising anyone-can-join parties, I have never attended one. I do not know what to expect when I arrive at Fitzgerald at eight o'clock to collect Daphne and her friend. Expectedly, the dorm has no elevator. I need to walk up to the fourth floor. But before I start climbing the stairs, one of the two girls at the front desk stops me.

"You need to be escorted to go up to the room."

"When did they change the rules?" This is unexpected.

"Well, there was a case of assault last week." She clarifies.

"What do I do to reach the resident I want to see?"

"Let me know the room. I can buzz her to come down." That is fine with me.

"Four sixty eight."

"There's no four sixty eight. The room numbers end at four sixty four." I am surprised. The girls did not seem to lead me up a blind alley. Perhaps I heard the room number wrong.

"Why don't you try four sixty four then?"

"Okay." We wait for a couple of minutes. No one comes down. We try four sixty three. Same result. An African American girl walks down the staircase when four sixty two is buzzed. I can only apologize for making her take the trouble. The girl behind the front desk is getting suspicious. When no one responds from room four sixty one, she cannot stop herself from asking me to name the resident I am looking for.

The question is deeply embarrassing. Forget the last name, I do not even know the first name of the girl Daphne is visiting. I kick myself for not enquiring the name of Daphne's passenger. Then I realize that the girl in front of me now is waiting for an answer.

"Actually, I'm looking for someone visiting from Saint Jo. I don't know who she's here to see." I reply, trying to look honest.

"Do you know who has a visitor from Saint Jo?" She asks her colleague sitting next to her at the desk, apparently believing my explanation. I sense my embarrassment ebb.

"Nope."

"There's nothing I can do then." The young lady I am speaking with shrugs her shoulders.

"Thanks for trying, anyway." I appreciate her effort. And her unsuspecting manner.

I walk out of the dorm feeling convinced that a couple of kids barely out of high school have thrown a curve ball I could not read. I curse myself for this utter gullibility in getting conned so easily. Of course, I am unhappy about missing the party I was looking forward to, but my wounded ego really hurts.

While getting into the car, I deliberate on the idea of calling Debbie over. I quickly discard it. My approaching her on the rebound may offend Debbie. And it will be an admission of my naïveté. As I pull out deciding to just go home and watch television, I notice the Audi parallel-parked on the right, Daphne's calling card scabbed-fender clearly visible under the street lights. It is 8:15 p.m.

The unmistakable car testifies the girls' presence in Fitzgerald. If they are going to the party, they should do so in the next few minutes. I park a couple of places down from the Audi and wait. After fifteen minutes no one has approached the car on my radar. May be the girls have walked to the party or been driven or simply dropped the plan. Playing a spook is no fun; it is making me restless. I decide to endure the role for another ten minutes and then go home if the girls don't show up.

I do not have to wait that long.

At eight thirty five, Daphne appears in my wing mirror, approaching the Audi. I get out of my car, walk up to her and say "Hi", just as she lowers herself into the driver's seat. On seeing me, she steps out. So does her host.

"You stood us up." Daphne complains.

"Actually, I thought you conned me with a fabricated room number. Fitzgerald doesn't have four sixty eight. And I don't know your name. So there was no way to find the correct room." I direct my alibi to the young brunette standing outside the passenger door.

Before she responds, my attention is drawn to the light make-up enhancing Daphne's beauty, the fuchsia lipstick highlighting her rose-bud pout. She has changed into a low-neckline collarless grey T-shirt and black trousers. Patent leather stilettos extend her Coke bottle figure by a good six inches. The alluring fragrance of her expensive perfume is strewn by the light breeze.

"I said four fifty eight. And by the way, I am Chris." The clarification interrupts my thoughts.

"Okay, Chris. I must've heard you wrong then. Let's get going." I want to bury the controversy and move on. We get into my car.

"Are you a Moslem?" Daphne enquires as soon as I pull out of the parking spot.

"Why do you ask that?" I need to know where she is coming from.

"Because I know Moslems are not supposed to drink. My friend from Iran stuck to the rule." She spells out the reason for her question.

"No. I'm not a Moslem."

"Then what's your faith?" Chris interposes.

"I'm a Hindu. My faith doesn't ban alcohol." I clarify.

Chris guides us to Larkin. House number one fifty six is an ordinary looking two-storey Dutch colonial revival bungalow that can do with a fresh coat of off-white paint. As Daphne opens the door and we enter, I hear Pat Benatar thundering her "Hit Me With Your Best Shot". I like Benatar. Hopefully they will play her other numbers as well.

Inside, the place is rocking. We are asked to contribute a dollar each and go upstairs. The suite of rooms, clearly a shared residence of a few students, is teeming with young men and women, probably about thirty five in all. The haze of floating smoke has further muted the already dim lighting. There is whiff of hashish in the air. In addition to Benatar, other high decibel chartbusters by Michael Jackson,

Alan Parsons Project, Queen, The Who, Led Zeppelin and Pink Floyd are lined up to whip up the frenzy. I would be happier if the list included Abba. Unfortunately, it does not. I notice that the entire crowd is Caucasian; I am the only non-white in attendance.

The party must have started some time back; several bacchants are already glassy-eyed. A blonde is rolling a joint in the corner of a room with two boys and a girl waiting in anticipation for her to finish. In another corner, a boy is sunk in a beanbag, passionately kissing a girl straddling him. Around the apartment, boys and girls are sitting or standing in groups of four or six, plastic glasses in hand. They need to shout to be heard over the loud music.

One of the bedrooms is the make-shift bar. But I have never seen anything like it. On a desk in the middle of the room are a couple of five-gallon punch bowls. One is less than a fourth filled with a yellowish brown liquid. It is depleting further as the revelers serve themselves with a ladle. An identical concoction is being mixed in the other bowl by two students, one male the other female, who seem to have consumed generous helpings from the first. The ingredients are beyond my wildest imagination: a bottle each of Jack Daniel's whiskey, Bacardi white rum, Smirnoff vodka, Jim Beam bourbon, Gordon's dry gin and Admiral Nelson dark rum; twelve cans of Michelob and a quart each of orange, grape and apple juice.

Back in India, we sometimes mixed whiskey and beer. A few of us thought the blend was more potent than drinking them separately and, therefore, more macho. But that seems like goat's milk compared to this vicious cocktail. I am not sure how much of it will be enough to knock me out.

Not much, I reckon. But I see my two new friends helping themselves and venture to join them. Glasses of the heady drink in hand, we wander to another room.

Chris introduces Daphne and me to Ian, a sophomore she works with at a restaurant. The four of us taste the wicked punch. Contrary to my expectation, it is potable, the juices and the beer taking some of the sting off the spirits. But a few minutes later, the acrid aftertaste bites my throat.

"Do you know 'punch' has originated from the Hindi word *paanch*, meaning five?" I quiz the three of them about a fact few Americans know, although punch is a well-liked beverage in this country.

"Really? Why five?" Chris asks before I complete.

"The Indian drink was made of five ingredients: liquor, sugar, lemon, tea and water."

"Logical. I didn't know that." Daphne admits.

"You're not alone. Most people don't." I comfort her.

"But how did it make its way into our lives?" Chris enquires.

"In the seventeenth century, employees of British East India Company learnt the recipe during their stay in India. They carried it back to England. From there, it spread to other European countries and finally to the remaining world." I explain, feeling a little proud that a product of my country has grown so popular around the world.

"Interesting." Ian nods.

"I think so too. But I'm sure the original formula wasn't even close to what we're drinking here." Daphne adds, wincing after sipping from the glass in her hand.

"True. This brew's lethal. Actually when I saw them mixing the second bowl, I thought it would be so. But now I find it a little less deadly than poison." I express my view.

"I don't think I can drink this. I'm not used to it." Daphne complains.

"What're you used to then?" I chide, not expecting an answer.

"Pink gin, actually." I have not even heard of it. I thought gin was always colourless.

"What's that?" I am curious.

"It's fruit flavored gin, dark pink in colour." Ian butts in.

"Normally, I prefer beer. I don't like more potent booze, especially spirits." I share my choice.

"Then why don't we go get pink gin and beer?" Daphne hopefully proposes.

The punch-drunk crowd is getting passionate. Boys and girls are increasingly hugging and even necking with every sip of the cocktail or drag of the joint. Two young women with massive tattoos on their arms are preparing to snort through a rolled-up dollar bill. The heat of so many bodies in the enclosed space is making the suite uncomfortably warm. I notice the clothes coming off; several guys are now bare-chested, some girls only in their underwear. The blast of music has reached the stratosphere. I wonder if this whole gathering will soon turn into an orgy fueled by alcohol, drugs and lust.

And then, all of a sudden, I hear a scream over the loud music, "Kill the fucking Iranians!"

I turn to look in the direction of the shout and find a completely wasted young man of about my height and build lurching towards me through the throng, his fist cocked to let loose a punch. He is too unsteady to even throw a hard jab, let alone connect. Handling him is no problem. But I am worried about the mob-mentality taking over and causing others to gang-up in a violent frenzy. If the entire smashed swarm pounces on me, I would have no chance. I try to think of my options, if any. Thankfully, Chris saves me the trouble.

Before the assailant can thread his way through the horde on his wobbly legs and reach me, Chris rushes to the music system in the next room, punches the stop button and returns to my side. The sudden silence hits the intoxicated merrymakers like chilled water, forcing them to take notice with a start. She then catches hold my arm and raises it.

"This guy's from India, not Iran. And he's not even a Moslem." She shouts at the top of her voice, stopping short of disclosing my religion.

The doddering attacker reaches me as Chris finishes her announcement. I am not sure if he has understood her. But mercifully, he drops his coiled fist, extends his hand to shake mine and says he loves India. I doubt if he can make out his own words, much less mean them.

"Thanks a lot, Chris. You probably saved my life tonight." I express my gratitude before the amplifiers resume the roar of hard rock.

"You wouldn't have been here if it weren't for us." She is magnanimous.

The deafening music is hurting my ears. I have a headache, either from the drink or the carbon monoxide in the exhaled smoke or both. The aborted attack on me is the last straw. In any case, Daphne wants pink gin.

"Let's go." I suggest to my new friends.

"I think I'll stay on with Ian. But you guys go ahead." Chris puts forward her preference, wrapping her arm around Ian's waist. The booze in their veins is obviously drawing them closer.

"See you later." Daphne tells Chris, then takes my hand to lead me down the stairs and out of the building.

The fresh night air and the quiet feel like heaven. We drive to the round-the-clock convenience store to buy a pint of pink gin and a six-pack of Michelob. When I prepare to pay for the purchase, Daphne is astounded. She protests, saying she wants to go Dutch.

"You're a guest here. So allow me to play the host." I justify the gesture that is taken for granted in India.

"Why don't we go for a drive? I don't want to go back to that party, at least for some time." Daphne expresses her wish as soon as we get into the car. The idea is also on my mind.

"You took the words out of my mouth."

We drive south down McGuire. In a couple of miles, we clear the inhabited areas and reach the countryside.

"It may be a good idea to park somewhere, drink and chat." I propose.

"Let's do that." Daphne sounds enthusiastic.

We come across a narrow dirt track heading east, turn into it, go up a furlong and stop. There are no lights in view. We are surrounded by the moon's pale glow and soothing silence punctuated by hissing insects.

"Try this. You'll like it." Daphne passes to me her bottle of pink gin. I take a swig of the sweet fruity beverage. The taste is infinitely pleasant after the brutal concoction at the wild party.

"It's nice. I like it." I hand the bottle back to her.

"You can have more if you want. I can't finish the whole bottle." She offers. I let it pass, at least for now and open a can of Michelob.

"Were you and Chris in high school together?" I ask in an effort to start the conversation, although the answer is obvious.

"Yes, right through high school in Saint Joseph."

"Why didn't you join Chris for college then?" I am curious.

"I can't leave my grandma in Saint Jo." Her reply is most unexpected. This is the first time I have found an American youngster making career choices around a family member.

"And why's that?" I cannot stop myself from asking. Daphne does not seem to mind my probing into her personal life.

"My parents divorced when I was two. The court handed me to Dad because my mother's an alcoholic. He married again six months later. At the time, my step-mother had two sons from a previous marriage."

"Did you stay with them?"

"Only a couple of months. They didn't treat me well. So, my grandma - my father's mother – brought me to her place when I was less than three. I've lived with her ever since." She shares her intimate private history as if she is letting a load off her chest.

"Your father didn't mind that?" It is beyond me how a father can leave his three-year-old child with someone else, even when that someone happens to be his mother.

"He'd to choose between my step-mother and me, I guess."

"Do they also live in Saint Jo?"

"No. Saint Louis. He rarely visits me. My step-mother and my grandma don't get along." Her effort to be matter-of-fact does not succeed; her voice gets lined with tremble of sadness.

"And your mother?" I hope this girl has a family other than her grandma.

"She married again and moved to Canada when I was four. Haven't heard from her since." Daphne is getting emotional now. She surely has reason to be but still I wonder if the pink gin is nudging her along.

"Too bad." I don't know what else to say.

"Let me show you my grandma's picture." She switches the cabin light on, pulls out a leather-bound pocket album from her handbag and flips through it till she reaches the desired photograph. She slides close to me to show the portrait of a woman with gentle eyes staring at me.

"She seems a very kind person." I remark and feel stupid as soon as I finish.

"Grandma's everything to me. There's no way I'll leave her." Daphne's longing for the only family member at home is perceptible in her tone. I notice her eyes getting moist in the cabin light. She wistfully turns a few pages and shows me the images of her cousins and friends.

"From what you've told me, you don't seem to have any siblings." I try to divert her attention from the album that holds no interest for me beyond the photograph I have already seen.

"Wish I had at least one. I feel jealous of friends with siblings." She openly admits.

"They're fun, not to miss great support." I speak my mind without realizing I may be adding to Daphne's misery.

"My father runs a business in Saint Louis. He's very well off. But he thinks his cheques compensate for absence of parental love in my life." Her candour surprises me.

"One can't have everything, I suppose." My remark does not alleviate her chronic regret.

"He thinks he's doing me a great favour by paying for my college, not expecting me to work like my friends. But actually, I'd be happy to work if I could live with my parents." Her mood is decidedly melancholy now; her voice seems to be cracking as if she is about to cry.

"Are you still seeing your Iranian…er…boyfriend?" I want to change the subject.

"No. His family wouldn't accept our relationship. They called him back to Tehran." Her tone sounds pensive, yet she seems resigned to the reality.

"What a pity!" I make a feeble attempt to sympathize with her.

"Well, I'd pretty much grown out of the relationship myself." She recovers some of her buoyant bearing. But I am amazed. This girl has already grown out of a relationship when, in fact, she is not old enough to grow into one.

Through her bravado, I can easily see she is starved of mother's doting and father's affection. In a country that provides abundant creature comforts, the basic human need of love is often left unfulfilled. I consider myself lucky to be born in a culture and family where caring parental warmth is a given. I try to imagine where I would be, had I been raised in Daphne's circumstances.

"How'd you land up getting here?" She breaks my chain of thoughts with her question. I briefly narrate my story. When I tell her I left home last November, she looks at me with her eyebrows raised.

"You mean you haven't met anyone from your family for practically a year? I thought Asian families were very close-knit." She is probably sharing the observation made during her now broken relationship.

"That's right. We're very close but it costs a bomb to travel half way around the world and back." I explain, trying to prevent my longing for home from seeping down to my tone.

"Don't you miss them?" I can hear softness in her voice. She snuggles closer, gently touching my face with her dainty fingers.

I lift her chin and kiss her. She frees her arms and hugs me, holding tight as if my life depends on it. We remain in that intimate position for a long time. The alcohol has now loosened our carnal inhibitions and weakened my good judgment. My unassertive mind is no longer ready to control my heedless body. It is 11:55 p.m.

We are down to the last beer can and the bottom fifth of the pink gin bottle. When we finish both off, we would not be able to drive home. I start the car keeping my right arm around Daphne's shoulders.

"Let's go to my place." I don't bother to check if she agrees.

"Whatever you say." I notice a pronounced lisp in her diction.

I need to focus on the road to make sure that the night patrolmen on the prowl do not find anything untoward in my driving. It is a risk I should shun but my beer-soaked brain has turned way too rash to really care. Once I am off the state highway and onto the city streets, I decide to swing by Hustle, the disco on Pine Street, instead of going straight to my studio. I park in front of its beckoning neon sign and ask Daphne to wait in the car without explaining where I am going. She does not ask. I wonder if she has guessed.

Inside the disco, the patrons are in high spirits, dancing to AC/DC's "Highway to Hell". I ignore them and head for the restroom. The two vending boxes are mounted on the wall opposite the sink. I insert three quarters in the slot, collect the pack of Trojans when it drops in the tray and return to the car. My apartment is a short two-minute drive across the rail line.

Daphne brings her bottle inside with her. There is more beer in the fridge. I rustle up a ham-and-cheese sandwich and we share it, alternately taking bites. We continue drinking, getting more intimate with every swig. My last memory is of her sitting on my lap holding my head pressed to her ample bosom.

When I wake up in the morning, Daphne is gone but the faint fragrance of her perfume is still in the air. Stuck on the bathroom mirror is a slip of paper with 'Thanks for the good time, foreigner' scribbled below the line sketch of an arrow piercing a heart. When I make the bed, I find the used up condom on the floor.

It occurs to me that despite spending a night together, I do not even know Daphne's last name. She is not likely to know mine either. And I may not see her ever again. The momentary malfunction of my moral compass pricks my good conscience and wounds my sense of responsibility.

Daphne would have been branded a slut, had she done in India what she did here last night. Perhaps her parents would have been blamed too, for pursuing their own happiness to the detriment of their daughter. But everyone would have overlooked the obvious fact that it takes two to tango; that I was a willing accomplice.

The thought leaves me with a feeling of unknown guilt.

Twenty Four

To counter the lingering unease, I try to occupy myself with the unavoidable weekly chores. By early afternoon, I am done with them. But my efforts to shake the previous night off my mind do not seem to work. On the contrary, the shame of reckless binge-drinking that led to perilous memory-loss, intensifies my feeling of disquiet. I reach the conclusion that one-night-stands are not my cup of tea and resolve to be more responsible with alcohol. Desperate to cure the gnawing restlessness, I decide to visit Hamzeh. In any case, I have not met him since he returned from Jordan.

When I arrive at his ground floor apartment, he is in an animated discussion in Arabic with another man I have never met. The stranger is much older than Hamzeh, possibly in his mid-thirties. He sports an athletic build, a celestial nose and thin lips. The lenses of his horn rimmed glasses make his light brown eyes look bigger than they actually are; he has a habit of frequently pushing the specs back on the bridge of his nose. He radiates the confidence of someone who knows he is smart and handsome, despite a receding hairline.

"Bassam Halaweh." The man stands up and introduces himself, offering his hand to shake mine.

"Bassam's also from Palestine. He's been here a long time." Hamzeh adds for my benefit and looks at Bassam, expecting him to quantify 'long time'.

"A little over ten years." Bassam defines the timeframe.

"Bassam, remember I told you about the guy who met Ronny Parton after being mistaken for an Iranian?" Hamzeh kindles Bassam's memory.

"Of course I do." Bassam replies with flourish.

"That's him. He's doing his MBA." Hamzeh points at me.

It takes us no time at all to become friends. Bassam comes across as suave and cosmopolitan, his understandably strong views on the Palestinian imbroglio notwithstanding.

He does not know much about India and is naturally curious, wanting to learn about my country's history, culture, languages and food. He is a very good listener, always paying close attention. He is surprised when I tell him that India has the world's second largest Moslem population after Indonesia.

"We hear so little about your country." He confesses.

"The television channels rarely cover our part of the planet." I lament.

"What did you study in India before coming here, Guru?" Bassam asks me when Hamzeh goes to the kitchen to make his popular honey-laced mint tea.

"Engineering. And after completing the degree, I worked at a steel forging plant for a few years."

"Wow. Adding a master's in business would make an unbeatable combination." Somehow Bassam's tone and manner does not make it sound like fake flattery.

"I hope the companies I approach think so." I try to sound casual.

"Well, the economy here isn't doing good right now. The job market's down." He turns serious.

"That's the word going around."

"The company I work for is cutting costs too. We expect pink slips soon." He uses the widely used slang for lay-off notices. I remember Ed McGovern telling me that no one knows why they are called so.

"Where do you work, Bassam?"

"At a plastic moulding company up in Sedalia." He points in the general direction of Sedalia.

Hamzeh enters the room carrying a tea-pot filled with his famous brew, three empty cups and a bowl of soft dates with toothpicks stuck in them. He seems to have an unending supply of the delicious snack from his country. The aroma of the drink fills the room as he pours it into the cups.

"You must meet my family one of these days. They'll enjoy spending time with you." Bassam suggests, lifting a date by its toothpick and mouthing it.

"Look forward to it."

"We'll have you over for dinner one night, along with Hamzeh and Ahmed." Bassam sounds gracious.

"That'd be great. I love Arabic food." I express my enthusiasm.

"I can't guarantee that. Sally's American, from Boonville, actually. She's learnt to cook a few Arabic recipes after we got married but obviously she's not an expert." He confesses frankly.

"That's no problem. How old are your kids?" I ask.

"Yassar's six, Fatima's four." Bassam appears to be a proud father.

"They're really cute. I play basketball with Yassar and take Fatima to the zoo whenever I can." Hamzeh butts in.

"Do they know Arabic?" I am curious. Children of many Indian immigrants here are not good at Indian languages. Perhaps it is the same with Arabs.

"They understand most of it but can't speak fluently." Bassam admits, a shade ruefully.

I am happy to learn that Bassam is a baseball buff and supports Kansas City Royals. They are playing Philadelphia Phillies at the Royals Stadium today in the fifth game of the World Series.

"I thought the Royals were down and out after losing the first two games, but they bounced back really well to level the series yesterday." He echoes the popular opinion, lighting another Marlboro.

"I agree. Hope they win today." I express my wish as Hamzeh switches the TV on although he has no interest in baseball.

"Today's game's crucial. I guess the team that wins today'll take the series." Bassam pops one more date in his mouth and drops the toothpick in the ashtray.

"Wasn't it weird for Phillies to start the first game of the Series with Bob Walk at the mound? I mean, how could they have a 'Walk' pitch at such a critical phase?" I highlight the funny side as the game begins. It would not be more amusing if a man named Will Byes is selected to keep wickets in a cricket World Cup final.

We have a hearty laugh and then settle to watch the ongoing fixture. The score remains nil-nil after the bottom of the third. Although neither Hamzeh nor Bassam have shown any displeasure over my presence, I decide to leave so that they can finish the discussion I had intruded into. While getting into my car, I feel convinced that I would enjoy talking with Bassam on a range of other issues.

About a month later, I need Hamzeh's help to complete my assignment in computer programming. He is studying computer science and should be able to sort out my problems effortlessly. I decide to visit him on a Sunday afternoon.

Hamzeh is watching TV. Kansas City Chiefs are playing Detroit Lions. Although I do not follow football, I know that Hamzeh is a Chiefs fan and likes to watch their games without distraction. He is, however, too polite to suggest it himself.

"I think I'll come back a little later, when you can spare some time." I consider it fair to let him enjoy the game.

"No, no, hold on. The game's getting over in a couple of minutes. And hopefully, Chiefs should win with a small margin." His happiness with the expected outcome is written all over his face.

I wait till the Chiefs beat the Lions 20-17 and Hamzeh switches the TV off.

"American football is beyond me. For starters, I can't see why it's called football when the players mostly use their hands." I express my position.

"Well, I love it. Had I been born in this country, I would've most certainly become a pro-football player." He responds with gusto.

"Your physique would've justified it too." I state the obvious. Yet he nods.

"Don't you think we need to celebrate the Chiefs' win with my special tea?" He gets up from the sofa without waiting for my answer. That is the best cheer he can have as a true Moslem.

"Sure. By the way, how's Bassam? I enjoyed meeting him the last time I was here." The mention of tea brings back memories of my previous visit.

"I thought he sounded low on the phone a few days back. Bound to happen if you're pink-slipped." He gives a thumbs-down.

"I'm sorry to hear that. Does Sally work?"

"Not anymore. I believe she used to but quit when Fatima was born." Lay-offs are almost unheard of in India. But this is America, a free-market economy. Just as I try to imagine how hard it must be for Bassam, he walks in through the open door of Hamzeh's apartment.

"Think of the Devil and the Devil's here." Hamzeh laughs and hugs Bassam, exchanging perfunctory kisses on cheeks in the traditional Arabic greeting.

"Don't you dare call me the Devil." Bassam threatens in mock anger. He is formally dressed in a dark suit, white shirt and maroon tie, an unusual choice for a Sunday afternoon.

"What's up, Bassam? How come you're all decked up on a week-end?" I ask.

"I just flew back from California." he lights a Marlboro.

"In that case, you should be in Bermuda shorts." Hamzeh suggests.

"Went there for a job interview with a Saudi sheikh. We met on Queen Mary, at Long Beach. What a hotel!" Bassam refers to the luxury ocean liner, converted to a hotel about nine years ago and permanently docked in California.

"So how'd it go?" Hamzeh asks the obvious question.

"Pretty good, actually. I think I'll get the job." Bassam sounds upbeat.

"Where'd you be located?" I want to know if Bassam will have to move.

"Riyadh, in Saudi Arabia."

We leave it at that and change the topic.

Twenty Five

The winter trimester begins with the euphoria of Ronald Regan's landslide win over President Jimmy Carter and the Republicans regaining Senate majority after twenty eight years. The American people expect their president-elect to turn the economy around and lift the pall of the past few years.

For me, the Reagan victory is significant for one more reason. The Iran hostage crisis that has shadowed me since my arrival in this country over a year ago, shows promise of resolution when the new administration takes over. I find irony of history in the date of Carter's electoral defeat: 4th November 1980, exactly one year, to the day, after American diplomats were taken hostage in Tehran.

Most of my friends are happy to see President Carter replaced but I feel sad for him. I think he is a decent man who tried the best he could. Unfortunately, he could not reverse the stubborn economic downturn and his re-election prospects eroded with every additional day of the hostages' captivity.

One of the subjects I have elected this term is security analysis. Edwin McGovern is the instructor. I catch hold of him after the first class.

"What'd you think of the presidential election, Ed?" He always has an informed and well thought out opinion. I am keen to know it.

"I normally vote for the Democrats but this time I voted for Reagan. Hope he gets better of stagflation." He mentions the portmanteau word of stagnation and inflation, coined a decade and a half ago by Iain Macleod, the former British chancellor of the exchequer. The phenomenon has defied conventional economic theory in recent years to cause headache for governments in many countries.

"It was interesting for me to witness the election up-close." I admit.

"I guess it's different from how you elect governments in India." The usual warmth is missing from his voice. Perhaps he wishes to maintain the distance appropriate for our new teacher-student relationship.

"Very. Remember we talked about it at the Mexican restaurant the day of the car crash?" I regret my thoughtless question the moment I finish asking it. Ed must already be blaming himself for the horrible mishap. Reminding him of it now is unfair. But he does not give me the opportunity to apologize.

"Oh yes. I do recall now. Hope you've a good Christmas this time." He sounds as if he is not looking forward to the annual festival.

"I intend to drive to California and back with a friend from my Indian engineering school, now working in Louisiana." I try to sound exuberant, hoping it will lift Ed's somber mood. The ploy fails to work.

"Interesting. Have fun." He sounds uncharacteristically abrupt, almost dismissive. May be he has had a bad day. I decide to leave him alone.

At the end of the fall term, Dr. Fingleton had mentioned that materials science would not be offered during the winter term. There are no other assistantships, teaching or research, on offer either. I need to speak with Ms. Jasper Hutton for an on-campus job. I decide to see her straightaway.

She is at her desk, preparing a chart, presumably matching students with positions.

"Good morning, ma'am. I was a TA in materials science up until fall but Dr. Fingleton tells me it's not offered this term."

"Yes, he told me so too." Her breathing is as heavy as ever.

"So, I'm looking for an on-campus job." I get to the point.

"Would you be interested in the Todd cafeteria?" She asks.

"It'd be nice if I can go back to Seymours. I know how the place works." I plead my preference.

"In that case, I'll have to speak with … let's see … John Racine if he's willing to trade." She states the position referring to the chart on her desk.

"Can you do that, please?" I ask, willing her to reply in the affirmative.

"Sure. Why don't you check with me tomorrow?" I feel grateful for her favour.

"Thanks, ma'am."

On the way to my apartment, I spot Donna sitting under a tree by the library, reading a book. I am seeing her after several months.

"Hi Donna, long time no see. How're you doing?" I smile.

"Okay, I guess. It's been a long time, isn't it? How're you, Guru?" Her face is drawn, mien gloomy. I wonder why.

"I'm good, thanks. How's Anissa?" I try to bring cheer into my voice.

"Well, Ed and I split. He won her custody. She visits me weekly now." Her eyes turn moist.

"What? I'd no idea." I can neither hide my shock nor think of saying anything more.

"It's been a few months. I've moved to Mitchell Street, a couple of miles north-east of the campus. Drop by when you can spare the time." She writes down her phone number on a page of her notebook, tears it and hands to me."

"Sure, Donna. Take care."

I leave Donna to her book but cannot stomach her disclosure, finding it hard to imagine such gentle individuals developing such irreconcilable differences. My lovely host family's split-up breaks my heart; its abruptness numbs my mind. Ed and Donna are both mature and level headed. They must have thought things through before reaching their decision. Yet I fail to see how they could take such a drastic step. A sense of deep dismay drains my energy. I need to stop by the library instead of directly walking home. On entering, I sit on the first available chair to recoup my strength. Once my lurching emotions settle down a little, I shift attention from my own feelings to the main players in the unfolding tragedy. I feel awfully sorry for Ed and Donna; sorrier for Anissa.

Depriving a three-year-old of her mother's uninterrupted care does not fit into my Indian norms of fairness. I come from a society where parents place their own interests on the back burner for their children's sake. I do not want to pass a value judgment on Ed or Donna and, in fact, fervently hope that they overcome the trauma soon. But I seek God's intervention to prevent emotional scars from permanently disfiguring Anissa's tender soul. And although I place my faith in the trio's resilience to be eventually happy, the disintegration of my local family does rob me of sleep at least for one night. Knowing the reason for Ed's distant demeanour is no consolation for the deflating loss I feel within me.

Mrs. Hutton keeps her promise when I meet her the next day. She has the folder of my documents on her desk.

"I spoke with John Racine about the switch. He's happy to work at Todd because it's closer to his home." She shares the good news with a smile.

"That's great. Can I start this evening?" I try not to sound impatient.

"Yes. You can follow the same routine as last winter." She suggests after opening the file and referring to my record.

"Is Ms. Maurer still running the place?"

"Yes. She'd be happy to see you." I wonder if Ms. Hutton really believes her own projection.

"Thanks, ma'am."

When I report for duty at the cafeteria in the evening, Ms. Maurer welcomes me with a smile.

"Nice to see you back. I don't have to brief you." She looks up from the paper on her desk and, in her trademark style, drops the reading glasses to hang on the neck cord.

"Me too. Is the crew the same as before?"

"The cooking staff's the same, not the students. But you shouldn't face any problem." She attempts to boost my confidence.

I take from her the sheet of paper listing the names of students on my shift and sit at the desk in the other corner to prepare the rota. At that moment, Sarah Walker enters the room, peeling her quilted jacket off. My heart misses a beat. Then it races as never before. I am seeing her for the first time since February and she looks even more attractive.

"Hi, I didn't know you work here." I strive to sound indifferent, hoping the quiver in my voice is not a giveaway.

"Are you assigned this cafeteria too?" She smiles, tossing back her bouncy blonde locks with a tug of her head. I am floored.

"Well, yes. Good to have you on the team." She will never understand how much I mean it.

"Great. Look forward to working with you." She appears to stand in front of the desk a bit longer than necessary. I am not sure if it is really so or my imagination acting up. Eventually, she leaves me with my chart and proceeds to hang her jacket on the wall peg.

While returning to my apartment that evening, I recall the numerous times Sarah had crossed my thoughts since the end of the previous winter term. I did not know where to find her but fate has cleared that hurdle from my path. Our working together at the cafeteria is manna from the heavens. Now I am not strait-jacketed by the earlier teacher-student relationship. That is a liberating change. I am keen to find out what, if anything, she feels about me.

Working together for a couple of hours every day provides a window of opportunity to interact, albeit small. It is just enough to discover vestiges of her life. She is from Trenton, wants to study chemistry and is a health buff. I find her interesting to talk to and like her easy laughter. I have never felt comfortable with people who do not laugh often.

About a week after the term commences, Sarah and I exit the cafeteria at the same time. She starts walking south while I head north.

"Where'd you stay?" I ask, pretending not to be very interested in her reply.

"Nattinger." She points to the south-west in the direction of her dorm.

"That's by the multipurpose building, isn't it?" I want to be sure.

"Yes. And you?" I am glad she asks.

"Off campus. On Madison, by the railroad."

"Bye then. I think I'll go jogging now." She waves her goodbye.

"Where do you jog? On the football field?" I persist.

"No. That's too boring. I prefer the street. A couple of miles around the campus starting from Nattinger." I make a mental note of the details.

"Have fun. See you soon." I mean it.

Two days later, Joan Zimmermann, the student slotted to work on the serving line does not show up. I need to take her position and am delighted to find Sarah on serving duty as well. We have a great time, standing next to each other and getting the opportunity to chat every time a gap appears in the queue of diners. I get to know that her father works for a transportation company, mother is a home-maker and brother is in pre-med.

The day's fare includes hamburgers.

"Why's this called 'fast food'?" Sarah asks a student opting for it.

"Why?" The student does not want to give the obvious answer, suspecting a trap."

"Because if you don't eat it really fast, you might actually taste it." We all laugh. I am glad neither Ms. Maurer nor the cooks are within earshot.

Sarah's wry sense of humour deepens my attraction for her.

On getting home, I change into a tracksuit and go out for a jog. I take the route that, in my estimate, would be in the opposite direction to Sarah's. Three blocks down that way I come to Houx Street that leads to Nattinger. By the time I cover two hundred yards on Houx, my chest is hurting. I am not used to sucking in such cold air; it is freezing my lungs. I slow down, trying to inhale as little air as possible.

Nattinger is within shouting distance and I am seriously tempted to enter it to let my lungs warm up. But I would look stupid if Sarah happens to see me hanging around in her dorm. I discard the idea before it takes root and continue on. Twenty minutes later, I am home without achieving my objective, my chest an ice bag. Worse, I am feeling like a deflated balloon.

My disappointment soon turns into anger. It is directed at me. I am upset with myself because I cannot decide if I should give in to my feelings for Sarah at all. She is from a different ethnicity, a different race and a different background, not to mention different religion. Moreover, I have no idea what she thinks of me.

I revile myself for going on a wild chase that I should not have and consider not finding Sarah a blessing in disguise. I resolve not to do it again, determined to shake her off my mind. I switch on the television in an effort to divert my thoughts, but soon realize that the news being presented is not registering at all. Luckily, Jung Nam drops by to seek help in deciding the topic of his research methods term paper.

I remain firmly committed to my decision the next day, hardening my will further before entering the cafeteria at four in the afternoon. On checking the day's roster, I find that Sarah is assigned the job of first loading the soda pop dispensers and then unloading the dishwasher as the washed tableware comes out on the conveyor. She would thus work far away from me most of the time. I reckon the distance would help me resist the onslaught on my will-power.

In order for the supper service to start at five, the chopping of lettuce and other salad ingredients needs to begin at four thirty. Fred Mikula is listed for the task today. But he is nowhere in sight till four forty. I cannot wait for him any longer and have to take over the work designated to him. By the time I take out the cucumbers, tomatoes, onions, carrots, radish, celery, mushrooms and heads of lettuce from the cold storage, it is four forty five. I need to hurry.

By five o'clock, the jars for salad ingredients and the large bowl for lettuce are only half full. I send them out to the salad bar in the dining area and continue to rush through the chopping so that the jars and the bowl can be quickly replenished. As I hasten to complete the task, Sarah walks in and assumes her position at the end of the dishwasher, barely eight feet from me. I struggle to ignore the distraction, my resolve notwithstanding.

With the timeline crunch on my back and Sarah on my mind, I wield the sharp knife on my index finger instead of a mushroom.

"Sucks." I shout and jerk my hand away from the cutting board to avoid blood from spilling on it.

"What happened?" Sarah turns to look at me, concern mirrored in her pretty eyes.

"Cut myself." I put the bleeding finger in my mouth.

"Show me." She insists, hurrying to get near me to inspect the wound. The dishwasher has yet to start spewing washed tableware but it soon will.

"Nothing much, really." I try to sound unhurt and take out the injured finger from my mouth. It starts to bleed profusely again, forcing me to stick it back in.

"Mind the dishwasher. I'll go get cotton wool and tape." Sarah runs to the first-aid box mounted on the wall at the other end of the kitchen, leaving me to unload the dishwasher with one hand.

She does not take long to return with a bottle of liquid antiseptic, a small roll of surgical cotton, a spool of sticking plaster and a pair of scissors. On taking out the finger from my mouth, I find the bleeding reduced to a hesitant ooze. It would probably heal on its own without any dressing. But

I enjoy the attention as Sarah dabs the antiseptic-soaked cotton on the wound and then wraps the strip of sticking plaster around the finger.

"Thanks, Sarah. The antiseptic should mend the cut real quick."

"Not the antiseptic, Smarty. It's my tender touch." She smiles, a little coyly I imagine. Then she looks straight into my eyes. If her words fail to torpedo my determination, the glance does.

"Can you chop the salad? I'll unload the dishwasher with one hand." I make a feeble attempt to bring myself to the mundane as the crockery begins to emerge on the dishwasher's carousel. But my thoughts continue to revolve around Sarah's words and actions.

As soon as I get home, I reach for the tracksuit like an alcoholic for the bottle. I jog along the same streets as the evening before, except in the opposite direction. The chilled air soon starts to hurt my lungs and I slow down to control my breathing. I turn the corner to enter Grover Street heading east, wondering if I should continue on Holden instead.

"Hi." I hear Sarah yell from the other side of the road before I make up my mind. She is wearing a purple training fleece and matching running shorts. I forget the ice in my chest.

"Hi. Good to see you." I react as if it is a chance encounter.

"Why don't you jog with me?" Her question appears natural.

"Okay, if that's what you want." I suspect I sound condescending without meaning to and immediately feel sorry for making the misleading remark. To be truthful, I would have suggested jogging together, had she not done so.

"Isn't your wound hurting?" She asks, looking at my taped finger.

"Nope. Your tender touch, remember?" I tease. She laughs, giving me that haunting look.

We jog in silence. Her company makes me ignore the pain in my frozen lungs and the throb in my injured finger. Her five feet six frame is just about an inch shorter than mine; we find it easy to match each other's step. In about twenty minutes, we go around five blocks in each direction and are back in front of Nattinger. I want to go in and spend time with her but do not have the gall to suggest it, uncertain of her response. Thankfully, she turns and waves me in while climbing the steps to the entrance. I eagerly follow.

Just past the double doors leading to the entrance lobby is a chesterfield upholstered in maroon leather. Sarah lowers herself on it and invites me to sit by her side, words sputtering through her still heavy breathing. Today is the first time just the two of us are by ourselves for an extended duration. I am awestruck by the occasion. But Sarah has no such difficulty.

"Tell me about your family." She coaxes me.

"Talking about them makes me homesick." I am not sure why I say it, but then go on to briefly describe my parents and siblings.

"And what religion do you practise?" She turns to face me.

"I'm born and raised a Hindu."

"I know so little about it. Who do you worship?" She sounds curious.

"Unlike Christianity or Islam, Hinduism is not monotheistic. It also doesn't completely fit the definitions of polytheism and pantheism. But Hindu religious texts are thought to be the oldest narratives of pantheistic ideas." I try to explain a profound concept.

"What does it preach?"

"Hindus believe in the Divine Being's all encompassing presence. It's embodied in everything that comprises the universe." I paraphrase an enormous philosophy.

"Do you pray often?"

"Not really. Do you?" I keep it vague.

"I go to church on Sundays, sometimes on Wednesdays too. And I read the Bible every day." She seems proud of her religiosity.

"Do you know I sold Bibles in Tennessee during summer?" How would she, I realize as soon as I ask the question.

"Really? My mom'll love you for it." That would be a help, I think to myself.

"I also managed to buy a 1973 Buick for one hundred forty dollars, thirty nine cents and a Bible." I boast, wanting to guide the discussion away from religion.

"Wow, that sounds like some deal. How'd you manage that?"

"I'll tell the story when we meet again." I sow the seeds of our next encounter and decide to leave. No point in overstaying my welcome.

Once I am alone, I get conscious of a warm glow in my heart. The cold breeze brushing my cheeks does not freeze my skin anymore. I have never experienced this feeling before. To be frank, I have had a crush here and a crush there since my late teens. But they were nothing more than that. This is different.

I have fallen head over heels in love.

Twenty Six

The intense craving for Sarah's company crowds out all my apprehensions over our dissimilarities. I unabashedly search for excuses to meet her beyond the daily cafeteria routine. The evening jog is the obvious low hanging fruit. I make it a point to join her as frequently as possible, not finding the need to justify the effort in terms of its health benefits.

But just the jog is not enough to assuage my yearning for Sarah; it does not accord the chance to talk with her. She is a serious fitness freak and wants to synchronize breathing with the rhythm of her pounding feet. Talking disrupts that harmony, so I refrain from the indulgence. Instead, I invent pretexts to stretch the time in her company, taking care to hide my wish to be invited to the chesterfield in Nattinger's lobby. My ego stops me from looking obsessed without knowing her feelings for me.

"I am going to the library to see Jung Nam. It shouldn't take long. I'll walk you back to Nattinger if you come along."

I suggest after our third jog, trying to make the offer sound spontaneous.

"Who's Jung Nam?"

"Oh, I should've realized you wouldn't know him. He's from Korea, my roommate at Seymours last year. A great guy." I explain.

"Okay. Let's go." Her response is heartening.

"Do you like Korean food?" I ask her as we turn the corner and head north on College Avenue.

"Never tasted it." She shrugs shoulders.

"I hadn't either, till Jung Nam invited me over. He's such cute kids, a son and a daughter. And his wife makes great *andong jjimdak*."

"What's that?" She asks with a quizzical look on her face.

"Chicken and vegetables steamed with cellophane noodles in *ganjang* sauce. The recipe is from Andong, a city in Korea." I flaunt my newly acquired knowledge.

"Never heard of *ganjang* sauce." She admits.

"It's a sort of Korean soy sauce made from fermented soybeans." I explain as we enter the library.

Jung Nam is frantically hitting the keys of a manual typewriter, trying to complete a term paper before the library closes for the night. He looks tired. The task is almost as hard for him as doing sums on a Korean abacus would be for me. I introduce him to Sarah, adding that she was my student last winter and now works with me at the cafeteria. They exchange pleasantries.

"Guru told me about your cute daughter and son. Can I meet them sometime?" I notice warmth in Sarah's tone.

"Of course. Of course." Jung Nam displays his oriental trait of repeating a short answer. His response reminds me of Cheng Jian. I wonder if he has become a monk in Taiwan.

Jung Nam needs help in writing his economics term paper. I collect his draft and promise to return it with corrections the next day. We are out of the library in less than ten minutes.

"If it's okay with you, we'll stop by at the students' union for a cup of coffee?" I propose, looking at my watch. The snack bar would be open for another fifteen minutes.

"Only if you promise to tell me how you bought a Buick for one hundred forty dollars, thirty nine cents and a Bible." She lays down her condition with a smile.

"Done deal." I shake her hand in mock seriousness. Then I am struck by her precise reference to the brand of the car and the exact price I had paid. Evidently, she not only listens to me carefully but also remembers the minutiae. A casual acquaintance would rarely do that, if ever. I feel encouraged.

For the next fifteen minutes, I narrate my encounter with Mrs. Maynard and the lucrative bargain I managed to wrangle out of her. Right through, Sarah takes in the story in rapt attention, barely touching her coffee.

"You're one smooth operator, Mr. Golden Tongue." She jabs when I stop.

"Well, I couldn't have paid more even if I wanted to. And she was free to turn down my best offer." I claim my innocence, taking umbrage at the connotation of the 'Golden Tongue' sobriquet. I am surely no con-artist.

"Tell me, would you've paid what she wanted if you'd had the money?" Her eyes are fixed on mine in a steady gaze. I suspect she is testing my integrity.

"I don't know. I'd most probably have negotiated hard. But I can't say how much I would've actually shelled out." I come clean.

"That sounds an honest answer. I like that." Her lips part in a grin. I sense relief and happiness in her eyes but I cannot put a finger on whether that is indeed so or my wish colouring my vision.

"Wouldn't you want to take a spin in my car to find out its real worth?" It is a perfect bait for a date. I hope she swallows.

"That's not a bad idea, but for my ineptness to put a price tag on a used car." Her tone is mischievous. I am not sure what to make of her ambivalent remark. But I do not want to let go so easily.

"It's worth a shot, isn't it?" I press on.

"Okay, let's try." Even though her reply is far from emphatically affirmative, my heart goes aflutter at the prospect of our first date. I want to seal the plan without wasting a moment.

"How about Sunday evening? We can drive down to Clinton. I hear there's a nice Italian restaurant just off the highway." It is a thirty-mile-run each way. Allowing for a leisurely meal, I would get to spend three hours with her. I wait expectantly for her response.

"Let's see… It should work for me." She confirms, after staring in space for a few seconds, trying to remember if she has other commitments.

"Great." I am ecstatic.

After finishing coffee, we walk to Nattinger. I bid her goodbye at the entrance to the dorm and wait on the sidewalk while she climbs the few steps to the double doors. Before reaching for the door handle, she lingers a few seconds longer than necessary to turn and look at me. The expression in her eyes reflects my sadness at leaving her behind. After she disappears inside the building, I begin the slow trudge home. Once I reach my apartment though, the anticipation of our upcoming date helps lift my spirits.

Yet the time till Sunday evening seems to last forever. It stretches even further when Sarah calls in sick for the next day's cafeteria duty. That pretty much rules out her jog too. Not seeing her is bad enough; the possibility of her not recovering in time for the appointment two days later makes it worse. And I would be mortified if the illness is a subterfuge for escaping the commitment. I cannot wait to get home and call to find out what is wrong with her.

By the time I look up Nattinger's number in the phone book though, I begin to question the wisdom in making the call. It may appear too pushy, if not downright obtrusive. The doubt holds me back from dialing Nattinger but cannot erase my disappointment at Sarah choosing Elaine Maurer to report her illness, not me. I try to force my heart to trash the feeling as sappy. Why should I expect her to reach me ahead of the others? I think it wise to get my mind off the episode and decide to go down to the multipurpose building for a swim in the heated indoor pool.

But just as I am leaving the apartment, the phone rings. At this time of the evening, it could be anyone. I reach for the receiver, trying to guess who it would be.

"My name's Rhonda. I'm Sarah Walker's roommate." My heart is in my mouth. Is Sarah so unwell that she cannot call herself?

"I don't think we've met." I involuntarily make the inane comment.

"No, we haven't. But Sarah asked me to let you know that she twisted her ankle; it's ballooned real bad." The girl at the other end delivers the message.

"Sorry to hear that." I suspect my tone conveys the concern that I would prefer to keep to myself.

"Well, she can barely stand right now but expects to be able to hobble around in a couple of days." I do not know if the prognosis is backed by expert opinion or just Sarah's hope. Whatever the case, I feel optimistic about Sunday evening.

"May be I should come and see her tomorrow. What's the room number?" I expectantly wait for her reply.

"Three twenty nine. And I'll have to escort you." I am reminded of my adventure at Fitzgerald last fall when I went to fetch Daphne and Chris.

"Tomorrow's Saturday. Would three in the afternoon be okay?"

"I guess so. We're not going anywhere."

"Okay. Room three twenty nine then." I don't want any misunderstanding, although it would be easy to fix it this time, unlike at Fitzgerald.

I hang up and find myself on Cloud Nine. Sarah did feel the need to inform me of her condition. Better still, she expects to be mobile again on Sunday. It is more than evident that I am on her mind, although it is hard to say to what extent.

The hands on my watch seem reluctant to move the next day. I will them to speed up but they stubbornly test my patience. At long last, the agonizing wait is over and I arrive at Nattinger. Rhonda comes down to the lobby to escort me upstairs, when the girl at the reception buzzes her. I enter the room expecting to see Sarah on the bed. Instead she is sitting on a chair with her crepe-bandaged right ankle propped up on the seat of another. Her infectious smile lights up her eyes, the dimpled cheeks adding to her allure.

"Why don't you sign this?" I ask her, pointing at a sheet of paper I extract from my pocket.

"What's that?" Sarah's forehead creases.

"An application to change your last name from Walker to Hobbler." I reply, pretending to be serious.

"That's mean." Rhonda screeches. We all laugh.

"Do you know how a grasshopper with a broken leg feels?" I quiz Sarah.

"How?" She sees the trap.

"Unhoppy."

"Very funny." Sarah comments with false sarcasm.

"This'll make you to feel better and give Rhonda the energy to take good care of you." I offer them a bar of chocolate each.

"Thanks, Guru. But I'm already fretting over lack of exercise. This'll surely add more pounds." Sarah keeps the chocolate on her desk. Rhonda peels the silver foil and bites into the bar, bliss spreading across her face.

"I'd be very happy if you eat it now. You can skip the dessert tonight." I want to see if she cares for my happiness.

"Okay, I'll take a bite if you finish the rest. I'll worry about my weight later." She eats half the bar and hands me the remaining portion. I am thrilled at her giving in to my wish.

"Well, I hope you're able to walk by tomorrow evening. I'd hate to cancel our drive." I express my fear after swallowing the chocolate and wait for her response.

"I look forward to it too. My will-power will heal the injury." She looks at her bandaged foot. Her comment warms my heart.

"Sounds good. See you tomorrow evening at seven."

One of the courses I have taken this term is reading in management. As part of its requirement, I have to read a pertinent book every week and submit its synopsis to the instructor the following Monday. I am always through with the book by Saturday, leaving the whole of Sunday for completing the abstract. This week I have chosen *Managing in Turbulent Times,* Peter Drucker's latest publication. I am a staunch Drucker devotee, convinced of the longevity of his ideas on business management. Normally, I look forward to reading his books, devouring every word like a starved pig. But this week has hardly been normal. I have lumbered my way through the pages, often drifting into a hypnotic trance filled with imagery of my as yet one-sided romance. And now I am on to Sunday. It is turning out to be different too.

Hard as I try to concentrate on writing the synopsis, my mind keeps wandering to the anticipated evening engagement. I eventually concede the futility of trying to complete the assignment and decide to return to it at night, when the dinner with Sarah would be behind me. In an attempt to cope with the sluggish clock, I visit the laundromat, spend another hour buying groceries and blow a tidy sum at the car wash. Finally, it is time to meet Sarah.

She is waiting for me in the lobby, elegantly dressed in a black pencil skirt and a white puff sleeved blouse with puritan collar, her middle-parted blonde curls carefully combed. A neatly folded winter coat is at her side on the chesterfield. She greets me with a bright smile and tries to rise with the support of her hand pressed against the padded arm of the sofa. The maneuver succeeds only partially, the stress on the buttressing elbow threatening to buckle it midway. But before it does, I step forward and hold her free arm, propping her up. The subtle fragrance of her French perfume tantalises my senses in the fraction of a second she is close to me.

Sarah is happy to regain balance but the walk to the car is not much easier. She has to hold my arm to take the few steps to reach it. When she sees the Buick, she's astounded.

"Wow! You must've really charmed the Japanese lady to get this beauty for a song!" Her reaction appears genuinely spontaneous.

"A song and a prayer, actually." We laugh at my off-the-cuff pun.

"Don't ask me to put a price tag on it though. I don't have the foggiest idea."

"That's okay. I'm sure I got a great deal." I act cool and open the door for her.

"Thanks for the gallantry. We don't see it often enough anymore." She eases herself into the passenger seat, letting go of my hand.

"Are you still okay with the Italian restaurant in Clinton?" I ask as we start rolling.

"No need to go that far, really. Why don't we try Valentino's on the corner of Market and Warren?" Her suggestion makes sense. After all, this car guzzles gas; the trip to Clinton will burn five gallons, a waste.

"Sure thing. You've been there?"

"No, but Rhonda said it's excellent." The reply gladdens me. At least Sarah will remember the first visit to the restaurant and, by association, me.

"Great. First trip to the restaurant on our first dinner outing. I like that."

Twenty Seven

Valentino's is a small eatery serving authentic Italian recipes cooked in the traditional mode. Sunday evening does not appear to be the restaurant's busiest time; barely a third of the dozen tables are occupied. We ask the *maitre d* to seat us at a quiet corner table. He happily obliges and hands us thick padded menus.

I am keen to get the ordering part quickly out of the way. That will allow more time to know Sarah's past and understand her personality.

"What'd you like to try for the main course?" I seek her preference.

"Why don't we split pasta and a pizza? That way, we'll get to try two different dishes." She speaks my mind.

In keeping with the American custom, we first order salads, panzanella for her and tortellini pesto for me. For the main course, we agree on ragu alla bolognese and pepperoni pizza. The *maitre d* wants to know if we would like to pair the pasta with a wine and recommends a dry Lambrusco.

"I'm a teetotaler, so I'll go for tomato juice." Sarah is quick to announce. I also decide to abstain from alcohol.

"I'd prefer ice tea, easy on ice."

"Are you also a teetotaler?" Sarah asks after the *maitre d* collects the menus and leaves the table.

"Not really. I enjoy beer but don't like spirits."

"Tell me more about your home. You were very brief the last time." Sarah changes the track.

I fill her in on my family. She appears impressed with their qualifications and wonders if I miss them.

"Well, I used to suffer unbearable pangs of what I named domusphilia. But now that I'm used to being away, I no longer do." I admit.

"Why domusphilia?" She does not understand the name.

"I wanted to coin a Latin label to make it sound impressive. Domus in Latin is home and philia, as you may know, means a strong feeling of love or admiration." I share my logic.

"Everyone calls it homesickness." She smiles.

"Not true. Homesickness is missing home, not hating the new environment. It afflicts a person immediately after migration." I explain.

"How is domusphilia different, Guru?" Her question is wrapped in a pound of mischief, garnished with a pinch of sarcasm. It stirs my intellect into action.

"One, it doesn't hit immediately on leaving home but after the foreign setting ceases to zap you. Two, you develop a temporary allergy for all aspects of the new surroundings. Three, you discover the virtues embedded in the way of life at home that you hadn't detected earlier. The discovery leads to adulation of previous lifestyle that you'd never thought possible. And four, domusphilia's far less common than homesickness." My own eloquence takes me by surprise. I had never dissected my anecdotal affliction in such clear terms.

"You could easily pass as a clinical psychologist presenting a research paper at a seminar. I'd be fooled." She laughs innocently. The mischief and the sarcasm are conspicuous by their absence.

"Don't make me an imposter, Sarah." I protest.

"No, I'm not. You've gleaned a facet of mental trauma that mankind has ignored all along." The mischief is back in her tone.

"Let's change the topic." I would like to know more about her.

Before we can do that though, the waitress serves our beverages and salads. The sight of good food whips up my appetite. Overcome by the exciting prospect of going out with Sarah in the evening, I had neglected to eat a proper meal during the day. Now I can enjoy both, the food and her proximity. After tasting the salad, I thank Sarah for choosing this restaurant and steer the discussion to her life.

"What about your family? What do you do when the four of you're together?" I prod her, remembering that her father works for a transportation company, mother is a housewife and brother is at pre-med.

"We're nowhere near as cerebral as your folks. In Trenton, our life revolves around the church."

"As a part of my Bible sales training, I attended a Sunday service at a Lutheran church in Saint Louis." I attempt to continue with the topic of her interest.

"How'd you find it?" She leans forward, looking serious, elbows planted on the table and palms supporting her chin.

I am reminded of Audrey Manning's similar question. Her face flashes in front of mind's eye, the fancy sinamay church hat standing out.

"Interesting." I repeat the reply given earlier to Ms. Manning as I cannot think of a better expression. And I refrain from mentioning Pastor Bell's shot at converting me.

"Are you religious?" She asks, locking her eyes into mine.

"I don't think so. I am Hindu by birth but I follow Holyoake's secularism." I state my disposition.

"Who is Holyoake?" She looks confused.

"George Jacob Holyoake was a British writer and lecturer. He's the last person to be prosecuted for blasphemy in a public speech. That was over a hundred and thirty five years ago."

"Never heard of him." She admits.

"Few have. Many people know secularism but not who coined the term." I share my observation.

"But isn't secularism separation of government from religion?" She asks the question that most would.

"Yes, as applied to state institutions. But in the context of individuals, secularism seeks maximum possible development of the physical, moral and intellectual nature of humans as the duty of life."

"So, you don't believe in God?" I sense her more-than-casual interest in the question.

"Not as the preachers of religion ask us to. All I would grant is that we can't adequately explain every occurrence using our scientific knowledge. So there must be reasons beyond our comprehension." I put forward my honest position, not sure how she would respond.

She does not get a chance to as our main course appears. Valentino's servings not only look prettier than Italian food I have seen so far but are tastier too. The tagliatelle is unlike any pasta I have eaten before, a little rough in texture. The cheese on the pizza is piquant provolone instead of the ubiquitous mozzarella. We welcome the change. After we split the pasta and help ourselves with slices of the pizza, we resume our conversation but shift the tack to friends on the campus and the courses we have taken so far.

"How'd you get to know students from so many different countries?" Sarah asks after I tell her about my multinational friend circle.

"At the international club. It's a colourful gathering, no pun intended."

"Can I tag along for one of the events?" She asks, looking sincere.

"Sure. I'll be more than happy to take you."

The restaurant seems to serve large portions. We take our own time savouring the delicious preparations. When we finish, the *maitre d* appears again.

"Hope you enjoyed the food. What'd you like for the dessert? I'd recommend panna cotta and cannoli, today's specials." He places the dessert menu in front of us.

"The entrée has stuffed me to my gills. I've absolutely no room left for the dessert or even coffee, for that matter." Sarah's tone is apologetic.

"Do you know that only Americans refer to the main course as 'entrée'?" I ask her after the *maitre d* goes to get the cheque.

"What do they mean by entrée then?"

"An appetiser or a starter." I add to her general knowledge.

It is almost nine o'clock by the time we get into the car. I have had a wonderful evening but am a little sad that it is about to get over.

"Thanks for a great dinner, Guru. I really loved it." Sarah reaches for my arm as I turn the ignition.

"My pleasure, Sarah. And thanks for keeping the commitment in the face of your hurtful foot."

When we meet the next evening at the cafeteria, I feel a new bond, as if Sarah has long been a dear friend. And the look in her eyes suggests that she shares my sentiment.

"Your ankle looks much better." Her gait is almost normal.

"Yesterday's date has healed it." Her face sports a playful expression. I find cheer in her choice of word to describe the outing. Surely she knows that 'date' implies greater intimacy than simply eating out together.

When the supper service is over, she does not leave the cafeteria immediately, preferring to chat with Ms. Maurer till I finish my work. On the way out, she joins me.

"Your foot clearly can't endure jogging today. But would you like to try my cardamom coffee and study at my place?" I wait for her response, wondering if I should have made the proposition at all.

"Wouldn't it be a hassle to drive me to and from your apartment?" She pops the question, rather than answering in terms of yes or no. I am delighted.

"Not one bit. If you'd be ready in half an hour, I'll come and get you."

"Should be okay."

We study till late. In between, we take turns brewing coffee. Although Sarah does not fall for its Indian flavour, preferring cinnamon over cardamom, she is polite enough not to reject it outright. She even suggests that over time she would develop a liking for the aroma. Her presence turns my otherwise austere apartment cozy and warm. I also realize that I am able to concentrate better. A little after midnight, Sarah wants to leave.

"What'd Rhonda and others think about your being at my place till so late?" I do not want Sarah's friends to harbour wrong ideas about her.

"They know I'll not sleep with anyone till I get married." She is blunt. I am stunned by her assertion. In a society where students rarely finish high school before losing their virginity, she is obviously the odd person out.

"Really?" I cannot hide my astonishment.

"They think I'm weird but I can handle the peer pressure. I'll do what I think is right." She sounds refreshingly nonchalant but her outlook is more conservative than that of many Indians I know. Apparently, Sarah's position is shaped by a strong influence of her church. This element of her personality adds to the list of our dissimilarities; I cannot be classified as anything but liberal, my own discomfort with one-night-stands notwithstanding. Yet I find succour in the scientific fact that unlike poles attract each other.

Spending after-supper hours together becomes a regular feature of our routine. We mostly study on our own but at times, I help her with physics and mathematics. Sarah lends her portable electric typewriter to me, eliminating the need to go to the library for typing my assignments and term papers. It allows us more time at my apartment.

After she comes over on several successive evenings, I am convinced that she reciprocates my feelings for her. By then we have talked a great deal about ourselves and our families. These exchanges seem to foster close understanding of each other. In the process, we have reached a level of comfort that has made formalities redundant. On perhaps the twentieth such night, we are done with our studies early and spend the next two hours sipping coffee over a chat about the differences between Indian and American cultures.

"I wouldn't mind living in a large household among a bunch of relatives." Sarah's opinion is based on imagery created by my description of a huge house occupied by a large joint family.

"You've always lived in a nuclear family. You can't imagine the niggles breach of privacy causes." I express my considered reservation.

"Don't underestimate my tolerance for people." She sounds confident.

"You may be right." I choose not to persist with my view.

It is well past midnight when Sarah reluctantly decides to leave. In keeping with our established protocol, I drive her to Nattinger. When I stop in front of the dorm's entrance, she does not get out of the car immediately. I sense her hesitation, switch the engine off and turn to look at her. She has a coy expression on her face.

"I've become habituated to you, Guru." She confesses, avoiding my eyes.

"It's not a habit you want to kick?" It is partly an expression of my hope, partly a question.

"No." She locks her eyes into mine.

I lean toward the passenger side, close my eyes and kiss her.

Twenty Eight

Sarah's passionate response turns my life into a beautiful melody. We meet for coffee between classes, go swimming in the evenings, watch films at night and take in sunrise at Lions Lake. On week-ends, I ask her to go with me to the parties I attend. And although she is a teetotaler, she enthusiastically joins in, truly enjoying the interaction with the international crowd. I soon feel certain that she would love a Saturday night at Ahmed's. The opportunity arises a few weeks after I return from San Francisco, having ushered in 1981 at a rambunctious New Year's Eve carnival in Union Square.

Born in Yemen, raised in Egypt and holding a Saudi Arabian passport, Ahmed Saleh is a psychedelic character. Standing on a slight frame a couple of inches shorter than five and a half feet, he manages to exude an aura that men enjoying far more imposing physique would find hard to match. Like everything else he does, Ahmed speaks fast, lending an Arabic lilt to English diction. The only action he takes slowly is stroking his full beard and he does it frequently. The lemon yellow Volkswagen Beetle he drives compliments his personality.

With a bulbous nose, small twinkling eyes and a wide mouth that reveals prominent teeth when he speaks, Ahmed cannot be described as good looking by any stretch of the imagination. But his sharp wit makes girls go crazy on his ready quips. He liberally spreads his considerable charisma on young women, often showering them with expensive gifts. His parties are extravagant, packed with lavish food and awash in exotic drinks that none other on the campus can rival.

A great votary of Giacomo Girolamo Casanova, Ahmed often tries to outdo the eighteenth century Italian playboy. After I got to know him well, I thought of needling him about his indulgence.

"Do you throw money around because you can't charm girls any other way?" I poked.

"Not at all. I know I can talk them into my den." He pompously declared, perhaps justifiably so.

"Why don't you do it then?" I prodded on.

"I believe in Casanova's two tenets." He was quick to reply.

"And what're those?" I could not resist the question.

"Economy spoils pleasure." He smiled.

"And the other?"

"The thing is to dazzle." I had nothing more to ask.

Ahmed's spendthrift ways are bankrolled by his research assistantship and the munificent Saudi Arabian government that pays him a monthly stipend of $700 on top of tuition fees, books and winter clothing. Benefiting from his government's largesse, however, has not debauched his thinking. He espouses civil liberties and democratic rights, openly criticising his country's oppressive monarchy. But when asked if he will fight against the Kingdom's rulers after going back, he is non-committal.

"May be I'll also be lulled by the creature comforts offered to me on a silver platter. Who knows?" He admits with a sheepish smile.

"But what about your claim to democratic values?" I hear myself push him.

"When in Rome, do as the Romans do!" He floors me with his unabashed candour.

Ahmed is famous for his exploits with girls, frequently laying bets on accomplishing impossible feats. I have learnt it the hard way, losing $10 last spring.

But for all the fun and flirting he indulges in, Ahmed manages to get very good grades. He is studying here for a master's in economics, having earned a bachelor's degree from Cairo University. Dr. Wilson, one of the decorated professors in the economics department, would have no other research assistant to work under him. Ahmed is proud of the fact and does not hesitate to flaunt it.

It is always interesting to see Ahmed in the students' union cafeteria. He is invariably surrounded by a group of students, girls outnumbering guys by at least three to one. He is always the focal point of the gathering, animatedly cracking jokes and sharing stories that throw his loyal audience into raptures. He is a heavy smoker but every time plucks the filter off his cigarette before lighting it. His bottomless cup of black tea is sweetened with six sachets of sugar. Most of his friends think a tea-bag is redundant litter in his sugar-syrup. I have yet to see anyone else with such peculiar habits.

On this particular night, Ahmed is host to students from half a dozen countries excluding the Americans. As always, he is tending his elaborate bar with rare panache, mixing exotic cocktails: Tom Collins, Tequila Sunrise, Manhattan, Spice Tree and Sidecar, among others. We are having a wonderful time, taking pictures of each of us in Ahmed's *keffiah*, the famous Arab headgear. By eleven o'clock, the party has truly warmed up.

At that late hour, Bassam walks in. He circulates among the group and reaches me after about fifteen minutes. We exchange pleasantries. I introduce him to Sarah and ask about the job in Saudi Arabia he had interviewed for.

"I did get the job. I knew I would." He is obviously proud of his accomplishment.

"So when do you start?" I ask the logical question.

"I just got the papers on Thursday. I'll go to Washington on Monday, get the Saudi visa and fly off to Riyadh on Wednesday." He declares with a flourish. The lay-off seems to have roused his urge to be occupied again.

"What kind of a job is it?" I ask as a matter of small talk.

"I'll be working in the chairman's office, setting management systems in the group companies." His tone echoes the pride in getting a senior position.

"And what does the group do?" My question is more to push the conversation in the direction he wants it to go than curiosity.

"Well, they've five companies. Three sell imported products, one's in construction business and the last one's a manufacturing company." He explains enthusiastically.

"Wow! You'll be working for a conglomerate!" Sarah expresses her admiration.

"Sort of, although some of the companies may not be very big." Bassam is honest.

"The varied experience will be good for you. All the best." I wish him.

"Well, it's going to be very different to what I've been used to so far. But I'll handle it."

"You'll miss baseball, I presume." I remember his Royals fixation.

"Absolutely. And many other things." He admits.

"Such as?" Sarah asks.

"Free news media, movie theatres, bars, freedom of all sorts." I sense a hint of ruefulness in his reply.

"You'll get used to it. And knowing Arabic would make life easier, wouldn't it?" I try to pep him up.

"Oh yes. That's a big help." His voice is buoyant again.

The conversation veers to politics. I express my relief at the resolution of the Iran hostage situation on the day of Reagan's inauguration.

"Right through my stay here, I've lived in the shadow of the hostage crisis. Now people should stop badgering me." I express my hope.

"The public mood should probably change, if it hasn't already." Bassam seconds my opinion.

"What do you think of Reagan's victory from the Middle East standpoint?" His view would surely reflect the Arab perspective.

"Jimmy Carter was considered credible by both, the Jews and the Palestinians. I'm not sure if President Reagan gets the same rating." He is candid. I notice his refusal to mention Israel, preferring 'Jews' instead.

"I suppose people also expect Reagan to turn the economy around. Incidentally, Dr. Dolecke's prediction came true." I try to tickle his curiosity.

"Which was?"

"The incumbent can't win the presidency again if the unemployment exceeds six percent."

"Well, now that I'm leaving, I don't much care for the economy here. The Middle East is booming and that's good news." Bassam shrugs his shoulders.

When he moves to another group, I spot Atif talking with Yves LaPierre, an exchange student from France, here to study American history. I join them and introduce Sarah. Yves and I have met a few times at the international club but never really talked at length. Like many Europeans, he is well aware of the geopolitical realities of the world and is fully conversant with the conflicts between India and Pakistan. He is surprised to see Atif getting along perfectly fine with me.

"Are you guys really friendly or pretending to be so?" His undiplomatic inquisition stumps us.

"Why do you question that?" Atif asks after recovering from Yves' tactlessness.

"Because your countries are always hostile towards each other." Yves puts on the table the point we have never discussed among ourselves.

"We're here as individuals from the Indian sub-continent. In many ways, we share a common culture. It's natural for us to be friends." I try to be polite in the face of his provocation.

"But you've significant differences too." Yves is unrelenting. I am getting angry now.

"That holds true for individuals from any two nationalities." Atif calmly argues.

"Not to the same level of animosity." Obviously, Yves doesn't want to let go.

"Look Yves, here we belong to the same community. Dr. Saran, an Indian professor, invites all of us during Indian festivals and Dr. Ismail, a Pakistani professor, has us over for Pakistani celebrations." I hope my clarification shuts Yves up.

"Will you remain friends after you return to your respective countries?" The Frenchman is impossible. I am on the verge of flying off the handle.

"We don't want to worry about it right now." Atif deftly steers clear. I want to tell Yves it's none of his business anyway, but am distracted by a tap on my shoulder. I turn around to find Bassam exhaling a cloud of smoke. His question comes from the blue.

"Hey, I know your credentials. Engineering with an MBA. Would you be interested in joining the group I'm going to in Riyadh?" He seems serious.

"I don't know, Bassam." I reply in all honesty.

"It's tax free income." Bassam dangles the carrot.

"I want to build my career in India. Whether I'd like to stop in Saudi Arabia on the way isn't something I've thought about." I choose to be frank.

"Give a thought to it. You don't have to commit right now." He sounds reasonable.

"I'll do that."

"Why don't you give me your phone number? I'm not sure I've got it. That way, I can call if I find anything interesting." Bassam dips into his pockets for a slip of paper.

He does not find one. But rather than asking it from Ahmed, he opens a new Marlboro pack and tweezes out the small piece of aluminium foil covering the cigarettes. The foil is lined with white paper. He hands it to me. I write my phone number and give it back to him. As far as I am concerned the matter ends there.

Once the party is over, I promptly forget the episode.

Twenty Nine

In consonance with my work hard, play harder maxim, I am always looking for a reason to celebrate during my free time. Ahmed's parties may be extravagant but I take pride in meticulously planning mine and cooking enticing food for my friends.

The occasion tonight, if we needed one, is Becky's twenty second birthday. She was born in February of 1959 at the tail end of the post-World War II baby boom that lasted a decade and a half. It must have been a good time to enter the American stage. The dramatic increase in births from 1946 drove an exponential growth in demand for homes, household appliances, roads, vehicles and services. The mushrooming demand enlarged the economy, creating more jobs and unprecedented prosperity. Becky is a beneficiary of those good times.

Frankly, I do not recall the first time I met Becky. She claims to have accompanied Debbie to my apartment one week-end several months back. From what she tells me, I had a bunch of friends and friends' friends at my pad that evening, all having fun. "The place was packed wall-to-wall with revelers", is how she once described the scene. Obviously, I must have missed her out in the jag. We got to know each other well when both of us took Dr. Engelmann's accounting course. I remember thinking of her as an amiable version of Ursula Andress. But in contrast to the famous Swiss-American film star's stern demeanour, Becky laughed easily. She wasn't great at crunching numbers and often asked me to help out with her sums. We have got along famously ever since.

Becky is one of the few Americans genuinely interested in the world at large. She has been to many countries in South America and Africa, an exceptional record among her peers. The exposure has helped her understand the human suffering caused by abject poverty and she is keen to do something for the affected people. To this end, she has joined Peace Corps, the American organization for international service set up to tackle burning problems of people in several countries. Despite our many differences on possible antidotes to stubborn socioeconomic challenges in the developing world, I respect Becky's views and enjoy our robust debates.

Hamzeh, Debbie, Atif, Ahmed, Dan, Marsha and, of course, Sarah have come in early to prepare for the celebration. Becky has no inkling of the party yet; surprise is the zing of a charming birthday bash. Marsha, Becky's roommate, has persuaded Becky to do their laundry in the dorm so that she does not go out. The plan is for Marsha to fetch Becky at seven o'clock and party till midnight to bring in her birthday. I am happy to play my usual role of the host.

Ahmed has arranged a mortarboard-shaped dark chocolate cake, complete with the square plate on top, adorned with a gold tassel. It is Debbie's idea; Becky is graduating in June. Ahmed specially ordered it at the local patisserie a week ago. It looks beautiful. And delicious. Hamzeh has brought shiny streamers, lanterns, confetti, balloons and a 'Happy Birthday' banner. As a Peace Corps volunteer, Becky is going to Kenya after graduation. All of us have chipped in to gift her a sturdy fiberglass suitcase to take on her trip.

As is our custom, I am the chef. And I have an enthusiastic new sous chef in the form of Sarah. The menu is a medley of international cuisine: Italian pasta, Mexican rice, Indian bread, Lebanese *hummus*, Irish stew and French vegetable *au gratin*. It has taken me the whole afternoon to cook. I enjoy performing the gratifying task. The bar is in Ahmed's deft hands. Hamzeh and Sarah, the teetotalers, have warned him not to spike their juice.

The entire scheme works to perfection. Becky has no inkling of the celebration awaiting her. She is floored when she walks in through the door. And thrilled. We have a great time singing, dancing, chatting, drinking and, of course, eating. At the stroke of midnight, we bring out the specially ordered cake and sing "Happy Birthday" as Becky cuts it with a festooned knife. She enjoys the heady cocktails, loves the international food and adores the apt birthday present. The satiated revelers reluctantly start winding down the party an hour or so later.

Hamzeh and Sarah stay behind to help me tidy up the place after everyone else leaves. Just as I get ready to take them to their dwellings, the skies open up. The thunder peals are deafening; the lightening flashes blinding. It is soon raining buckets. We scamper into my modest old Buick. But before I pull out, the engine sputters, then dies. 'What a screw up. Must be the moisture in the carburetor,' I silently blame the weather and try the ignition a few more times. The engine refuses to kick in. The freezing rain is coming down harder now. There is no way Hamzeh and Sarah can walk in these conditions. I have no option but to steal Reufey's car.

Reufey Akhtar is my next door neighbour, also a graduate student. He doubles as a medical technologist at Clinton General Hospital from three in the afternoon till eleven at night, thrice a week. He has returned from work and gone to bed. As usual, his apartment is not locked. I run to it, pick up the car keys on the dining table and take his Dodge Charger to drop my friends. It is a short drive. I am on my way back ten minutes later. The rain is heavier, if anything. The time is approaching 2:00 a.m.

The road is very familiar; I have driven on it a zillion times. I am in the westerly lane on Grover Street, approaching College Avenue running north-south. Suddenly, the empty car makes me shiver. It did not feel so cold when Sarah was on board. Now I need to heat the cabin up a bit. My chilled hand gropes for the thermostat. But my subconscious is not attuned to this car; I cannot blindly reach its knobs and levers. I am forced to take my eyes off the road to look down and locate the heater control as the car approaches the intersection. There is no need to slow down though; College has a stop sign, not Grover.

I locate the thermostat toggle, slide it to hot and shift my gaze back to the wet road, expecting to see the shiny tarred stretch again. Instead, I am blinded by the reflection of the Charger's headlights in the drenched side panel of a silver coloured station wagon barely ten feet ahead. It looks like a Chevy Impala, moving across my way from left to right on College. 'Asshole!' I curse the offending driver in my mind, instinctively slam the brakes and at the same time spin the steering in a desperate attempt to clear the station wagon's tail. I am hopelessly late. The Charger's right front end takes out the Chevy's right tail portion. The clamour of shattering glass and crushing sheet metal is drowned by the loud thunder. The rude shock stuns my mind into a stall.

I cross the intersection in a daze, pull over and look back through the rear windscreen. My heart is pounding in my chest. The Impala has only one taillight burning now; I have killed the other. It hangs in there for a moment and then moves on, disappearing behind the building occupying the corner plot. The Charger has four headlights, a pair on each side, recessed in the projected chrome trim framing the front. The beam of the right unit is split into two; one is lighting up the road, the other falling on the house to the right. Obviously, the light unit is bent, but not broken. That is a relief.

Slowly I recover from the debilitating jolt, trying to think straight. The driver of the Impala should have obeyed the stop sign and waited before crossing the intersection, not me. He did not. His fault. The disappearance of the Impala suggests he knows he is the culprit. I have nothing to worry. My mind is made. The rain has no intention of slackening.

I drive home, drop the keys back on Reufey's dinette and hit the sack. Reufey and I inspect the damage in the morning. The trim around the right headlight unit is torn and twisted. So is a portion of the fender. The right parking light has vanished. A strip of sheet metal has snaked on to the wheel. We yank it clear of the tyre. Our attempts to restore the headlight unit fail. Reufey is gracious. He does not as much as bring up the topic of fixing the wreckage.

Reufey is a very dear friend, his Pakistani nationality notwithstanding. His looks often remind me of Asif Iqbal, the famous Pakistani cricketer. Like all outspoken men, Reufey is not a popular figure among his peers but we get along very well. I respect his integrity, sincerity and thought process while he reposes his complete and implicit trust in me. He lived in Florida for seven years before enrolling in the MBA programme last spring. His father in Karachi has a heart condition. Reufey dreads the possibility of his family failing to reach him quickly in case his father suffers another stroke. To mitigate this risk, we have one phone connection with parallel lines in each of our apartments. If he is out, I may be in to take and relay an urgent message.

A couple of days after I dismiss the accident as a forgettable fender-bender, the phone rings in the morning when Reufey is at school. I answer.

"This is Sergeant Ray Goodwin from the police department. Can I speak with Mr. Reufey Akhtar?"

"He's not in right now. But I can take a message or have him call back." I have a sneaky suspicion this is about the car accident.

"We've impounded his car. It is a 1975 Dodge Charger with Florida license plates." He reads out the license number. Although I do not remember the number on Reufey's car, the mention of Florida registration is enough. My fear is coming true.

"Is it in connection with an accident over the weekend?" I try to be absolutely sure.

"Yes. The vehicle was involved in an incident at about two o'clock on the twenty second morning. Mr. Akhtar needs to see us as soon as possible." The time and date mentioned by the police officer is the night spanning Saturday and Sunday. There is no doubt now.

"In that case, I need to see you since I was driving the vehicle at the time." I give my name and address with a promise of reaching the department in the next ten minutes.

I collect Reufey's car keys from his dinette before walking across the rail line and into the police department. Sergeant Goodwin is waiting. He is a tall man in his early thirties with a round rosy face thatched with crew cut auburn hair. His hard blue eyes, thick eyebrows and bushy moustache soften the prominence of the parrot's beak nose. He stands imposing in his dark blue uniform, the three inverted chevrons testifying his rank. I wonder if he was a football player before joining the force.

The sergeant has no time for pleasantries. He leads me to a warehouse by the police station, rolls up the shutter and walks in. Reufey's damaged Dodge is parked inside, looking sullen. Ray Goodwin takes out a paper from his shirt pocket and gives it to me.

"Will you please sign this before taking possession of the car, sir?" I do what he has asked me to and return the paper to him. Then I drive the car out and into the police station's parking lot.

When we are back in the sergeant's office, he neither bothers to sit nor offers me a chair. We are going to have a standing committee meet, I surmise. He comes straight to the point.

"What happened on the night in question?"

I describe the episode as it happened, stressing my right of way as Grover has no stop sign. The sergeant is not convinced.

"That isn't what we're given to understand, sir." He is courteous but sounds suspicious.

"I am sure of what happened, officer." I press my point.

"If you weren't at fault, you should've come and reported the incident. You didn't."

"It was raining heavily and the other car involved in the accident drove away without stopping. I thought it's a minor fender-bender and went home." I speak the truth, hoping it will prevail.

"The other car in the incident was driven by Mr. Robert Wooley. He came and reported the accident, claiming to be in the clear." The officer refers to the piece of paper in his hand before mentioning the driver's name. Then he glowers at me.

"My version's contrary to his." I defend my position.

"There're no witnesses, so we've to be guided by the available evidence. The paint scrapings from the Charger match with the Chevy's paint. The front of your car hit the Chevy's tail. That's inculpatory." He has made up his mind.

"What're the consequences?" I need to know the outcome of his inference.

"Since you did not report the accident, we've to go by Mr. Wooley's charge of hit-and-run."

"I didn't run away." I argue, knowing it is superfluous.

"Only if Mr. Wooley accepts it." He smiles. The sergeant is rubbing salt on my wound. It hurts.

"Where can I find him?"

"That's his phone number. You're free to call him." He hands me a piece of paper.

I have no idea how serious hit-and-run is; I need legal advice. Edwin McGovern should be able to tell me where to look. He does not want to scare me but cannot hide his concern from his deep voice. He suggests I meet Gerry Fink.

Several months earlier, Ed had introduced me to Gerry and his wife Susan at a party Ed had thrown. I remember thinking of them as an odd couple. Gerry is a large rotund man whose age is hard to guess while Susan is a petite, delicate lady in her mid-thirties. Gerry had given me his business card, a gesture I considered unusual for the occasion.

I call Gerry's office and find Joan, his secretary, on the line. She insists on knowing the purpose of seeking an appointment with Mr. Fink. After I explain the reason, she confirms it for the same afternoon at four o'clock.

Gerry's office on Holden Street is a ground floor suite of three rooms. Joan sits in the reception area that also has sofas for waiting clients. Of the two doors leading to the adjoining rooms, one is closed. The small hand painted wooden board at the eye level simply reads 'Records'. The other opens into Gerry's office. He is ready for me when I enter.

Unlike for Ed's party, today Gerry is formally dressed in a black suit, white shirt and a red striped tie in a Windsor knot. He has a mane of thick black hair, large dark brown eyes and a small squat nose that seems unable to hold up his round wire-framed glasses. Yet it is hard to say if pushing them back to the base of the nose is his pastime or necessity.

Gerry's mahogany-paneled chamber is appointed with heavy matching furniture. His certificates and expensive framed paintings gild the walls. Each is spot-lit with a tubular picture light in gold mat finish. He sits behind a large desk cluttered with several stacks of papers and yellow manila envelopes. Across the desk from him are two arm chairs upholstered in crimson leather and placed facing each other along the edge of the desk. The afternoon sun filtering through the wide casement window behind Gerry is diffused by off-white vertical strip blinds. The plush tan rug on the floor helps mute the sounds in the room. Gerry Fink must be a successful lawyer.

I expect Gerry to be surprised by my visit. He is not. Joan seems to have briefed him.

"Tell me everything that happened, without jumping over any scraps." He suggests after we exchange pleasantries. I tell him the whole story, in minute detail, including the visit to the police department.

"Hit-and-run! That's not good news. And the cops have all the proof they need."

"I see that, Gerry. But what does hit-and-run mean in practical terms?" I am eager to know the penalties.

"Well, if you're found guilty, you face a fine and lose twelve points on your driver's license. That means suspension of the license."

I notice he has avoided the term 'convicted', preferring less menacing 'found guilty' instead. There is no way to know if the choice of words is to make me feel better or his normal style.

"That'd be terrible. Losing driver's license in this country's like losing legs. I graduate in three months. A driver's license is a must to start on a job."

Joan brings steaming coffee I am in no frame of mind to enjoy. But I do not wish to be rude. I thank her and turn my attention to Gerry again.

"There could be a way out, Guru." His tone sounds reassuring.

"At long last." I am not sure if my comment is warranted but I hear myself making it just the same.

"This guy you hit," he looks at the sheet of paper I have handed him, searching for the name.

"Robert Wooley." I save him the trouble.

"If Wooley doesn't press charges, the matter shall go to the public prosecutor. In that case, I can talk the prosecutor into changing the hit-and-run to careless driving." He sounds as if he does this all the time.

"How'll that help?" I am hopeful now but not sure why.

"Careless driving attracts far less fine and costs only four points. That means you save money and keep your license." Gerry makes the deal sound like a flea market bargain. If nothing else, it helps ease my tension a little.

"It's a no-brainer then, really." My mind is made.

"I suggest you talk to this Robert Wooley. We'll take a call after that." Gerry stands up to signify the end of the meeting.

Thirty

I phone Robert Wooley as soon as I get home. He is happy to hear from me. It transpires that he works in the Accounting Department of the university. We decide to meet the next day in his office.

From the way he sounded on the phone, I expected Mr. Wooley to be older than what I find him in person. He is barely thirty five, his reed-thin frame making him look taller than he actually is. With his long nose, thin lips and receding hairline, he resembles Stan Laurel but the famous comedian's endearing innocence is missing in Wooley's countenance. I am grateful to Laurel and Hardy for the joy they brought to my childhood and feel guilty of associating the delightful duo's memory with the sly individual standing behind the desk. Robert Wooley is sporting a tan I am certain is fake. I suspect he wants to hide his anemic complexion. He greets me with a limp handshake. I hate limp handshakes.

"I presume you know why I'm here." I start the discussion.

"Yes."

"Both of us saw what happened the other night and why. Only College has a stop sign on the Grover-College intersection. You should've obeyed it but didn't. That slip caused the incident. Do you agree?" I want him to own up his mistake first. The move is nothing short of naïveté.

"That's irrelevant. I went to the cops, you went home. That's what matters now." I am outraged by the man's audacity. Anger is of no help, I tell myself. The law is on his side.

"You're right but I'm charged with hit-and-run when the accident wasn't my fault." I hope against hope he sees my point.

"Didn't I tell you it's irrelevant now? We need to decide where we go from here." I do not agree with him but have no choice but to continue the negotiation.

"All right, where do we go from here?" I ask. May be, just may be, he is kind enough to let me off the hook.

"I've no particular interest in pressing charges if I don't take a hit."

"Okay, what'd you want me to do then?" I wish he will say "Nothing", we will shake hands again and I will leave. I am ready to forgive his listless handshake.

"Simple. I want my car repaired. I'll get three quotes and you pay the lowest of the lot. I get my car fixed, drop the charges and we're both happy." He demands his ransom with a straight face.

I feel vilified yet relieved. Surely Reufey's insurance will pay the third party damages. Without wasting an extra minute, I agree to Robert Wooley's proposal. He says he will have the quotes ready in three days. That suits me fine.

Not that my seeing Wooley's bruised car is likely to change the situation in any way but I take up his offer to walk down to the parking lot and take a look. Thankfully, it does not appear so bad. Reufey's Charger is much worse. I do not want to be there long.

"We'll meet again after you receive the quotes." I am happy to get away from the crook.

On reaching home, I call Gerry and brief him on the distasteful meeting.

"When you're ready to pay Wooley up, give me a holler. We'll have him sign the document that I can take to the public prosecutor."

"I will, Gerry."

I meet Reufey in the evening. My mood is upbeat. I have found a way of escaping the hit-and-run. Reufey senses the cheer when I tell him about my deal with Wooley. He turns serious.

"We've a problem here, Guru." He comments. I am perplexed.

"I thought I had a problem, Reufey. Past tense, not present."

"I wish you were right. Unfortunately, insurance's not mandatory in Florida. I chose not to buy it." He lets me in on the problem. This is bad news but I am yet to learn how bad. I have to wait till Wooley comes up with his quotes.

The three days till then seem like three years. I am dying to get the problem out of the way and get on with my life. After the fidgety interlude, the D-day finally arrives. I reach Robert Wooley's office with trepidation, not really knowing how much I will have to pay. My guess is three hundred bucks.

Wooley is prepared. Even before I sit in the chair opposite him, he takes out an envelope from his desk's top drawer and tosses it to my side of the table. He has a triumphant air about him.

"Sheet metal repair's a slow, painstaking job. It needs highly skilled workers. They don't come cheap." Wooley has a wicked smile on his face. His preamble sounds ominous. Worse, he is clearly enjoying it.

I ignore his comment and take out the three quotes from the envelope, unfold them and look at the first one. Parts and labour add up to a whopping $1,495.00. My hands begin to tremble. I somehow manage to muster enough nerve to see the next, $1,540.00. It is pointless to bother with the third, but I take a peek anyway. The amount is not less than the lower of the first two.

I am ready to pass out. Three hundred would have stung like a sharp uppercut, yet I could have survived it. Fourteen ninety five is a knock-out punch.

My mind goes blank, body cold. I sit there like a mannequin staring at Wooley. After a few moments my brain switches on. I am tempted to throw the three quotes on the face of the cheat in front of me, ask him to shove them up his posterior and walk out. But I feel too spent to utter even a single word. I hang in there for the debilitating blow to wear off. Eventually, I gather enough wit and all the strength in me to speak. I am not sure if Wooley's offer is up for negotiation but I must try.

"I suppose you can buy the bumper, panels and taillight at a junkyard for fifty bucks and replace the damaged ones.

They may need a paint job to match your car's but all put together, the entire cost shouldn't go beyond three hundred bucks, three fifty tops." My friends have told me that no one gets mangled panels repaired. Everyone cannibalises junked cars. Robert Wooley need not be an exception.

"What I do with my car is my business. I want to get it done the right way." Although he is a consummate liar, his claim sounds unconvincing. But he holds all the aces; I am trumped. If I do not want to forfeit my driving rights, I must pay him $1,495.00. My bank account held $39.57 that morning.

"The car's not insured. I'll have to shell out the cost from my pocket." I make a feeble attempt to garner sympathy despite doubting its effectiveness.

"What a pity! But I'm not responsible for it, am I?" He is ruthless. There is no gain in further pleading for discount. But I need to try and buy a little time.

"Be that as it may, your lowest quote is still a large sum, especially for a student. I need a few days to arrange the amount." I dip into the negotiation skills learned during the training at Saint Louis.

"I'd be flexible on the timeline but not by more than a couple of days." The thief is lusting to pocket his immoral pay-off this minute. Two days may be a long time for him but not me. I need the week-end to raise the debt.

"I'll call on Monday to let you know about the money." The negotiation has gone nowhere. All that is left to do now is get up and leave with the three quotes. I am not interested in the pathetic handshake.

I call Gerry from home. He is no help.

"Do what's necessary, but arrange the money quickly, Guru. The case comes up for hearing in a fortnight. We want the guy to drop his charge within a week." He is hurrying me up.

"I'll try and do that, Gerry. For now, can you indicate the fine for careless driving?" I will have to be ready with it too.

"I know Judge Melvin Cooper. He's not known to be kind to traffic offenders. You can expect two hundred dollars. If he's in a foul mood, he might go up to two fifty."

"Let's hope he doesn't get up from the wrong side of the bed that day. And what about your fees?" I cannot ignore that burden either.

"Joan works out my fees but I'll ask her to be reasonable and not charge more than one fifty an hour." Reasonable at $150 an hour? This is highway robbery. I pretend to be calm.

Over the week-end, I call my Indian friends who came to the US immediately after graduating from engineering college. They completed their master's programmes while I was rotating shifts at the steel forge. A few of them are still at school writing dissertations for their doctorates but most are working at large corporations for some time now. The conversation during each call is pretty much the same: the hit-and-run, no insurance, huge damages, how much money can they lend?

Most of them started jobs at twenty two grand a year, give or take ten percent. Being single, they attract a higher tax slab. They also incur heavy outgoes on car installment and house rent or mortgage, not to mention holiday trips to India. They save little, if at all. But they generously agree to send whatever they can. I am grateful for the help.

By Sunday night, I am confident of collecting enough to cover Robert Wooley's opportunistic greed. I call him on Monday to confirm that we will settle the matter by Thursday. Gerry needs to draw out the document for Wooley to sign. He says he will be ready with it by Tuesday. That fits well with my schedule. If Wooley can clear the draft by Wednesday, Gerry can get the paperwork ready on Thursday. I am surely not handing the cheque without having Wooley sign Gerry's paperwork in return.

Come Thursday, Wooley is off my back. I am certain he is pocketing at least a thousand dollars after a visit to the junkyard. His devious smile drives a wedge in my heart. Instead of facing penalties for jumping a stop sign, he is laughing his way to the bank. What an irony!

Getting Wooley out of my hair is a relief but a short-lived one. I need to start worrying about Judge Cooper's fine, Gerry's fee and Reufey's car. They are likely to cost another three grand. I scrounge, asking my Indian friends to be more generous. I also cut all expenses to the bone although my small income does not stretch much. I hunt for cheap groceries, walk as much as possible to save on gas, turn the heater down, put in twenty hours a week at the cafeteria on minimum wage and quit eating out to save two bucks thirty five for hamburger, French fries and soda pop. It is tough.

Gerry calls on the Monday after we get Wooley out of the way. He has spoken to the public prosecutor. The charge will be changed to careless driving. The case is scheduled for hearing on Friday.

"We need to meet before that, Guru. I've to brief you on what to do in the court." Gerry suggests.

"How about Thursday? That'll allow me enough time to digest the briefing." I have never been to a court in India, let alone one in America.

"Sounds good. Four o'clock?"

"That'll work, Gerry."

"All right then. I'll ask Joan to put you in the diary." He hangs up.

My friends send me more cheques. I am also able to save a few dollars that I never thought feasible. The target of collecting three thousand more dollars is now within reach. I start feeling less insecure.

On Thursday, Gerry tutors me on my impending court appearance. I need not have gone to his office; it could have easily been done on the phone. Gerry's company hurts; his two-and-a-half-dollars-a-minute fee is wringing me dry. I strive to keep the meeting brief, downing the coffee in one gulp and quickly setting out for the door.

"One more point." Gerry says to my back. I stop and turn. He continues, "Joan's kept a tab on the time we've devoted to your case. You may want to talk to her on the way out. She's good at emptying clients' pockets." He laughs. I feign a smile.

Joan is ready when I step in front of her. She slides a sheet of paper across the desk. The invoice is for nine hours and forty minutes. I have been dreading this moment. But I am prepared. I take out the cheque book from my pocket, sign a cheque for $1,450 and hand it to her.

"We'll raise another invoice after the court appearance tomorrow." She gives the bad news with a grin.

The county courthouse is one block from Gerry's office, on the opposite side of the street, at the corner of Holden and Gay. I meet Gerry in his office and we walk together from there. The courthouse is an imposing three story stone building with sloping tiled roof, arched wooden windows and a clock tower rising behind the façade. Once we enter the building, Gerry asks me to wait in the courtroom and disappears. Apparently, he is talking to the public prosecutor. He is not gone long.

The clerk of the court orders everyone to rise as Judge Melvin Cooper, looking dignified in his black robe and silver hair, enters from his adjoining chamber. He nods in acknowledgment and sits down behind his elevated bench. He is probably in his late sixties, with features of a Greek God. He could easily have been a Hollywood hero in his younger days, but for his stern look. The clerk calls my name. Gerry prods me to step into the box. I oblige. The clerk reads the charge. I let him complete and turn my gaze towards Judge Cooper. He looks at me and raises an enquiring eyebrow. I nod as instructed by Gerry. The judge then turns to the public prosecutor and asks if he has anything to say. The public prosecutor replies in the negative. The judge proclaims me guilty and slaps a fine of two hundred dollars. Presumably, he has risen from the right side of his bed in the morning. My first and hopefully last appearance in an American court is quickly over.

I step out of the box and leave the room. Gerry follows. We meet in the anteroom. I sign a cheque for two hundred dollars and give it to Gerry. He says I can collect the written order and the fine receipt from his office at four in the afternoon. I stroll out of the court premises wondering what Robert Wooley is doing right then. Planning his paid holiday, I imagine with rising bitterness.

When I get to Gerry's office at four, he is not in. But Joan has the court order and the receipt neatly folded in an envelope. I ask her if she is ready with the balance amount of Gerry's fee. She is. I sign and hand over another cheque for four hundred and seventy five dollars. It is painful.

When I meet Reufey in the evening, I bring up the topic of getting his car fixed. Knowing him, he would never mention the subject on his own. He is reluctant to discuss it but I insist.

"I was at the junkyard yesterday." he finally relents.

"And what'd you find there?" I am anxious to know.

"Fortunately, they've a couple of Chargers we can strip. So we'll get all the replacements we need, except that the panels are a different colour." He tries to make it seem simple.

"The garage can re-paint them, I guess."

"I checked with Shelley's for fitment and paint job. It all adds up to seven thirty five bucks. I wish it was lower but that's the best." He is almost apologetic.

"Well, the damage on your car's much more than on Wooley's. You need to replace a lot more parts. So my guess was right; he would not pay much more than three hundred dollars, three twenty five on the outside.

"It's best not think about it, Guru." Reufey is far more philosophical than me.

On Monday, I force him to get his car fixed. The workshop returns it in two days. I am finally done with my most traumatic brush with the law. My ignorance has set me back by a crippling $4,355 and left me worried as to how I am going to repay this mountain of debt.

Thirty One

Three Sundays later, the phone rings at nine in the morning. All my friends know it is a bad time to call. I rarely sleep before the small hours on week-ends, generally waking up around noon. I ignore the ring. Barely five minutes later, it rings again and keeps ringing. I curse under my breath, get up and answer. I am still in a fog.

The person at the other end of the line sounds like Dr. Saran, the Indian professor who teaches psychology at the university. Apart from inviting me for Divali, the annual Indian festival of lights, Dr. Saran and his Puerto Rican wife have never felt the need to contact me. And Divali was barely five months ago. I am surprised to hear Dr. Saran's voice.

"Yes, Dr. Saran." I try to escape the fog.

"Hey, I'm not Dr. Saran. This is Bassam speaking."

"Bassam, you were to go to Saudi Arabia weeks ago. What're you still doing in the states?"

"Listen, buddy. I'm calling from Saudi Arabia." I am not sure this is real. I pinch myself.

"Look Bassam, you know I was partying till late and my head hasn't cleared yet. But that doesn't mean you can kid me with this baloney." I am getting annoyed with his Sunday morning intrusion.

"I'm not kidding. If you want to be sure, take my number down and call me in Saudi. It's six o'clock in the evening here."

He sounds ready to swear by his God. Besides, I am in no mood to blow money calling long distance.

"Okay. What can I do for you?" I want to finish this insane discussion and go back to bed.

"I may've a job for you here. One of our group companies runs an aluminium extrusion plant. They can do with some help in marketing."

"Bassam, I'm not sure if I'd want it." I hide behind subterfuge. Actually, I am not sure of Bassam's story although the year has yet to progress to All Fools' Day.

"You can decide that later. Why don't you note my address and post your résumé as soon as you can?" It sounds a fair proposal. So I write down his address, hang up and return to my bed.

I get no time that day to go down to the library to type out my résumé. But I make sure to make the document ready the next afternoon. There is no point in holding on to it, so I decide to go to the post office straightaway for sending it to Bassam.

While exiting the library, I run into Tom Weber. He seems to be in a hurry but looks mighty pleased to see me. We have not seen each other since our escapade in Chattanooga.

"I'm so glad I met you. What're you doing right now?" His expression clearly suggests he wants me to spare time for him.

"Nothing much. Why?" Not only am I happy to do what he wants me to but also think it wise to keep to myself the plan of going to the post office. Why talk about a job that is still in the application stage? With that thought, I put away the folded résumé in my pocket before Tom answers.

"I need your help. My car conked off just as I set out for an important appointment. Can you take me there?" He spells out his problem in a single breath.

"For you Tom, any time. You know it. My car's over there." I laugh and point at the parking lot by the Administration building.

"Let's run." He takes off.

"Where to?" I ask as I turn the key in the ignition, springing the motor to life.

"Morgan Cermets, just off Route 50 west." He sounds edgy.

"We'll be there in twenty minutes." I assure him.

"Perfect." He leans back in his seat, appearing to calm down a little.

"How've you been?" I change the topic, hoping to ease up his nerves.

"Looking for a job, now that I'm graduating in May."

"At Morgan Cermets?"

"Yup. One of my teachers told me Morgan's hiring and suggested I call them. By the way, do you know what a cermet is? I should've checked the encyclopedia." He still sounds a little tense. Understandably so.

"Of course. I taught materials science, remember?"

"Then tell me. Quickly."

"Cermets are composite materials made from ceramics and metals. The aim is to harness good properties of both. Sort of making the best of both the worlds. You want more?"

"Nope. That's good enough."

"Relax now. Morgan needs you." I again attempt to purge his tension, without even knowing the position he is being interviewed for. But before I ask, we reach the burnt-clay bricks façade of the office block fronting the factory shed behind. I swing the car into the parking lot and stop in the visitor's slot. The burnished brass plaque nailed to the wall by the entrance declares Morgan Cermets to be manufacturers of high quality sintered magnets.

We step into the entrance lobby enclosed by light green walls lined with chrome chairs padded in deep tan leather. Enlarged photographs of sintered magnets of various shapes surround the area. I am familiar with this product range, having interned at a sintered magnets production facility during the summer separating my second and third years at the engineering college.

"My name's Tom Weber. I've an appointment with Mr. Don Morgan at three." He informs the young woman sitting behind the reception desk. The clock on the partition behind her shows 2:55.

"Why don't you talk with Leigh in his office down the hall?" She points in the direction of our destination.

We walk down the corridor flanked by glass-partitioned offices occupied by staffers busy with their work. The place exudes quiet efficiency. The chamber we are asked to go to is monochromatic: white wallpaper, white carpet, white cotton window blinds and white painted birch wood furniture upholstered in white twill. It reminds me of a hospital waiting room, except that the monotony in this case is punctuated by more blow-ups of magnets on every wall.

A middle-aged lady sporting a mane of salt-and-pepper candyfloss is sitting at a credenza in the far corner. Thankfully, she is wearing a navy pant suit, providing semblance of colour to the place. The wall on one side of her workstation has a door fitted with Don Morgan's name plate. It also carries his designation: president.

"Good afternoon. How can I help you today?" Her eight-hundred-watt smile competes for brightness with the stark surroundings. She cannot be anyone but Mr. Morgan's secretary.

"We were asked to wait here for Mr. Morgan." Tom sounds nervous. In a hushed tone, I ask him relax and take a seat.

"You must be Mr. Weber, scheduled for the three o'clock meeting. I expect Mr. Morgan to be back any moment. He's never late for an appointment."

Even before she finishes making the claim, a tall hefty man with a shiny bald pate, snow white whiskers and a sharp nose breezes in, smiles at us and continues on through the door to the president's office. Leigh follows him.

"The guy's in a hurry." I comment on his gait.

"He had better, if he wants to retain his unblemished record of keeping appointments." Tom murmurs in my ear, looking at the hands of his wrist watch approaching a perfect right angle.

Leigh returns in less than a minute and asks Tom to see Mr. Morgan. He stands up as if Leigh has administered an electric shock, straightens the front of his clothes and goes in to meet Don Morgan. I have never seen Tom so jumpy before. Perhaps he desperately needs this job. Pressure affects people in strange ways. I silently pray for him.

As seconds tick into minutes, I start gaining confidence in Tom's song and dance in front of Don Morgan. My logic is simple: if the president thinks it worth his while to stretch the interview, he must be seriously interested in the candidate, increasing the chances of the candidate passing muster. With that soothing thought, I reach into my pocket and extract the résumé I had finished typing just before bumping into Tom. It would be a good idea to go through it one last time for spotting any errors.

Before I am able to go down half the first page though, Tom reappears, his complexion as pallid as the surroundings. He looks gutted. The interview has obviously gone awry. I search for comforting words to cheer him up. He never gives me the opportunity.

"He wants to see you." Tom points to Don Morgan's office and sinks in the chair beside me even before I can manage to open my mouth.

"Me?" I cannot hide my astonishment.

"He asked me to send you in as I was stepping out of his office." Tom's dejected voice is barely audible. I feel for him.

The forced interview means little to me, if anything at all. Yet I feel uncomfortable to go through it in faded jeans, plaid shirt and sneakers. Since no option is available, I walk past Leigh and into Don Morgan's office, the unfolded résumé still in my hand. The president's office is spacious and exquisitely appointed, befitting his position. The absence of white in the entire décor is a welcome relief. Soft shades of blue and grey have taken its place. Don Morgan is sitting in a padded high-backed swivel chair at a carved wood executive desk. The matching hutch behind him proudly displays handsome golf trophies.

He gestures to suggest I take one of the three chairs on the opposite side of the desk from him. Then, seeing the unfolded sheets in my hand, he stretches his arm, expecting me to pass the papers to him. When I meet his expectation, he pulls his reading glasses down from the barren dome of his pate and carefully goes through my credentials. I have no reason to be tense, but the fact that we have not spoken a word for several minutes does make me a little restless.

"Why should I hire you?" He eventually snaps, just as I start wondering if his office is a silence zone. He raises his eyes to meet mine, drilling me with his piercing gaze.

The question is an obvious ruse to shock and awe, to test my reaction to pressure. Yet I notice a hint of childlike curiosity in his tone, shorn of arrogance of power. The observation relaxes me even further. From my standpoint, this exchange is redundant. I think of telling him that he should not hire me, that he is talking to a wrong guy. But I do not wish to sound rude. Besides, I can treat this as a dress rehearsal to prepare me for a real encounter sometime later. I decide to play along.

"Because I can help Morgan Cermets grow." I hear myself say, even to my own surprise. If Don Morgan is a true American, my words should be music to his ears.

"Really?" His eyes widen; eyebrows jump up. I sense a shade of sarcasm underpinning his question.

"I guess you focus on the local market here in the US, perhaps extending it to Canada." I pause for his response.

"Pretty much." I interpret it as 'correct'.

"There's a huge market out there beyond the borders of North America, in India, for example. Millions of audio and video tape recorders, radios and television sets are made there each year. Every one of them needs magnets. I can help you tap into that demand." I spell out my proposition.

"How?" I feel his interest getting ignited.

"I know the weaknesses in the magnets currently available in that market. I suppose Morgan Cermets have a better product to offer." My assessment of the products in the Indian market is backed by my internship study. The claim about Morgan's product, however, is a calculated gamble with odds stacked better than even.

"What do you know about sintered magnet production?" He leads me into familiar territory.

Although my brief tenure at the magnet plant was several years ago, I clearly remember the materials used, the processes employed, the properties sought and the parameters checked. I relish Don Morgan's question like a piece of cake. My articulation leaves him dazzled. He seems unsure of what more to ask and goes over my résumé again.

"You collect stamps." He lingers on philately mentioned as my hobby. A mischievous smile appears under his bushy silver moustache.

"I used to in high school. Haven't really kept up since." I state the truth.

"What's a black listed stamp?" His eyes bear the 'gotchya' look of an urchin playing a wicked prank.

When I was in the seventh grade, my high school had organized a hobby workshop where reputed philatelists had been invited. One of them had explained the term to us and it stayed glued to my memory. I can easily access it now.

"One that's not used for postage but is sold to collectors for earning a profit. It's of no value to a true philatelist." My confident reply is the clincher. Don Morgan stands up and proffers his hand to firmly shake mine.

"You're hired. We're not the top paymasters in the industry but we're not at the bottom of the pile either. I'll have Len Brown, our HR chief, issue the appointment letter." He steps around his desk, presumably to walk me to the door. I hold my ground.

"What position am I being offered?" I ask, not fully comprehending the impact of his statement.

"Executive assistant to the president."

Thirty Two

"What'd he want?" Tom enquires as soon as I come out of Don Morgan's office. I look for a narrative that would be more palatable to him. But there is no way to soft-pedal the issue.

"He wanted to interview me; couldn't have known I was only chauffeuring you, could he?" I pause, not sure how to proceed.

"Did he?" I notice impatience in his question.

"Yes." I cannot meet his eye.

"And?"

"I think he wants me to join." There is no gentler way of sharing the truth.

He sulks as if he has just heard his fiancée is eloping with his best friend.

"As what?" He asks after gathering himself.

"His executive assistant." I try to sound disinterested, hoping it will make Tom feel a little less threatened.

"So you're not stealing my job. I'm looking for a sales position." He smiles, without anxiety leaving his eyes.

His disclosure is a great relief. I would have hated to spoil a dear friend's party, however unintentionally. Had I been offered the job he had applied for, I would have found myself in a no-win situation. Accepting it would have attracted blame for cheating Tom and refusing it would have seemed a shot at martyrdom. After all, the economy is still not creating enough jobs to employ all.

"I'm glad we're not competing for the same slot. But even then, I'm not sure if I want to accept it." I express my indecision during the drive back to the campus.

"Why? I think it's a good company to work for." He cannot understand my position.

"In fact, the company I interned at in India also offered me the job on graduation but I declined because that's not my field." I try to clarify.

"What'd you mean?"

"I interned thinking I'd get trained in powder metallurgy. But after spending three months there, I realized it wasn't so. The same reason applies to Morgan even though this isn't a manufacturing job."

"It doesn't. An EA to the president is an EA to the president; doesn't matter what business the company is in."

"There're other reasons too, Tom. An EA enjoys the president's reflected power but is really a glorified gofer. And his access to the boss makes other employees either jealous or suspicious of him." I share my observation made at the steel forge back home.

"You're probably right." He agrees and gets out of the car in front of his dorm.

Once I am alone, I realize that the copy of my résumé meant for Bassam is now with Don Morgan. I need to type another one. Unfortunately, there is not enough time left today to do that and still reach the post office before it closes. I go to the library nonetheless and type out the résumé again. The next morning, I visit the post office and dispatch it to Saudi Arabia.

I consider it to be the end of the matter. I am wrong.

Within a week of the unscheduled meeting with Don Morgan, I get the appointment letter from his company. A little under a fortnight thereafter, a thick envelope arrives in the post from Al Daba'an Aluminium Factory in Riyadh, Kingdom of Saudi Arabia. On opening it, I find an employment contract for the post of sales engineer.

At the end of an amazing chain of incredible coincidences, I have landed two jobs without ever asking for them.

Frankly, I am not able to decide which of them to accept. So I sit on the letters, trying to figure out what to do. I need to think through my options before getting back to the two willing employers.

The purpose for which I came to America is largely served. Well over a year into the master's programme, I now have barely three months left for receiving my degree. I have so far scored very good grades and can see myself maintaining that record till the end. The management education has surely been valuable but equally importantly, I have tasted a slice of the world that I could never have in my own country. I have been exposed to a wide variety of nationalities and cultures, met with traumatic yet educating mishaps, received practical training in personal selling and have learned to deal with daunting challenges on my own. The journey has immensely boosted my self-confidence.

I have not only seen the bright side and disciplined work ethos of America but also experienced her unsavoury underbelly. In the process, I have understood the hereto unperceived facets of my emotionally beneficent and spiritually complex society. If I can blend the virtues of the two cultures, it will create an elixir to achieve professional success and personal happiness.

To be fair, I could not have asked for more.

I arrived in America with the plan of returning to India after completing my education. That option is theoretically open but practically closed. For starters, I do not have the thousand dollars needed to buy a plane ticket to India. But even if I did, the skyscraping debt would still pose an insurmountable hurdle. Given my professional credentials, I can expect to get a job in India paying in the vicinity of two thousand rupees a month, a decent sum to meet the Indian cost of comfortable living. But it converts to a paltry two hundred dollars in American currency. After taxes and other unavoidable outgoes, I would struggle to set aside thirty dollars to repay my enormous borrowings. It will take more than a decade to pay back all my Indian friends living in America. I can never ask them to bear with me for so long.

That leaves two options: either remain in America or go to Saudi Arabia. On the one hand, my deep involvement with Sarah is a huge incentive to pick the former. But on the other, the financial imperative of my indebtedness mandates the latter. I am in a quandary.

Although Ronald Regan has not had much time in the White House to fix the economy and pare the unemployment, I have accidentally landed a decent job at Morgan. But after taxes and living expenses, I would be left with little to reimburse my benefactors. And not doing so quickly would be unfair to my friends who bailed me out without batting an eyelid. In contrast, the job in Saudi Arabia will enable me to easily repay my supporters within a few months. However, that will result in a long separation from Sarah, a thought I find hard to bear.

It is a tough call.

Hard as I try deliberate, I cannot make up my mind. Yet I am reluctant to discuss the issue with Sarah because she would undoubtedly be averse to my going away. I need a sounding board that can bring some objectivity to my decision. Debbie Smith is the perfect choice. She knows me well, has a ringside view and, most importantly, is sensible.

She seems hard to get to. I keep trying her phone for three days but continue to get no answer. Somehow, she is always out. I am left with no choice but to gatecrash her home. It happens to be the afternoon of the fourth Sunday in March.

The sight of her red Mustang in the driveway, with the signature poodle dangling from its rear view mirror, is a great relief. I ring the door bell hoping Debbie has not gone out in someone else's car. I get lucky. She is in and quick to open the door. Her eyebrows rise when she finds me in the doorway. This is the second time I have arrived unannounced at her place.

"Sorry to barge in like this but I got no answer to a million calls I must've made over the past few days." I think an explanation for my intrusion is in order at the very outset.

"You're not the first one with that gripe. Actually, I was away for a couple of days. After I got in, the phone's wire popped out of the socket but I didn't know it. The repair crew fixed it fifteen minutes back." Her tone is apologetic, needlessly so, I feel.

"I'm so glad you're home. I wasn't sure I'd find you." I choose to articulate my feeling although she must have sensed my relief.

"Come on in. You're not going to stand there all afternoon long, are you?" She laughs and steps aside for me to enter.

We discuss a few topics of small talk. She asks me about my host family and is understandably shocked when I break the news of Ed and Donna's separation.

"They seemed such a lovely couple, not to mention their cute daughter." She echoes everyone's opinion.

"Anissa." I volunteer. Debbie and I baby-sat Anissa last year when Ed and Donna wanted to go for a film.

"That's the name. Such a bright kid! Who gets to raise her?" An obvious question.

"Ed. He won the custody after a nasty court battle." I feel sadness return even as I say it.

"What a pity! Coffee?" She tries to line her question with cheer.

"Cream, no sugar. Thanks." I specify, although it is unnecessary.

"I know. Be back in a jiffy."

She hurries to the kitchen leaving me to browse through the news magazine on the coffee table. I am engrossed in the article on Walter Cronkite's retirement a little while earlier, after nineteen years as the *CBS Evening News* anchor. I am an admirer of Cronkite and his avuncular voice, agreeing with the multitude who voted him the most trusted man in America. The mention of Saint Jo as the place of his birth brings back the guilt-spiked memory of my amorous encounter with Daphne. I promptly brush it off.

"The coffee smells refreshing." I complement Debbie when she places the mug on the side table.

"I'm glad you like it." She lowers herself on the ottoman on my left.

"Debbie, I want to pick your brain a little." I sip from the mug.

"Oh my my, Guru. I didn't know you thought I had brain." She smiles.

"Jokes aside, I need your advice." I want her to be serious.

"Shoot. I'm all ears." She looks straight at me.

"I'm in a relationship, pretty deep too." I begin.

"Who's the unlucky girl? Sorry, let's be serious." She cannot resist the temptation to pull my leg. Then she leans forward to pay closer attention.

"Sarah Walker, a sophomore. She was my materials science student last year. Now we work at the Seymours cafeteria. We've been spending a lot of time together." I try to be brief.

"So? You're not on a one-way street here, are you?"

"Oh no, not at all. It's both ways. Last week, her aunt drove through town. We took her to the garment store on Main. Thinking I wasn't within earshot, she asked Sarah if I was a friend. I overheard Sarah say we've gone way beyond just friendship." I pause to sip coffee.

"Where's the problem then?" Debbie looks baffled.

We're so very different, in every way. Including, of course, our religions." I come to the point.

"Do you really care? I remember you telling me that you aren't religious." She squints.

"Not me, but I suspect she does." I wonder if Debbie will see my point.

"You'll have to talk it over with her then, I guess." Debbie shrugs her shoulders, suggesting the problem is solved.

"That's not all. There's something else."

"What?" She doesn't understand where I am coming from.

"I want to go back to India at some point." The information confuses her further.

"I've heard that. So?"

"India's not a place where an American woman can feel comfortable. Life out there is so very different. It'd be unfair to expect Sarah to adjust." I hope Debbie is able to appreciate the reasons for my apprehension.

"What's her view?"

"It doesn't count because she can't even begin to imagine what it's like." I admit the reality.

"Well, Guru, if she feels strongly about you, she'll adapt." Her point is logical.

"I'm not sure she knows how strong her feelings are." I see no harm in being frank.

"Her true feelings will be known if and when you're not around." Debbie shares the female perspective. It is priceless.

"That makes sense. If the fondness remains undiminished over an extended separation, then the feelings are strong enough to make compromises; otherwise not." I outline my understanding of Debbie's inference.

"Bull's-eye." She mimes firing a handgun.

Debbie has provided the answer I was looking for. Instead of looking at the separation as a problem, I need to think of it as a solution. It will be hard, but that is the right thing to do. If Sarah and I don't endure the separation, the bond would not be strong enough for Sarah to withstand India.

"You've been a great help, Debbie. Thanks a million." I get up from my seat to leave.

"I wouldn't let you off so cheap. You owe me an evening of six-pack and home cooked Indian food." She walks with me to the front door.

"You choose the time." I step out and close the door behind me.

Once I am back in the car, it occurs to me that I have ignored the professional considerations of Bassam's job. True, it offers tax-free income inflated by handsome perquisites, but how would it contribute to my career prospects? I recall one of my professors asking us to think of the value of a job in terms of improving our résumés. His advice was simple: don't accept a job just because it looks good at the time of joining; think of how it will look on your résumé at the time of leaving. I must evaluate the Saudi employment from this angle.

The best person to consult on the issue is Ed McGovern. But I hesitate to approach him, not sure if dragging him in this decision would appear insensitive to his recent family problems. On second thought though, I reckon the distraction may actually take his mind off the unpleasant development, albeit for a short time. He is most forthcoming when I call, inviting me over straightaway.

As I park in front of his house, the days spent there after the hospitalization over a year ago come back to me. It was then a happy home of Ed, Donna and Anissa. The world has gone around a few hundred times since. Not only has my host family disintegrated but I am in a different state of mind too. How quickly has life changed for all of us!

I realize that I would meet Anissa for the first time since her parents' separation. The prospect is not enticing. Obviously, losing the proximity of her mother would be hard on her. More so, since her preference must not have been considered in the court of law. My Indian sensibilities find it all so unnecessary and perhaps avoidable. I ring the bell feeling more than a little morose.

Ed opens the door and when I enter, switches off *60 Minutes* he is watching on TV. Anissa is nowhere in sight.

"Where's Anissa?" I involuntarily pop the question.

"She's with Donna on week-ends." I take the matter-of-fact reply as an indication of his adjustment to the new life. Yet I deem it courteous to shift the focus away from his broken family.

"I need your advice, Ed." I begin.

"You can try but I can't guarantee a whole lot of wisdom." He smiles.

I tell him about the jobs I am offered by Morgan here and Al Daba'an Aluminium in Saudi Arabia, then go on to explain how my precarious financial situation makes Al Daba'an a preferred choice at the moment.

"I'm not sure how it'll benefit me in my future career though." I add.

"In what way, Guru?" He does not seem to understand what I am getting at.

"See, the other option is to join Morgan here in the US. In your assessment, which is better for my résumé, working in the US or in Saudi Arabia, given my plan to return to India after a few years?" I spell out my dilemma.

"Let's see……If you were to work in the US, you'd probably be a small cog in a big wheel. And perhaps you also need to think as to whether the experience here would be relevant for a subsequent job in India."

"The company in Saudi's small so I'd shoulder some serious responsibilities. And a few years of Saudi work experience would probably be more relevant for later employment in India, would it not?"

"I've an uncle who's been working in Jeddah for the last five years. He tells me he's gained immensely from the truly multinational business culture over there."

"That's good to know."

"He goes on all the time about working with Egyptians, Jordanians, Indians, Philippinos, Germans, Brits and, of course, Americans. A real melting pot."

"Sure sounds like one." I endorse his assessment.

"But from what he describes, it's an oppressive place. Nothing like the US of A." I remember hearing it from Bassam.

"Not like India, either." I am sure of it.

"In my view, your work experience in a truly international cauldron would add greater value to your résumé." He offers his wisdom.

"Well, the US is also a melting pot as far as I can see." I don't bother to disclose that the main reason I chose to study here was precisely this character of America.

"As a society, probably. But our business culture is largely unidimensional, if you ask me." His opinion is valuable. He worked as an accounting assistant with a construction company before taking up the teaching assignment.

"You've a point, Ed." I admit.

"I guess you can figure out the importance of a Middle East experience vis-à-vis American from the standpoint of employers in India." He adds.

"From what Bassam, my Jordanian friend, tells me, I'd be entrusted with a wider range of duties in Riyadh than what I can expect from Morgan here." I wait for his reaction.

"That should be the clincher then. You'll definitely fast-track your career if you get to handle greater responsibility at an early age." I think I have got my answer.

"Thanks, Ed. I'm so glad I chose you to bounce my thoughts. The clutter in my mind's all tidied up now." I get up from my seat.

"I'm happy I could offer my two pennies' worth." He laughs as I prepare to leave.

"You can go back to whatever is left of *60 Minutes* now." I step out.

I am no more in a quandary. But I consider it wise to talk with Amit, my classmate at the engineering college in India. He has been working in Shreveport for a couple of years. I call him later that evening.

"You've got to be crazy to leave this place and go to Saudi Arabia." He spontaneously reacts on hearing my plan.

"Well, the income's tax-free and the perks are great." I put forward the positive angle.

"May be. But listen Guru, half the outside world's trying to get into this country, even illegally. The other half's tried but failed. And look at you, all set to throw away the advantage of being here." He sounds really upset with me.

"Eventually, I want to go back to India. So why don't you tell me if your experience here would be useful for a job in India?" I plead.

"In technical matters, yes. In non-techincal, no. I'm used to doing things the way they're done here. India's a different kettle of fish. I'd need to unlearn much of what I know and start all over again." He admits.

"Thanks for the input. It proves my point. Working in Riyadh will get me a truly international experience, something I can use when I get back to India." I argue, knowing he is never going to see it that way.

"I wouldn't be able to comment on that. But I've a very fundamental question. Why'd you want to go back to India in the first place?" I sense exasperation in his voice.

In my view, I would be able to add more value in India than over here. Besides, deep down at my core, I would deem myself a mercenary if I worked all my life in a foreign country. That would be too heavy a cross to bear. But sharing my beliefs and preferences may seem like running down Amit's decision to settle in America. It is not a risk worth taking. I consider the choice of where to spend one's life an intensely personal one, not to be judged in terms of right or wrong. That is the simple truth.

I decide to put forth other reasons, equally genuine.

"Listen Amit, if I settle in the US, I'll never be able to spend enough time with my parents and siblings. I benefited immensely from them. Being so far away would be unfair to them and to me, not to mention my kids, whenever they're born." I am treading on treacherous ground here because my point also applies to Amit, although I do not think he should necessarily feel the same way as I do.

"I'll grant that. But your kids can get a lot more opportunities in a developed country than in India." He mentions the reason cited by many immigrants.

"You're probably right. But I can't ignore a million ways in which I've gained from my background and upbringing." I argue.

"So have I. Yet I think you'll be better off here than there." He seems to have run out of his reasons.

"I respect your opinion. But we're different. At least you should accept that." I want to conclude this discussion.

"Accepted. You're your best judge, Guru."

"Thanks for sharing your views. I think they've provided enough insights to make the decision." I hang up.

The idea of seeking out Debbie, Ed and Amit has been very useful. The plan is in place now. I only need to implement it. Easier said than done, I fear.

Thirty Three

I simply do not know how to get Sarah to agree with my decision to go to Saudi Arabia. Every day I set out to talk it over with her but each time I duck when the opportunity arises. A week goes by without my mustering the necessary courage to spill the beans. On the eighth day, I am determined to share my plan.

"You're quiet today, Guru. Is something bothering you?" She asks half an hour after we meet at the union cafeteria in the evening.

"No, no. Just thinking about life in India." I try to sound casual, pretending to stir the coffee in my cup.

"What about it?" She leans forward and places her hand on my forearm.

"It's so very different, Sarah. Hard to imagine for someone who hasn't experienced it." I avoid meeting her eyes.

"You've said that before." She reminds me.

"And it's enriched me in so many ways. It's also provided a firm anchor to my life." I beat around the bush.

"Let's talk about what we're going to do in summer, now that we're almost there." She changes track, trying to sound cheerful. Inexplicably, her move makes me feel relieved.

"Good idea. Tell me, what've you decided to do?" I take the topic forward.

"I'm going to follow your footsteps and spread the gospel." She has twinkle in her eyes.

"Wow! Really? You've everything worked out already?" I cannot hide my surprise.

"You bet! I didn't want to tell you till I got the letter from the company. It arrived today." Her tone is soaked in pride.

"So when does the training start?" A pang sears through my midriff at the thought of our looming separation. I knew it would hurt once the deadline got frozen. But the intensity catches me off guard.

"In six weeks. Same place in Saint Louis where you trained last year." She squeezes my arm in excitement.

"Okay. And have you thought of a territory to flog the testaments?" I want to know if she would be around when I leave.

"I'm thinking of Kansas City. That way, I can cover eastern Kansas and western Missouri." She justifies her preference.

"And visit your parents every now and then." I add.

"And visit my parents every now and then." She echoes me.

"Smart plan."

"Why don't you work with me for a few days? Morgan won't have a problem if you join in August, will they?" She pops the question, putting her other hand on mine, hope spread all over her face. I had never indicated any preference for Morgan but she seems to have concluded that I will pick them over Bassam's company in Saudi Arabia.

"Don't be silly, Sarah. I haven't even enrolled." I offer a plausible excuse to avoid further discussion on her suggestion.

"Guru, I'm not talking about the training. I'm asking you to sell Bibles with me." She blows my excuse to pieces.

"I don't think it's appropriate to do it on the sly." I throw the ethical issue at her.

"Who's asking you to do it on the sly? I called Midwest Bible Sales as soon as I received their letter. They said those trained earlier can get a territory allotted and start selling Bibles straightaway." Her triumphant smile lights up her transparent blue eyes.

"You've covered every base, haven't you?" I smile back at her.

"You're joining me then, right?" She does not want to let go.

I am not sure how to respond. On the one hand, I have no heart to prick her bubble of enthusiasm. But on the other, I do not want to commit right now and back out later. That would be so unfair. I need to buy time.

"Excuse me. I need to run to the restroom." I rise from the chair and leave the table.

The restroom is about fifty yards down the hallway. I walk slowly, taking my own time to allow myself a few extra minutes to invent a ploy to dodge Sarah's question.

My focus on the problem at hand makes me oblivious of the other people milling past.

"Watch out!" I hear Janette Helmuth scream. We barely avoid a collision.

"Ouch! Sorry. I didn't see you coming at me, Janette." I apologize.

"You sure you haven't snorted something wicked?" She jokes.

"I was immersed in my thoughts." I offer my justification.

"Guru, have you seen *Ordinary People*?" She suddenly shifts to films.

"No. Why do you ask?" I am unable to see where she is coming from.

"Because I saw it today. It's a very good film that you might find interesting."

"Why do you think so?" I ask, not able to figure out the reason for her contention.

"Because you'll be able to appreciate the difference in the culture here and in your country." True to her character, Janette pinpoints the intellectual dimension of her cinematic experience.

"I want to see it then." I express my wish without knowing when it will come true.

"You'll have to hurry. Today's the last day. The show starts in another half hour." She resumes her clump past me.

While I am in the restroom, it suddenly dawns on me that Janette has saved me. Again. She seems to enter my orbit exactly when I am in need of her perceptive inputs. After the thought she has planted in my mind, I don't have to walk slowly on the way back to the cafeteria.

"Have you seen *Ordinary People*?" I ask Sarah as soon as I reach her table.

"No. Why?" She is as surprised as I was when Janette popped the same question in the hallway.

"I'm told it's a very good film. I'd like to see it." I spell out the decision I made a couple of minutes earlier.

"I wouldn't mind if that's what you want. When? Saturday?" I notice enthusiasm missing in her tone. I ignore it.

"Today's the last show at Highlander. We'll have to go now if we don't want to miss it." I try to bring urgency to my voice.

"Okay. Let's go." She gathers her books on the table and rises. I am scared the issue of selling Bibles will come up during the ten-minute walk to Highlander. I want to preempt the possibility.

"We've a little less than half hour. Why don't I run home and get the car while you change and wait for me in your dorm?" I resort to chicanery.

"Sounds good. See you in twenty minutes?"

"Twenty minutes it'll be." I start walking.

I know nothing about the film until I enter the theatre's lobby. The posters on the walls reveal Mary Tyler Moore and Donald Sutherland in lead roles and Robert Redford directing them. I did not know Redford directed films.

"This is Robert Redford's directorial debut." Sarah educates me as we enter the auditorium.

"That's why I did not know him as a director." I explain my ignorance.

"Now you do, Mr. Know All." She squeezes my hand. We laugh.

The film turns out to be a simple but powerful depiction of cataclysmic emotional upheaval during the disintegration of an otherwise perfect upper-middle-class family. The plot vividly brings home the harsh realities of crumbling American households. The riveting story, Redford's brilliant direction and the entire cast's histrionics keep me completely engrossed till the very end.

But when we exit the building and get into the car, the last minute decision to see the film after a chance meeting with Janette, strikes me as one more strange coincidence. At a time when I am weighing a life in America vis-à-vis in my country, the film inadvertently uncovers the importance of the emotional safety-net the close-knit structure of the Indian family offers, albeit at the cost of some privacy and freedom. To my Indian psyche, it is a crucial factor that cannot be ignored. The decision to eventually settle down in India is now sealed.

"Why don't we go to Dairy Queen for a cup of coffee?" Sarah's question brings me out of my thoughts.

"Good idea." I turn the car onto McGuire, heading north.

"I liked Timothy Hutton's acting a lot." Sarah returns to the film.

"Me too. A tough role." I add.

Once we are seated in the restaurant and the waitress leaves the table after taking down our order, Sarah brings up the topic I had skirted in the union cafeteria.

"We're going to spread the gospel together in summer, aren't we?" Her pitch is lined with anticipation.

"I'd love to, but I think I'll pass." The words come out, in spite of my reluctance to utter them.

"Why? It'll be so much fun!" Her tone is persuasive. I hate to turn her down but my mind is made.

"I believe Bassam's job in Saudi Arabia will benefit my career more." I sound too serious for my liking.

"I thought you wouldn't want to leave me. Don't do this to us, Guru." She pleads. I feel a tug in my heart.

"I wish I didn't have to, Sarah, but it's not so simple. If I take up a job in America, I'll need ages to repay my huge loan. I can't do that to my friends who helped in my hour of need." I defend my decision.

"If you penny-pinch for some time, you may be able to repay earlier." She suggests a weak solution.

"There's one other problem. The longer I live in the US, the harder it'll get to re-settle in India. I'll be torn between the material comforts I enjoy here and the emotional yearning for my folks back home. It's happened to a lot of Indian immigrants." I try to explain my apprehension.

"You can't be in two places at the same time. But that's okay." She counters.

"Whether it's okay or not depends on one's personal outlook. As for me, I won't be able to go through life with my body in America and half the heart in India." As soon as I finish saying it, I recognize the possible unfairness of my argument. Would it not be the same for her if she were to settle in India? I hope not.

"I think I'm a little more pragmatic about dealing with such opposite pulls." She looks straight in my eye. I find comfort in her adaptability.

"I know. You've always maintained that you're fine with the idea of living in India." I set aside the spoon her fingers are fiddling with and place my hand on hers.

"Why'd you want to be so complicated? Isn't it simpler to face life as it comes?" Although she sounds earnest, her eyes reflect a glint of mischief. I am relieved that my fear of discussing our separation is proving to be unfounded.

"Now you're talking Indian philosophy." I smile.

"So when do you start Bassam's job?" She turns serious.

"I'm not sure although he wants me there as soon as possible. My Saudi visa's under process in Riyadh. When it's issued, I'll go to Washington to get my passport stamped and proceed from there." I suddenly feel sad at the thought of leaving her behind. I suspect my face mirrors the emotion.

"I can't bear the idea of you not being around, Guru." I sense a faint tremor in Sarah's voice and notice her eyes turning moist.

"Neither can I. But it's a test for our feelings for each other." I verbalize the thought I have waited to since my chat with Debbie. I refrain from elaborating further.

"I guess you're right." She dabs her eyes with a paper napkin from the stack on the table.

We sit holding hands in silence. It is a poignant moment I knew we would have to face sooner or later. But the presence of other patrons in the restaurant forces us to rein in our emotions. After several minutes, the waitress appears with the carafe of coffee to refill our cups. I cover my mug to suggest I am done. Sarah does likewise. Both of us realize it is time to go.

We walk hand in hand to the car. I have mixed feelings as I get behind the wheel and drive out of the parking lot. I am relieved of the burden of selling my plan to Sarah. But the looming separation is deeply saddening.

"Do you plan to go to India before joining in Riyadh?" Sarah suddenly asks as we near her dorm.

"I wish I could. The company'll send me a ticket up to Riyadh. So I'll have to pay the fare from there to Bombay. I don't have the money for it." I tell her the sad truth.

Sarah is in no hurry to get out of the car when I park in front of Nattinger. On the contrary, she slides closer to me, pulling my chin to make me face her. The weak smile on her lips is just a ploy to hold her tears back. It does not work. She hugs me, uncontrolled tears rolling down her cheeks. My determination to hold my emotions in check dissolves too. The wave of heart-rending sadness sweeping over us threatens to wash away my resolve of leaving America. It takes a long time to ebb, but ebb eventually it does.

I wipe Sarah's eyes before she reluctantly steps out and runs up the steps to the double doors without looking back. Just a few months earlier, she had lingered on the same steps a wee bit longer than necessary. The gesture had set my heart aflutter.

Much water has flowed under the bridge since then, I reckon before turning the ignition on.

I receive my master's degree in the last week of May. I am ready to leave for Saudi Arabia. Bassam calls to inform that he would come to the US in the first week of June with the papers for my Saudi visa. I can collect them while he is with his in-laws in Boonville. That suits me just fine.

Thirty Four

After Sarah goes to Saint Louis for the Midwest Bible Sales training, I am overwhelmed by a feeling of emptiness. All my friends save Reufey have taken up summer jobs elsewhere. For the first time in months, I have nothing to do. I cannot travel because I am flat broke. I have no option but to wait for Bassam to get my visa papers and air ticket. I must stay put until he arrives.

The best use of the idle time on my hand is to catch up on my extra-curricular reading. Several works of fiction have been published since I joined graduate school, some of them by my favourite authors: Michael Crichton, Roald Dahl, Jeffrey Archer and Robert Ludlum, among others. I also go for Salman Rushdie's *Midnight's Children* primarily because of its Indian context.

From the time I arrived in America, my thirst for news about India has remained largely unquenched. The media have been almost totally unmindful of the goings-on in my country. The only TV clip covering India appeared last summer, a twenty seconds piece showing Sanjay Gandhi's funeral procession. Ignorance about India runs deep in this country; my American friends needed to be told that Sanjay was the son of our Prime Minister Mrs. Indira Gandhi and, in fact, had no relation to Mahatma Gandhi, the father of our non-violent freedom struggle. Other than the clip, there has been complete black-out. It would take another two decades for the Americans to locate India on the world map.

I expect Saudi Arabia to provide a welcome change on this count. Unlike here in the US, the demand generated by a large population of Indian expatriates in the workforce must drive abundant supply of Indian news, food, music and films. I consider this proximity to my homeland a small compensation for enduring Sarah's void. The thought alleviates some of the sadness in winding down my stay in this country.

The disposal of my meager possessions is easy. Hakim Haddad, a student from Jordan, is renting my apartment from fall. I am leaving all the household effects for him. Not that I have much, but whatever there is will be useful to him. The Buick LeSabre bought in Chattanooga is already given away to Sarah. She has taken it to Saint Louis. That leaves two suitcases full of clothes and mementos of my stay here: photographs, gifts, books, notebooks and letters. These are going with me.

Bassam reaches his in-laws' home on the second Friday in June and calls me the same day. We decide to meet the next morning. I borrow Reufey's Charger to drive up to Boonville, taking extra care to avoid the repetition of February's harrowing incident. Bassam is enjoying a breather with his family. Sally, Yassar and Fatima had not joined

Bassam in Saudi Arabia; the four of them are naturally happy to be reunited. He is planning to take them to Riyadh in fall. That is good news. It will be nice to have them around. Bassam hands me the papers. He says I should get the visa in two days, three on the outside. I book myself on Sunday's flight to Washington, DC, with the hope of continuing on to Riyadh on Thursday.

It is time for me to leave the place I called home for close to two years. Until the date of my departure was fixed, it somehow seemed a distant prospect. But now it looms large, dousing my spirit in melancholy. The days and months are replayed in my mind over and over again. As happens every so often, the hardships have faded from the memory while the happy occasions have crystalised into fond nostalgia. I have a heavy heart, not knowing when I will be able to visit this place again. And whenever I do, it will not be the same without the people I have enjoyed the company of.

Reufey drives me to Kansas City airport. We cannot think of much to say, silenced by the improbability of ever meeting again. He plans to return to Pakistan after graduating at the end of fall. The relations between India and Pakistan have always been strained, a reality throttling passage between our two countries. We are unlikely to visit each other.

Sarah meets us at the airport, looking pretty in fawn slacks and a white tank top. She has driven in the Buick LaSabre, accompanied by Veronica, her cousin. The four of us go up to the cafeteria on the mezzanine to talk over coffee until my flight is announced. After fifteen minutes, I come up with the excuse of driving my Buick one last time and ask Sarah to come with me. Reufey and Veronica understand our need for solitude and graciously offer to wait in the cafeteria.

The brave veneer we have held up so far crumbles once we are in the car. Sarah hugs me and we hold on to each other for a long time. It is going to be hard, she complains, trying to hold her sobs back. Thankfully, before we start having second thoughts about my move, the time is up. We kiss goodbye and return to the cafeteria.

My flight is announced within minutes. I walk up to the gate without looking back, unable to bear the sight of tearful Sarah.

Shiela meets me at Washington National. She had seen me off at the same airport when I proceeded to join the B-school. It seems like yesterday. The time has flown quickly. She finds me a different person to the one she knew before. I have endured a lot and learned a great deal. She is interested to know everything I did at school. On getting home, Vinay joins us. We talk late into the night.

The next morning, I am ready to go to the Saudi embassy. Vinay drops me at the Pentagon metro station before carrying on to his office next door. I take the Blue Line to Metro Centre and change on to the Red Line to get to Dupont Circle. The embassy is a short walk from there.

The visa section is housed in a small room located on one side of the building. It is sparsely furnished with seats along two walls and a rectangular desk next to the entrance against the third. The fourth wall has an opening, like the ticket window at a cinema hall. It is fitted with a heavy steel grill, presumably to guard the office inside.

Two men, one Caucasian and the other Arab, are at the desk completing their visa applications. No embassy staffer is in the room. I wait facing the grill, expecting an employee to show up and assist me. After several minutes, a sumptuous lady in a full-sleeved purple garment printed with large pink and white carnations appears on the other side. Surprisingly, her face is not veiled. Even her hair is not draped in a scarf. She is not pleased to see me. I ask her for a visa application form. She tears one from a pad and pushes it through the grill, exposing her hands decorated with dark brown leaf and flower motif in henna.

It takes me fifteen minutes to fill the form. One of the boxes requires my name to be written in Arabic script. I obviously have no idea how. The Arab visitor in the room comes to my rescue. I only hope he has not made a mistake. I go back to the ticket window.

This time the lady is not willing to appear in a hurry. I wait for almost ten minutes before she finally turns up. I hand her my application, passport and the papers Bassam brought from Riyadh. She does not touch the passport but yanks the remaining documents towards her and drops them, seemingly on a desk I cannot see.

"Come tomorrow." She barks. Her voice is unusually hoarse for a woman, accent clearly Arabic. No 'please', no 'sir'.

"When'll you need my passport?" I want to be sure she has not inadvertently left it untouched.

"Not until your visa's ready."

I collect my passport lying on the sill and leave the embassy.

The way back to Sheila's home is a bit more cumbersome. I walk to Dupont Circle station to take the Red Line to Metro Centre and change on to the Orange Line to Ballston, the last station on the route. From there, I need to hop on to a bus for the hour-long journey to Tyson's Corner where Shiela can pick me up on her way home for lunch. I kill a couple of hours at the shopping mall before she arrives.

As ordered, I am back at the embassy before ten o'clock the next morning. A solitary man, probably Palestinian, is in the visitors' room. After a few minutes, the unfriendly lady appears behind the grill, wearing a shiny blue and yellow satin dress styled on a sailor's tunic. Her face does not reflect her attire's brightness. She immediately recognizes me.

"Your visa's not come from Riyadh." Her manner is dismissive.

"How'd I know when it arrives?"

"Check with us on Friday."

There is nothing else to talk. I run my Dupont Circle-Metro Centre-Ballston-Tyson's Corner routine and find myself in the mall well before noon. By the time Shiela turns up, I have seen every item Macy's have on offer.

On Friday morning, I call the Embassy and ask for the visa section. I am put on hold. I wait. And wait. After twenty minutes, I hang up and call again. The experience is no different. I get lucky the third time. A lady in the visa section answers. She is the same person who had cold-shouldered me from behind the grill. I give my name and that of my Saudi employer. She puts me on hold and goes to check. Just when I am ready to hang up again, she returns with the bad news. My visa has not yet arrived.

"Check again on Monday." She tersely orders. I have stopped expecting courtesies from her.

There is no progress on Monday. The visa is untraceable. I am getting frustrated now. And bored of doing nothing.

The rude lady from the visa section tells me to check again on Friday.

I decide to go to the embassy on Friday. The lady has still not found my visa. I am getting impatient now. I have lost two weeks chasing the visa and gone nowhere. I want to know if there is anything I can do to help her locate it.

"Get the visa number and date of issue." She is petulant as ever.

Friday is the weekly holiday in Saudi Arabia. I wait till Saturday and call Bassam. He gives me the phone number of Milad Boutrus, the Egyptian secretary to the chairman of Al Daba'an Aluminium Factory. I call Milad. He is polite to a fault. I ask him to give me the information the embassy wants. He promises to find out and call back.

Milad takes his own sweet time to cull the information. But he does obtain it. He calls on Thursday to give me the visa number and the date on which it was issued. I am sure the embassy will be able to trace it now.

Armed with Milad's information, I am at the embassy again on Friday morning. Even before I open my mouth, the lady, this time dressed in a brown collarless dress that matches her complexion, tells me my visa has not been received.

"I've brought the visa number and date of issue you asked for. May be that'll help." I pass a piece of paper through the grill.

"Check on Monday." Although I find it hard to see why she cannot look at her records and let me know right away, there is no appeal here. But I sense a trace of politeness in her tone. The fact that I could get the information from

Riyadh may have impressed her a little. Her manner raises my hopes.

Sadly, my optimism is misplaced. Monday is no different, except that the gruff lady conveys the bad news with just a shake of her head, without a word. I am getting worried now. The few dollars I had arrived in DC with are fast running out.

In desperation, I call Milad immediately on reaching Sheila's home. With false bravado, I warn him that I am fed up of this suspended animation and will find a job in America, unless he solves the mystery of my missing visa by Friday. I hope he does not call my bluff.

This time Milad acts fast. On Wednesday, he calls me with more information: the date the visa was sent to Washington, the date it was received by the embassy and the name of the person who acknowledged the receipt. I note down the details.

I am back in the embassy on Thursday morning. The brusque lady is ready to dismiss me with her regulation denial.

"I've got more information on my visa." I pip her to the tape.

"Give it." She orders. I share the dates. They are almost a month old. The embassy has had my visa all along.

"The name of the person who received the visa is Hafiza Malik." I am sure that is a clincher.

"We've not received the visa on the date you mention." Her brazenness is shocking.

"In that case, can I talk to Hafiza Malik?" I need to check with the person who was delivered my visa.

"That's me."

"And you've not received the visa?"

"No. I told you already." Her eyes turn angry.

"Can I meet the person in charge of the visa section then?"

"I'm in charge of the visa section." She leaves the window.

I am convinced that Hafiza Malik does not like my face. The entry to the Kingdom of Saudi Arabia is, therefore, barred for me. Period.

On leaving the embassy, my thoughts veer to the other possible option. I seriously contemplate calling Morgan Cermets to convey my willingness to join them, contrary to the letter of non-acceptance I sent weeks ago. But I question the wisdom in such a move. Approaching them again would look utterly unprofessional. Besides, Don Morgan may have hired an executive assistant for himself by now. The other important consideration is the test of physical separation my relationship with Sarah needs to pass. I do not want either of us to be blinded by the lure of uninterrupted togetherness while making decisions of long term ramifications. And that is a definite risk if I do not avoid Sarah's close proximity over the coming months and perhaps a year. A much smaller concern, but a concern nonetheless, is my loss of face in returning after having packed up. Most of my friends would treat the story of denied visa as subterfuge for my chickening out. I do not relish the possibility. My mind is made. Morgan is out.

When I reach Tyson's Corner at noon, I remember that Shiela is attending a day-long seminar today. The programme includes lunch. There is no way I can afford the luxury of taking a cab to her home on Malraux Drive. I have to hang around the mall till five in the evening. By then, it would be midnight in Riyadh.

So I call Milad from a public phone in front of Bloomingdale's, the ticking minutes fast eroding my wafer thin liquidity. I hurriedly narrate my last encounter at the embassy and express the fear of not getting the visa till Hafiza Malik is running the department. I inform him of my planned trip to New Jersey to look for a job around New York City, expecting him to appreciate the urgency in resolving the matter. I hang up without waiting for his response.

In spite of my precarious finances, I must go to New Jersey to improve my prospects of getting a job. I check my wallet. It holds just about enough money to take the Greyhound to New Jersey and return to DC in case Hafiza Malik decides to change her attitude towards me. In my assessment, the chances of that eventuality are slim.

I pack my bags and board the bus to New Jersey on Friday morning. Arun and Sujata are happy to see me. The change of scene buoys up my mood too. Arun and I spend the week-end plotting my job-hunt. The economy has yet to pick up. Finding employment in the field of marketing would need a lot of legwork and a generous dollop of luck. I decide to give it my best shot.

When the phone rings on Monday morning, I am going through the 'positions vacant' page of *The New York Times*. No one is likely to call me. I ignore the ring as Sujata answers. She speaks for a few seconds and shouts for me. My surprise turns to astonishment when I hear Hafiza Malik at the other end.

"We've traced your visa. Can you please come and collect it, sir?" The 'please' and 'sir' sound discordant in her voice and tone. I am stunned.

"I'll submit my passport tomorrow. When can you return it?" Despite my shock, I think of making her commit before losing interest in me.

"We'll stamp the visa and give it back immediately, sir."

I pinch myself. Surely this is not for real.

"That's great. I'll see you tomorrow."

I hang up, fold the newspaper away and call the airline to book my seat on Friday's flight to Riyadh. I am astounded by the incredible turn in my fortune. More so, when I cannot remember giving Arun's phone number to Hafiza Malik. She must have taken the trouble of calling Sheila to get it.

Ms. Malik smiles broadly on seeing me the next morning. I am not used to anything but her frown. Today is different. She takes my passport and disappears, actually asking for my forgiveness to do so. I can hear the thud of a stamp. She returns a few seconds later, my passport in hand.

"Your visa's issued, sir. You can go to the Kingdom of Saudi Arabia any time now. And please inform the prince that everything's fine here." I have no idea who she is referring to. But asking her would be unwise, if not downright stupid.

"I'll do that." I promise her, not knowing if I will be able to keep it.

As I pocket my passport and leave the embassy for the last time, my first lesson on Saudi Arabia dawns on me: it's not what you know, but who you know that counts.